Sail With Me

LJ MAKENZIE

ISBN: 978-1-963807-00-4
Amazon Ebook: B0CR9YB2P4

To Drury and The Breakers.
Let's do this again sometime.

Map of Wild Shore

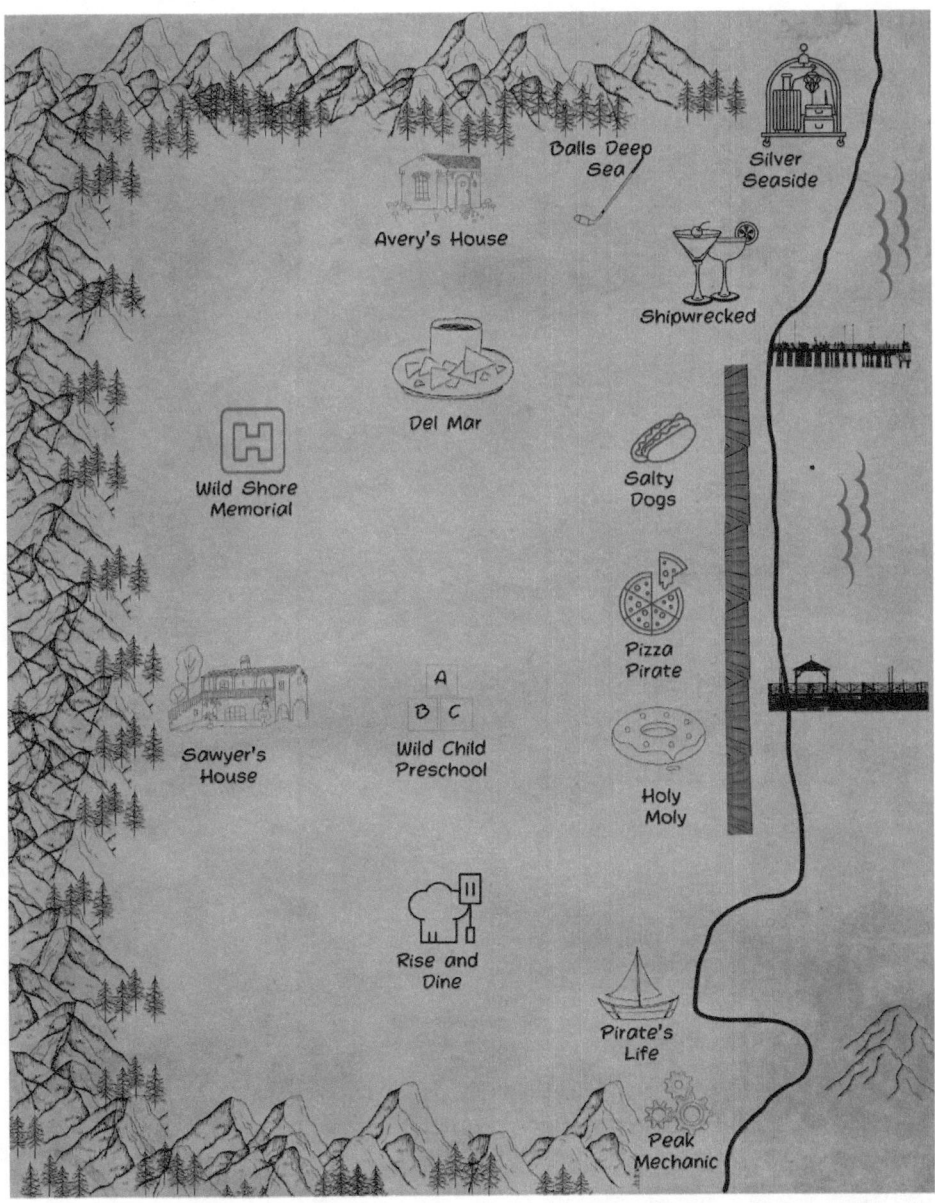

CHAPTER 1
THE ILLUSTRIOUS OXPECKER

Avery

"Oh my God, Riley! Have you finished that book yet?" I ask my best friend as soon as she answers the phone.

"I just finished it this morning before I opened the shop. I almost called you, but I knew you were shaping little minds and didn't need the distraction of my full-on fan girl excitement. I was totally blown away."

"That plot twist!" we both say at the same time. "Jinks!" We giggle before breaking out into full-on laughter. For being so different, our minds work the same.

When we finally calm down, Riley asks, "What are you doing tonight? We need to meet and discuss. I never saw that coming, and I'm usually pretty good at figuring out what is going to happen."

"The only thing I had planned tonight was to finish this book, but now I need to decompress. Del at six? Will that give you enough time to wash the oil and grease out from under your fingernails?" I quip.

"I'll probably just come as I am. Adds a little extra flavor to the salsa," she says sarcastically.

"I'm glad they changed to everyone getting their own small dish," I reply with my own sarcasm.

"We are still going to share the basket of chips, ya goof." She laughs.

"Ugh. You are terrible. Why are you my best friend?"

"Because everyone else in Wild Shore met their best friend in preschool, and there were no other options for us transplants. It really helped that you were the first person I met in this town. Holding each other and crying our eyes out within a half hour of meeting pretty much sealed the deal. You are stuck with me for life."

"Those are excellent points, so I guess I'll accept your vow of forever friendship," I respond.

"Wow. Thanks," Riley deadpans.

"Six? Yes or no? I need to put my clothes back on and brush my hair before I leave."

"Did we read the same book? I didn't think it was one-handed reading material worthy."

"I'm done with you. I will be eating my emotions at Del Mar at six with or without you."

"See ya then!" she bursts out as I press the red end call button on my cell.

Riley is without a doubt my other half. Which is a good thing because at twenty-eight, I don't think I am going to find a man in Wild Shore to occupy that position.

After browsing book groups on social media to see how other people reacted to the book, I glance at the clock and see it is time to get ready to leave.

I walk through my small Cape Cod to the single bedroom. Rifling through my closet, I pull out navy skinny jeans and a white short-sleeved Henley leotard top. I slip into tan ankle booties and walk across the hallway to my bathroom.

My dirty-blonde hair still has the curls I put in it this morning, so I add a swipe of mascara to accent my blue eyes and touch up my lipgloss. With one last glance in the full-length mirror, I decide I'm good to go. I grab my light blue denim jacket and purse from the hanger by the door and walk out to Chili, the red Volkswagen Beetle convertible my parents bought for my sixteenth birthday. I love this car and will drive it until it dies.

Since spring is barely upon us, traffic is not a problem. From the first summer breeze until the last leaf falls, the main streets in Wild Shore and The Drop, the only road into town from Magnolia Ridge, will be bumper-to-bumper traffic with tourists wanting to take in the scenery and outdoor adventures the locals provide.

Most of the citizens of Wild Shore depend on tourism income to keep them financially stable, but they breathe a sigh of relief when the last vehicle hits The Drop and heads out.

I, on the other hand, do not depend on tourists to keep me in a job. Quite the opposite actually. My job depends on the inhabitants having nothing else to do in the winter but populate the area with the next generation.

After graduating college with a degree in Early Childhood Education, I knew I wanted to move near my parents since we have always been close. My dad is the manager of Silver Seaside, one of the most upscale resorts built into the north bluff, so I applied for a job at Wild Child and got hired. I have been in charge of the four-year-old classroom ever since.

I make the trip to Del Mar in five minutes. I see Riley's motorcycle parked in the lot beside the building and drive over there too. I glance down at my phone: 5:58.

I walk through the glass doors set in a beige stone archway to the waiting area. Miguel sees me and points at Riley sitting in a booth along the far wall.

"I'll bring your drink right out, Avery," he says as I walk toward Riley, and he slips behind the dark wooden saloon door. We have been coming here a couple times a month for the last six years, so he has my order memorized.

Riley looks up from her phone as I toss my purse on the bench opposite her.

"'Bout time you show up. I about ate all the emotions without you," she razzes me, grabbing a chip from the almost empty basket.

"It's just now six. I can't help it you show up fifteen minutes early everywhere we go, and I show up on time," I state as I pour salsa into my bowl.

Miguel stops at our table with my frozen strawberry margarita with sugar on the rim, Riley's lime margarita on the rocks with salt on the rim, and a fresh round of chips and salsa.

"Thanks, Miguel," I say.

"Thanks for bringing my marg now that Avery is finally here," Riley ribs.

"You know she is always right on time and not a minute earlier," Miguel defends me.

"Thank you," I say, smiling at him.

"Chicken on the Beach for both of you tonight?" he asks with his pen poised on his notepad, ready to write.

"Yes, please," I say.

"Yep," Riley answers.

"I'll have it right out," Miguel responds with a smile.

Riley starts our conversation off with, "I have been thinking about that plot twist since this morning. Normally, I see it a mile away and want to scream at the main character for not seeing what is right in front of her face. This time, I would have been standing right next to her ready to be killed. Between customers and waiting on parts, I went back through the book to look for clues that I missed. They were buried in the action scenes. I was so focused on who was killing who and who was rising into the power role that I didn't notice them."

"That's brilliant. I read a few blogs after I talked to you, and so many people are saying the same thing as us. Of course there were a couple people who were all 'I DNF'd this book.

That was terrible writing. I don't see why you would want to read something like that.' Were they even reading the same book? That is going on the list as one of the best reads of the year, and I'm not usually into your psychological thriller, unreliable narrator crap. Give me all the hunky billionaires in charge or pro athlete playboys who fall deeply in love with unattainable women," I say, dipping a chip in my salsa.

"That's why we suit each other so well. You make me read the light, fluffy stuff so my brain doesn't start playing tricks on me, and I make you read the crazy stuff so you know you can't trust everyone. We have a weird symbiotic relationship. Like Nemo and his an-anemone." She grins as she pronounces it like the movie.

"I'm surprised you didn't choose the water buffalo and the oxpecker," I say, taking a drink of my perfect marg.

"Hell no. I would be the water buffalo in that relationship, and I'd rather not draw the similarities."

"So that would make me the oxpecker?" I ask.

"Guess so," she replies as she scoops a chip through her salsa.

"You would be so out of luck in that relationship. I wouldn't even know where to start using my pecker to keep you happy."

Riley stuffs her salsa-laden chip in her mouth and says, "Sounds like most of the guys I've gone out with recently."

"Touché, my friend. Touché."

Miguel walks up with our chicken, cheese, and rice and two glasses of water. I will never understand how he carries that many things without dropping anything.

Riley and I dig in and move our conversation back to the book we read this week, discussing which characters we liked, which characters we didn't, and what we think is going to happen in the next book of the series.

After we pay our bills, we walk outside. The nights are still a little chilly, so I slip on my jean jacket as we walk to the side lot.

"So what are we reading next? I think I need a palate cleanser from the dark books I have been reading. What do you have for me?"

"Well, I'm not sure yet. I have several on my TBR, but I need to look through them again. Any specific trope you are feeling?" I ask.

"Spring training is getting ready to start, so I could do a baseball rom-com. Bonus points if he is a catcher. NHL playoffs are right around the corner, so I could do a hockey romance too. Just make them professional players. I'm getting too old for college book boyfriends."

"Gotcha. Let me look through my list, and I will send you a link," I tell her as I get in my car, and she puts on her helmet.

We wave at each other, and I take off out of the parking lot. One of the most pristine, white sand beaches I have ever seen sits nestled in the semicircle created by Magnolia Ridge, so I decide to take a drive down Ocean Boulevard to see if I can catch the sunset.

The Boardwalk is dotted with cute clothing stores, ice cream stands, and surf shops. I continue driving down Ocean Boulevard after The Boardwalk ends. The shoreline dips in to create a cove that has several boats moored to a long dock. A footpath leads from the dock to a charcoal brick two-story building. The front of the building has a cream door with large windows on each side. The large cream lettering above the door says "Pirate's Life." One side of the name says "Snorkel and Catamaran." The other side says "Excursions and Lessons." Two emerald green Adirondack chairs sit in front of one window, and a large planter that matches the chairs sits in front of the other window. In front of the colorful spring flowers, a sign is stuck in the planter that says "Sailing Lessons Start Next Saturday! Inquire Within or Call."

A small shiver passes down my spine at the thought of being on the open water. I return my focus to the road and keep driving as the sun sets over the water.

CHAPTER 2
LOOKING FOR THAT BROASIS

Avery

I flop on the couch in a move that would make my teenage self proud and grab my Kindle from the end table. I look through my TBR for our next read. A grumpy-sunshine, baseball romance about a catcher and the new PT catches my eye.

Let's be honest. The magnificent arm porn on the cover catches my eye, and it just so happens to be what Riley requested. I can tell from the blurb it is going to be super angsty until the characters explode with chemistry in a bit of forbidden romance. My favorite, and I can't wait to start reading it.

I send Riley the link and change into my sleep shirt while it downloads. I get situated in my bed and press my finger on those forearms as I select the book.

I need to get out more if a book cover is getting me worked up. I begin reading, and the next thing I know, my cell phone alarm is blaring my wake-up call.

I pick my Kindle up from its prominent position on my forehead and put it on my nightstand. *Geesh, I hope I don't have a bruise or a dent from that thing lying on my face all night.*

I get out of bed and walk across the hall to my bathroom. A quick check in the mirror above the sink confirms I don't have any adverse side effects from my osmosis reading trial. It also confirms the possibility of a family of rats living in my hair.

I crank the water all the way to hot. I need full dragon breath to get me going this morning.

After drying off, I blow-dry my hair and braid it into a single long plait over one shoulder. I apply effortless makeup and walk back across the hallway to look through my closet. I decide on a pair of green tie-waist crop pants and a white blouse with a black sunflower seed print. I slip on my black ballet flats and walk to the kitchen for a to-go cup of Keurig cappuccino, even though every atom of my being cries out for a Rise and Dine latte.

I put on a black cardigan and grab my purse off the coat rack. My elderly neighbor is sitting on her porch in her bath robe, waiting for the newspaper to be delivered.

"Good morning, Mrs. Shorter!" I greet her as I walk to Chili.

"Morning, dear. Drive safe on your way to work," she replies, and I wave as I reverse out of the driveway.

The tree-lined streets are just beginning to come out of dormancy. Witnessing the once barren branches fill with buds reminds me that I am stuck in a season of life. There is no better time for change and growth than spring.

I sit down behind my desk ten minutes before drop-off starts. Instead of using the last few minutes to prepare for the day ahead, I click on one of my social media accounts. A sponsored advertisement quickly brings me out of my aimless scrolling. A sleek charcoal sailboat topped with a vibrant green sail adorns my phone screen. "Pirate's Life," in the same font as the building I saw last night, is written in the upper corner of the ad. Below the sailboat is an advertisement for four sailing classes for six hundred dollars.

My heart starts to beat a little erratically, and I jump as Candace, the three-year-old classroom teacher, raps her knuckles on the door.

"Sorry, I didn't mean to scare you. I didn't know you were wrapped up that tight in your phone," she says before pausing.

"Wait. Are you reading something that good this early in the morning? You hussy. You are about to get bombarded by children," she continues with a laugh. It is the running joke around here that if one of us is ultra-focused on our phone, we are probably throat deep in literary porn.

"Shows what you know. I was on social media," I sass as I stand up and walk to my door.

"I need to follow who you follow because you were focused. I could use that kind of inspiration."

"You have been married for almost ten years and have three kids who I have had the pleasure of teaching. You should probably lay off the inspiration before you have to buy a transport van to haul around your progeny," I respond.

"That ship has sailed. You have met those heathens. I need to live vicariously through a young, hot twenty-something to stay sane. Wait, don't you fall into that category?" she hints as she bumps her shoulder into mine as we walk through the front entrance to assist with drop-off.

"The only people living vicariously through me succumbed to boredom ages ago," I tell her as the first car pulls up and a kid hops out.

The kids did the Wild Child Preschool name justice today. No one wanted to stay on task, and there was a steady stream of kids going to the bathroom all day. The only thing that trumped my excitement for the afternoon rest break was my excitement for pickup.

The three-year-olds must have been just as bad because as the last car pulls away, Candace looks at me and pleads, "Can I retire yet?"

"Well, you are getting up there in years…"

"I'm thirty-five!" she yells at me.

"Don't use shouty capitals on me. I'm not old enough to have hearing loss, unlike some of us."

"I really am going to retire and leave all these kids to you," Candace taunts as she walks into her classroom.

I laugh all the way back to my classroom. I love working here. I hit the job lottery when I got this one. My coworkers are amazing, and I can see my parents whenever I want to.

Speaking of my parents, I pull my phone out of my purse to see what I missed while it was on Do Not Disturb all day.

A couple texts from Mom and Riley.

MOM: I'm going to the nursery to get spring flowers today. Lunch at SS then head over?

MOM: Ignore that last message. Today is Tuesday, and you're at work. Now I have to go figure out why your father is home at 10 a.m. on a Tuesday.

MOM: He decided to take a few days off before the tourist season starts. I'm making him go to the nursery with me for not telling me. I'll get something that looks nice for your planters. Love you!

Oh, Lord. My dad will never live this one down. He better have taken her to lunch and carried the flowers.

ME: Whatever you pick out will be great! Thanks!

Let's see what Riley wanted.

RILEY: Why do you always pick the books with arm porn? <eye roll emoji> It's a good thing I don't have to read this as a physical book. I'd never live it down.

RILEY: OMG. This book. It's all the things. My dad keeps grouching at me to put my phone down and get to work. I had to lie and tell him I was trying to figure out which tampons I need to put on my grocery pick-up, extra heavy or super heavy. He stopped harassing me after that, but now I feel guilty and have to get back to work.

RILEY: Lunch update. Their angst is giving me angst, and there's no one here I would even consider having angst with. Can tourist season start already? Can we please go out soon?????

ME: Yes! Shipwrecked Saturday?

She replies immediately with a string of cocktail emojis.

I set my phone down and pick up the stack of worksheets from today. Since the kids seemed to be falling prey to the pull of the full moon, I had them draw their favorite thing to do when it warms up.

The first one on the pile is a picture of a sailboat on blue water with a sunny sky. That's a weird coincidence. The rest were as expected. Pool, beach, baseball, ride bikes. I put stickers on them and put them in their mailboxes to take home tomorrow.

I stand up to leave, and my phone dings. It is a picture of my front porch with my newly filled planters and a message from my mom.

MOM: I had your dad plant these for you. Make sure you water them tonight.

ME: Thanks, guys. They look amazing!

I put my phone back in my purse and get my keys out.

I walk out the back exit and get in Chili. I'm really feeling fresh seafood for dinner tonight, so I drive down to the wharf.

There is only one person standing under the large pavilion where fishermen sell their catch of the day and tourists book excursions. I'm assuming the boat moored to the end of the extensive dock belongs to him. I have never seen him or his boat before.

When I get a little closer, I can make out the name of his boat. Bro and Tell. I'm suddenly not so sure about this, but I'm committed since I already walked halfway to the pavilion from the parking lot.

"Yo, bro. Sup?" he calls when I get close enough to hear.

I'm not sure how to answer that. Is he asking me what I'm doing or what I need? I'm going to go with the latter.

"Hi. What fresh catch do you have left?"

"I got a couple sick snowy grouper and a nasty swordfish. Thing pulled like a modded out Cummins."

Now I'm even more concerned for my life if I eat these fish.

"I'll, uh, I'll take the snowy grouper," I stammer.

"Bet," he acknowledges as he wraps the fish up and hands it to me.

"Are you from around here? I don't think I have ever seen you down here before," I pry as I hand him some cash.

"Nah, bro. I go where life takes me until I find a broasis to stay for a while. Just gonna do a little brobalization 'til then."

Is he even speaking English?

"Well, good luck to you," I say, hoping that was the right response. I walk to Chili to make the drive back across town. On my way, I see a new billboard went up today.

A sinfully sexy model is standing on the deck of a charcoal sailboat with a vibrant green sail. If that were a book cover, I would read it based on his vibe alone. Do these guys even exist in real life?

"What is with all these sailboats? I get it, universe! I have been holding onto this fear for far too long. I better get rewarded with a night spent with that guy when I conquer my fear," I say to my car.

I drive through the picturesque neighborhood, waving at parents of former students as they tend their flowerbeds or mow. I pull in my driveway and shut off my car. The red poppies and impatiens with raven ipomoea filler really did wonders with the curb appeal. I painted the door a deep red when I moved in to give the gray home a little character, so the flowers really add to the whole look.

I grab my purse and the possibly spoiled grouper and walk inside. Looking at the fish on my kitchen counter, I decide you only live once. I pull out a baking sheet and some spices and get to work.

After I close the oven door on the fish, I sauté some asparagus. The oven timer dings, and I sit down to a delicious meal for one.

A little thought in the back of my mind wonders if it will always be like this.

CHAPTER 3
LIKE A PIRATE FABIO

Sawyer

"Well, if it isn't the cover model himself. I'm glad you got back from location in time to hang out tonight. Do I need to start booking a slot with your assistant to see you?" Mason chuckles as he walks in the front door of my house carrying a six-pack.

I look up from the white oak hardwood flooring I am nailing down in my living room. "Fuck you, asshole. It was supposed to be a picture of The Emerald under full sail. I had just trimmed the mainsail and was waiting for everything to level out before I went below deck so the photographer could take some pictures. She must have taken that one while I was waiting to make sure my boat wasn't going to sink without anyone steering her."

"Then why weren't you wearing a shirt?" he fires back at me.

"Because the photographer spilled her drink all over me when we hit a wave on the way out," I defend myself.

Mason bursts into laughter as he opens a beer and puts the rest in my fridge.

"I don't even want to know how many times I overheard people asking if they thought your abs were airbrushed or how much you work out."

"Seriously?" I ask.

"I also heard more than one mom wondering if you do private lessons. From the way they said it, I don't think they were actually interested in sailing." He snorts as he hands me a board off the stack.

I take it from him and look up at the ceiling. "Ugh. I'm going to fire Emily." I fit the tongue and groove board into the next spot and grab the floor nailer. "This is all her fault. She convinced me that we needed to up our advertising to draw in more tourists before they book excursions on The Boardwalk. I finally told her to go for it so she would leave me alone. She set up the photo shoot and made all the decisions on the final ads. The first time I saw any of it was when I drove to Pirate's Life today," I complain as I swing the mallet, nailing the board down.

Laughing, Mason replies, "I saw the billboard on my way to the clinic this morning. I about dumped my coffee when I saw my best friend posing on his boat like some sort of Pirate Fabio. Luscious locks blowing in the wind, bare chest gleaming in the sun. Looking like he was about to rip the bodice off some eighteenth century virgin."

I give him a one-finger salute, and he laughs harder.

I take a measurement for the last board on this row and go outside to cut a piece of flooring. On the way back inside, I stop at the fridge and grab one of Mason's craft beers. Beer always tastes better when you don't have to buy it. Maybe Mason's beer just tastes better because he buys the expensive stuff.

"You drink that, and you're going to have to do extra crunches to keep the ladies drooling over your next sailing magazine cover. I never thought I would see the day Sawyer Davis had to sell his body to keep food on the table. Didn't the SEALs teach you any useful skills you could have turned to?"

"If I told you, I'd have to kill you using one of those skills," I tell him as I put down the cut piece of flooring.

He just laughs and takes another drink of his beer, unfazed by my threat.

"This is coming together really nicely, Saw," Mason says, looking around the unfinished house I started building last year. I have only finished the master suite and the four season room. The rest of the house is barely functional. "Your mom and sister did a good job picking the paint and finishes."

"Who knew Savannah was good for more than mixing drinks and slinging beer?" I ask.

"Everybody has a hidden talent somewhere," he remarks as he takes another drink of his beer.

I put the last board down in this section of the living room and stand up, stretching my back.

"I'm starving. I'm going to throw some burgers on the grill. Do you want one?" I ask.

"Only if you take your shirt off while you grill them, Fabio."

When I walk into Pirate's Life the next morning, I consider turning around and going straight to the dock. Emily is talking to someone on the phone, and the front desk is littered with Sticky Notes.

She sees me walk through the door and mouths "Stop." I hold up my lunch and motion to the small storage room off to the side of the main area that we use to store snacks and drinks for excursions. I installed a kitchenette so we can have a sink, coffee pot, and mini fridge to keep our lunches in as well.

When I walk back out, she is off the phone but still clicking around on the computer.

"Morning, Em. Busy day already?"

She pierces me with a peeved look. "This phone has been ringing off the hook, and the messages are piling up in our socials. I've just been deleting the ones from girls asking you to call them and the ones that are just boob pictures. What is wrong with people?" she asks.

"Well, to be fair, you did plaster my bare chest on a fourteen-foot-tall billboard in the middle of town."

"You have lived here your entire life. Don't people know you look like that?" She motions up and down my body.

"Before joining the Navy and going through BUD/S, I wasn't this flashing display of masculinity you see before you. My discharge became official two years ago, and I moved back right after. I have thrown my entire life into opening Pirate's Life and building a house. I pretty much gave up partying before I came back, so I haven't exactly been Mr. Social Hour here."

"Well, it's a good thing I went with the thirst trap then. At this rate, Pirate's Life is going to be fully booked this season, and your social life needs the boost. I'll start forwarding the decent ones your way," Emily cackles as the phone rings again.

She answers cheerfully and goes back to clicking away. I could never do her job. When I opened this place, she was the only person who applied for the front desk job, so I called her in for an interview. She had just graduated high school and wasn't sure what her future held. Her only plans were to get a job and never be dependent on anyone ever again. From the way her worn-out clothes hung off her body and her long blond hair looked a little dirty, I could tell she was slightly malnourished and could only guess at the reasons for the rest of her appearance.

With her show of determination and a little sympathy, I hired her on the spot. I gave her a five-hundred-dollar sign-on bonus that I hadn't planned on being part of the job offer, and she has been my right hand ever since. We have built this place together, and I couldn't do it without her. It scares me a little that I let someone who can't legally drink be in charge of my business, but she manages this place down to the tiniest detail.

I walk over to my office and sit behind my desk. I pull up the schedule for this weekend. I am starting a new program this year. It is a four-week introductory sailing course that will start on the first Saturday of each month. I spent quite a bit of money buying four Portland Pudgies, so I hope I can get enough interest to make my money back.

Looks like there is one spot left for the first session. The rest of the season is about half full. That is promising. I took a gamble since only locals or people who live relatively close will want to do this class. It's not geared toward tourists, which is where the majority of my income stems from. I may be able to compress it into two days for someone on vacation, but I will have to see how people do.

I see Emily has already printed out all the forms and materials each person will need and placed them in charcoal folders with the cream and emerald Pirate's Life logo on the front. They are in a box labeled *Saturday Sailing Class* in her neat handwriting.

I check my email to see if Emily has forwarded me anything from the Pirate's Life email. There is a technical question from a past client and someone looking for a lesson on a specific sailing technique. I reply to the two emails and my phone starts dinging. I look down as it dings again. The family chat is going crazy. I open the thread to see what my parents or sister want.

SAV: You owe me a car detail for the vomit on my floorboard from seeing you almost naked on my way to Shipwrecked to do inventory this morning.

MOM: Your dad and I are traveling this week. Sawyer, why are you almost naked in public in the middle of the morning? What's going on?

SAV: Sawyer put his half naked self on a billboard on Ocean Blvd.

MOM: Oh, honey. I know you haven't dated since you got back home and didn't date while you were in the service, but this isn't how you put yourself out there.

SAV: He put himself out there all right. <vomit emoji>

DAD: Don't you kids use Nugget for that kind of thing these days?

SAV: Tinder, Dad.

DAD: I knew it was some chicken thing.

SAV: <facepalm emoji>

ME: I didn't put that picture up there! Emily wanted to do some advertising for Pirate's Life, and I told her to go for it. She approved the final ads.

MOM: Does Emily have a thing for you? You're entirely too old for that sweet girl.

ME: Emily doesn't have a thing for me, and I'm not that old.

MOM: Good because if you dated her and broke her heart, she would have to quit, and there is no way you can manage the office like she does.

MOM: You aren't getting any younger and neither am I. I'm ready for some grandbabies, so you need to find someone who has a thing for you. Just not your barely legal office manager.

ME: I have a sister who can have kids too. Why are you putting this on me?

SAV: I'd love to pop out some mini-mes. Got any hot, single friends?

ME: Stay away from Mason.

MOM: ...

Why are they this way?

My phone rings. Pirate's Life is calling me.

"What do you need, Emily?" I answer.

"Do you have anything going on this afternoon? Someone just called and asked if you could take them on a ride around Twin Peaks. There isn't anything on the schedule, but with your newfound popularity, I wasn't sure if you had a personal appointment."

"No, Emily. I don't have a personal appointment," I say snidely. "I can take them out whenever they want."

"They said one o'clock."

"Sounds good," I tell her.

"They said you can leave your shirt on since it's a little nippley today."

I hang up on her without responding. I can hear her laughter from here.

CHAPTER 4
THAT'S WHAT SHE SAID

Avery

I am determined to conquer my deep-set fear of water. This has gone on long enough. I live by one of the best beaches in the world, and I need to be able to enjoy it to the fullest.

At least that is what I tell myself in my bathroom mirror as I blow-dry my hair and get ready for work. I leave my hair in flowing waves and slip a short-sleeved cream sundress over my head. I pair it with cute leopard flats all the little girls in my class love.

I grab my to-go cappuccino, jean jacket, and purse, and I'm out the door. The sky is overcast and dreary, so Mrs. Shorter is waiting for her paper inside this morning.

The first few raindrops are sprinkling my windshield when I pull into my parking space at Wild Child. I hurry inside before I get drenched.

The rain shower lasts most of the day, keeping the kids subdued. The grey sky has them yawning with droopy eyes for most of the morning. I give up on keeping them awake and turn off the lights to let them have a longer than normal rest period after lunch. The sound of the rain pattering against the window is the perfect background melody.

With the kids snoozing, I decide to make a pros and cons list for taking the sailing class.

Cons
1. Deep water
2. Fall off the boat and drown
3. Panic and make a fool of myself in front of other people

4. Dredge up memories I would rather not relive

Pros:

1. Conquer fear of water

2. Get a new hobby that will give me a suntan

3. See more of the crystal clear blue water

4. Meet a hot sailing model

After I write the last one, I scratch it off as unlikely. Where am I going to sail this boat? A Sailing World photo shoot? Not likely.

I waffle back and forth, talking myself out of the class then getting inspired to see it through.

Right before I wake the kids up, I add another line to the Pros column that pretty much seals the deal.

5. Aspen would want me to live my life

When I get my after-school work done, I gather my things and step outside. The storm has cleared, leaving behind a fresh smell to the air and a magnificent double rainbow over the town. I take this as a good omen and drive to the cute charcoal building by the shore.

I make sure to drive under the speed limit as I pass by the billboard advertising Pirate's Life so I can stare a little longer. Where do they find these models?

I park in the large gravel lot to the side of the building. From this angle, I can see the dock where the boats are parked. Three small yellow boats that look like rubber duckies are moored to one side of the dock.

A large black catamaran with two relaxing nets on the back, a curly slide on the front, and some sort of swinging line in the middle is docked on the opposite side. There is a green flag attached to the top of the pole in the middle of the boat with the Pirate's Life logo waving in the breeze. That boat looks like a lot of fun. I would love to spend an afternoon drinking rum punch with Riley as we sunbathe or try out the slide.

A small cream dive boat with charcoal and green intertwined accents is moored by the catamaran. It looks like there is some scuba equipment on board.

Beside that boat is a sleek sail boat with a charcoal bottom like the one used in the advertisements. I bet it is beautiful up close. Maybe one day I will book an afternoon sail on that one.

Hold up there, Gilligan. You need to sign up for the class and actually get on a boat before you start making big plans to sail one.

I walk around to the front of the building and go inside. There is country music playing in the background, and a cute blond girl wearing a Pirate's Life tee and short jean shorts looks up from the desk when she hears the door shut.

"Let me guess. You want a private sailing lesson," she huffs with a snooty voice.

"Oh, umm. No, I don't want a private lesson. I saw an advertisement," I falter.

"Everyone saw that advertisement." She cuts me off with an eye roll for emphasis on how inferior I am.

I can feel my cheeks getting a little warm as I think of what advertisement she is talking about. The one I have most definitely drooled over. Twice.

"No, I saw an advertisement on social media for a four-day beginner sailing course. I am interested in that one. With other people," I stammer through my thoughts.

I don't know if her off-putting nature is making me nervous or if the thought of what I am signing myself up for is getting to me now that I'm actually seeing it through.

Her demeanor instantly changes, and she smiles. "Well, you are in luck then. There is one spot left in the class that starts Saturday."

"This Saturday? Like the day after tomorrow?" I ask like a dunce.

"Uh, yeah. That is the first Saturday of the month. Will that work for you?"

"Yes, sorry. I was just a little surprised you could get me in so quickly," I reply as I muster my confidence.

"Sawyer just started the weekend program this year. You will be in the inaugural class, so there might be kinks to work out," she explains as she starts clicking around on her computer.

She must see my face fall as my anxiety ramps back up.

"Don't worry, though. He is an excellent teacher and takes any and all safety precautions when on the water with clients."

I try to calm myself down enough to finish the sign-up process. I can do this. This is just paperwork. No water involved.

"Okay. I will take the last spot."

She asks for my information, and I give her my card to pay for the class.

"The payment cleared, so you are good to start this Saturday. The first week is an indoor class. Sawyer will go through boater safety and laws. It will likely take around three hours. The next week you will learn how to handle the Pudgies on the beach behind this building. You won't see any water time until week three."

She must see my face relax with the realization that I have two more weeks to prepare myself to get in the water.

"You sure you want to learn how to sail?" she asks me with concern.

No, I'm not sure at all. I'm freaking out on the inside more than I'm freaking out on the outside, which is apparently a lot.

I tell her the exact opposite. "Yes, I am looking forward to trying something new."

She doesn't look convinced as she hands me my receipt. "We will see you Saturday at nine then. Thanks for coming in, Avery!"

I walk out the door and back around the side of the building to the parking lot. My heart is racing, and I need to calm down.

The whole process took less than fifteen minutes and probably shed that many years off my life.

I get to my car, sit down, and close my eyes. I try to clear my head of all thoughts and focus on my breathing. After a few minutes, I can feel myself returning to normal.

I get out my phone to text Riley.

ME: SOS I need to talk to you.

She responds immediately.

RILEY: Call, text, or meet up? What's your status?

ME: I am good enough to wait until we can meet. Salty Dogs for dinner?

RILEY: Sounds good. I can be there in 45 minutes. I have to get this carburetor put back together. Is that soon enough?

ME: Yes

I start my car and drive to the gourmet hot dog stand on The Boardwalk. This place is a Wild Shore staple. There is always a line no matter what time of day you go.

I secure us a table and people watch until Riley shows up. A group of young teenagers must have thrown some bread or other food on the ground because a flock of gulls is swarming them. The gulls are screeching and diving at the kids, causing them to scream and laugh.

I remember those days, messing around on the beach with Aspen and our friends. Not a care in the world. I look away as sadness washes over me.

The breaking of the waves invades my consciousness. I try not to think about being out on that water in the near future.

"Okay. I'm here. What's the SOS situation? You look equal parts like you are going to cry and have a meltdown. Which one do we need to address first?" she questions as she slides onto the bench across from me.

"Let's get food first since there are only three people in line," I declare as I stand up and walk to the stand.

"Whenever you are ready, we can talk. Or you don't have to talk and we can just hang out. You know I'm always up for having dinner with my bestie," Riley assures me as she hugs me to her side.

"I'm not quite ready to talk yet."

Riley nods, not pressuring me anymore.

When it is our turn, Benny asks, "What can I get you, ladies?"

Riley says, "I'll have two New Yorkers and a Coke."

He gives her the total, and she pays. He looks in my direction.

"I'll have the Georgia and a Coke," I decide. I can see Riley's eyes bug out. We only get the Georgia if we are at DEFCON 1.

"Yep. It's been that kind of day," I confirm as I hand over some cash and put the change in the tip jar.

Benny turns to fix our dinners and then hands them over.

"Thanks," we both say, and we walk back to our table.

Riley digs into a hot dog with mustard, sauerkraut, and onion sauce, while I unwrap a fork to eat what is basically hot dog nachos.

"So I signed up to take sailing lessons," I say.

29

Riley chokes on her hot dog and coughs to dislodge her food. She takes a drink before saying, "You can't say things like that when I'm eating. Were you trying to make me choke on this wiener?"

I look at her and banter, "That's what she said."

"I'm only allowing it because you did something huge today," Riley gripes.

"That's also what she said. Maybe what he said," I try to get out between laughs. Riley just rolls her eyes.

"But seriously, how are you feeling? That is a huge step."

"Honestly, I was terrified when I went into the office. The girl at the desk was mean, and that made it worse."

"Where is this place? I'm going to show that bitch a little something about how to treat customers," Riley explodes angrily, cutting me off.

"It's fine. I think she has been really busy with people coming in and not scheduling anything or something. When I told her I wanted to take the four-week course, she changed her attitude."

"So where are you taking this course? I want to check it out before you go out on the water with someone whose boat isn't sound enough to make it back."

"It is a place just down from here called Pirate's Life."

"Wait. Is that the place that just put up the new billboard on Ocean Boulevard everyone is going crazy about?" Riley asks.

"Yes. I'm not real sure why everyone is freaking out about a shirtless male model on a boat. Do these people not read magazines or watch TV?" I reply.

"I don't know. He is pretty good-looking in a pirate of the high seas kind of way. Maybe everyone else is as starved for hot men as we are, and seeing him on that billboard has their imaginations revving. They don't make them like that in real life. Photoshop to the rescue!" Riley mimics a superhero voice.

"More's the shame because he's pretty much perfect. I don't know if I could be held responsible for my actions if I were alone with him."

"Great. I can see it from here. Our next book is going to feature a pirate who steals a demure scholarly woman, a teacher if you will, from a small seaside town and has his way with her on his boat until they fall madly in love. I'll go ahead and get my corset and pantaloons ready."

I burst into laughter at her antics. I knew she would make me feel better about my day and less anxious about starting this class.

"Thanks for being my best friend," I tell her sincerely.

"Right back at you, Avery. You aren't getting rid of me anytime soon.

CHAPTER 5
WELL-BALANCED CHAKRAS

Sawyer

I get to Pirate's Life a little earlier on Saturday morning than I normally do. I am a bit nervous about teaching this class. I have taught several people how to sail, but I have never done it in a group setting before. I am worried about juggling a racehorse, a snail, and a few in between.

I walk up the narrow staircase at the back of the building. The upstairs used to be an apartment. When I started teaching sailing lessons, I needed a place to do boater safety and laws of the sea, so I slowly remodeled the upstairs to fit our needs.

Emily left the box of folders, a cup of pens emblazoned with the Pirate's Life logo, and a stack of koozies on the desk beside the laptop and projector. I put one of each on the white plastic table in front of every chair.

I can't think of anything else the clients would need, so I turn on the laptop and link the projector. I open the slideshow I made for this class and click through the slides to make sure everything I need to cover is there.

The presentation looks fine, but I am still a little anxious. I have invested a lot of time and money on this venture, and it would be great if it worked out.

I hear footsteps walking up here, so I look over when Emily reaches the top of the stairs.

"I figured I would find you up here way too early this morning freaking out about things that we have checked, rechecked, and checked again just for good measure," she chides as she hands me a large coffee from Rise and Dine.

"I had mixed feelings about getting this for you. I couldn't decide if you would be a zombie this morning from not sleeping at all last night or if you would be bouncing off the walls freaking out about this class going as planned. From the look of you, it's a little of both. You are pretty much a hyperactive zombie."

"Thanks, Em. You truly are a sweetheart," I say sarcastically as I take the first drink of java.

"I see you already got the swag passed out." She notices as she takes a drink of her coffee. She looks around the room, taking in the remodeled space. "I'm glad you went with the open, airy concept and tore all the walls down. Those rough beams where the walls used to be really add character."

She walks over to the far corner to look inside the bathroom. "Oh! This is nice! The dark grout really brings out the marbling in the tile. Oh, and the square sink. I like the modern touch to the natural theme you have going on. I haven't been up here in a while, so I didn't know you finished this," she says as she walks back over to me. "Just in time to use for this class."

"Yeah. No one can say they need to use the bathroom, slip out the front door, and never come back if this sucks. They are trapped up here until it's over."

"We already have their money, so it's their loss if they did," Emily utters with a shrug.

Always business. The way she grew up really did a number on her outlook on life.

"The class starts in an hour. You need to get out of here for a little while. Burn off some adrenaline. You are going to make me nervous about today, and I just run the front desk. Go take a Pudgy out in the cove. Recenter yourself," Emily urges.

"Fine, but only because I don't have anything else to do, and I haven't checked the boats this morning," I declare as I grab my coffee and walk to the stairs. "It's not because I need to 'recenter myself,'" I grouse.

I continue muttering as I walk out the back door. "When did she turn into Buddha? Center myself," I scoff. "Next she'll be telling me to do some downward dog bullshit and have well-balanced chakras."

The sun is shining in a blue sky dotted with puffy clouds, and the wind is blowing off the water strong enough to make the Pirate's Life flag on the Jolly Rodger flap. It is the perfect day for sailing. I untie a Portland Pudgy and use an oar to maneuver away from the dock.

The single sail system goes up in no time. I have sailed every one of these small boats to make sure they are ready for the class to sail in a couple weeks.

I play around in the cove, releasing stress and anxiety and having some fun. I race from one side to the other a few times, do some figure eights, and perform some awesome quick stops because these boats are so small.

It is almost time for the class to start. It probably won't look too good for the instructor to be late to the first class because he was out screwing around on a class boat.

I dock the Pudgy and throw the moorings on. I will have to come back after the class and stow the sail. It will be fine for a few hours.

I jog the path to the back door, a little out of breath from the uphill climb.

"You are almost late. Everyone showed up, and I sent them upstairs," Emily shouts at me as I take the steps two at a time to reach the second floor.

I take the last step out of the stairwell and stop to slow my breathing when I am ambushed from behind. I turn instinctively to defend myself when someone grabs my bicep with both hands. I have to lower my gaze to see who is holding on to me tighter than a barnacle and smells like vanilla and wildflowers.

The first thing I notice is a head that barely reaches my shoulder covered in light blond hair with some darker strands mixed in.

The hair shifts, and my eyes connect with eyes as blue as the deep water on a sunny day with a ring of amber around the pupils. I take a small step back to take in the rest of her.

My Mars crashes into Uranus. If my chakras were unbalanced earlier, they are not even on the same plane now. I could definitely go for some downward doggy style.

She is wearing a pink V-neck T-shirt that gives me a peak of her more than a handful tits. Her short jean shorts show off lean, lightly tanned legs. I wonder if she will let me find out what she has on underneath her clothes after class.

As I return my gaze back to her face, I stop on her shiny, full lips. The mental images of them wrapped around my cock about do me in.

It takes a few seconds before I return to her eyes, and the emotion there almost stops me in my tracks. Pure anxiety. I don't know how I missed that the first time.

It is then that I realize the grasp she has on my arm isn't merely to keep her from falling on her ass, which is probably as sexy as the rest of her. It's more of a "Save me from this situation" full-on grab. Her pupils are becoming more dilated, which I highly doubt is with desire.

Here I am thinking about getting her naked, and this poor woman is about to have a panic attack. My SEAL training kicks in, and I go into medic mode.

"Hey, my name is Sawyer. Can you tell me your name?"

"Ave-Avery," she stutters as her breathing starts to quicken.

"Nice to meet you, Avery. You are safe with me. Is there anything I can do for you?" I ask softly.

"Ju-Just give me a minute. Can I keep holding on to your arm?"

If any other woman did this to me, I would call bullshit. *I wasn't paying attention to where I was going and slammed into you. I'm so scared. Let me run my hands up and down your bulging muscles until I feel better.*

With Avery, I can tell this is a fight-or-flight response, and I will do everything in my power to help her get through this. I want to keep her safe and close to me.

That thought startles me almost more than the lightning bolt of desire from a few minutes ago. It's not like I haven't ever seen an attractive woman. Granted it has been a while, but I'm a grown-ass man. I can control my reactions, but something about this woman brings my protective instincts screeching to the surface.

My back is turned to the class, so no one can see what is happening in front of me. My focus is on Avery. I don't even know if they are looking this way, but I want to shield her from their curious gazes just in case.

After a couple minutes, the hold she has on my bicep loosens and her pupils begin to shrink back to normal size.

"Thank you. I am really sorry I ran into you and interrupted the class. I should probably leave. This is so embarrassing," she admits as she looks around me at the people sitting in the classroom.

"Hey," I say, making her look back at me. "You don't have to leave on my account. You didn't interrupt anything. The class hasn't even started. If you are comfortable, I would like you to stay. I can't guarantee the quality of my public speaking or how entertaining the material will be, though. I can only do so much with boater safety and the laws of the sea," I plead, hoping to lighten up the situation and make her stay.

Every part of my being needs to spend more time with this woman. I want to know what caused the attack and what I can do to prevent another one. I know if she steps out the door, I will never see her again, and that doesn't sit right with me.

"Everyone in the class just saw what happened. What are they thinking about me? *That desperate woman will try anything to get close to him.*"

"I'm not worried about what they think. You and I both know what happened, and that's all that matters."

"This is a new season in my life, and I need to learn to sail," she says.

"Well, then let's get started."

"I hate to delay class anymore, but could you give me a minute to compose myself?"

"Sure. Take all the time you need. I'll entertain everyone with my charm and wit until you get back."

The anxiety in her eyes turns to relief. I want to protect her so that emotion never clouds the deep blue depths again.

"Thanks, Sawyer."

And just like that, the sound of my name coming from those lips is making it really hard to focus on sailing. I watch the sway of her hips until the bathroom door closes. I inhale deeply and exhale slowly, trying to calm myself down.

I walk to the front of the classroom and perch one hip on the desk by the projector. They start to notice me one by one and stop their conversations to face forward.

"Hello, everyone. I'm Sawyer Davis. I own Pirate's Life and will be teaching this course. There are a few topics that I have to follow a strict guideline, but for the most part, I like to cater to what you guys want to know. First off, you probably want to know a little more about me and Pirate's Life," I start.

A middle-aged lady interrupts, "Yeah, like if that billboard is photoshopped."

Everyone starts laughing.

"He said he would tell us what we wanted to know. Well, that's a pretty hot topic right now," she says with a chuckle.

"A man never tells his secrets," I respond as Avery walks to the front of the classroom and sits in the middle seat right in front of me.

"I will tell you that I have been sailing since I could push a dinghy off the bank. Most of my sailing knowledge has been trial and error, so lucky for you guys, you can learn from my mishaps."

They all chuckle.

"I have sailed every nook and cranny of the shoreline around this town and a lot of the deep water when I got a little older. After I graduated high school, I joined the Navy. I was honorably discharged two years ago.

"I came home to Wild Shore and decided to open Pirate's Life. We have been steadily growing and adding more excursions and activities. This is the first group sailing class, but I have taught many private sailing lessons before this. Pirate's Life offers private sailings on a Saffier SE 33, party cruises on a 45' catamaran, snorkel tours, and sightseeing tours, and my office manager, Emily, is a Rescue Diver and Emergency First Responder. She is working on her Divemaster Certification so we can add scuba tours and conduct refresher scuba training as well.

"After you complete this class, let us know if there is anything in particular you want to do. We can likely accommodate you," I finish my introduction and business plug.

I pick up the remote from the desk and start the slideshow.

CHAPTER 6
MORTIFICATION, NO BREATHING

Avery

I am slightly mortified. And by slightly, I mean I will probably keel over from embarrassment at any time, causing my corpse more embarrassment.

I arrived at Pirate's Life about fifteen minutes before the class started. I was doing fine, looking through a window at a car driving across Magnolia Ridge headed to The Split.

Two people walked up the stairs chatting about the sailboat in the cove and how whatever maneuvers the person was doing about flipped the small boat.

They started talking about all the stories they had heard about sailboats capsizing or getting caught out in storms and torn to pieces.

My palms got clammy, and I could feel my heart pounding in my chest. I stood up and went to the room across from the stairs I was hoping was a bathroom to splash some cold water on my face.

The anxiety I have had since Thursday was giving way to a panic attack. I decided I should just leave since I'm not ready for this big of a step.

I stepped out of the bathroom and walked face first into a brick wall. Luckily, the wall had a muscular arm I could grab ahold of to anchor my mind and body.

When I calmed down enough to really see who I was holding onto, I almost fainted. I couldn't be totally sure since he was wearing an emerald green, short-sleeved, button-up shirt, but the model from the billboard was standing in front of me. Clove and sandalwood engulfed me in a cloud as masculine as him.

My eyes were drawn to his face. His melted chocolate eyes filled with concern and maybe something deeper. Darker. My emotions went haywire as desire took the place of anxiety deep in my stomach.

And I just clung to his arm like a baby koala bear. Every meet-cute fantasy I had in the last few days crashed and burned, the fire feeding my humiliation.

Luckily, his smooth voice worked some voodoo magic on my panic attack by inciting my libido, and I was able to reel it in. After calming myself down in the bathroom, I exit, more aware of my surroundings this time.

I return to my front and center seat just as Sawyer finishes his introduction.

He is currently going through a slideshow about boater safety. I missed the first part since I was basically held hostage by his over-the-top handsomeness and virile masculinity.

The combination of light brown hair bleached by the sun and cut a little longer on top and shaved on the sides, milk chocolate eyes, and a scruffy beard framing his square jaw is swoon-worthy. I could do things to him a preschool teacher shouldn't even know about.

That catcher has nothing on Sawyer's arms. All those years of pulling ropes have definitely not gone to waste. His khaki cargo shorts pull against his muscular thighs as he moves around the front of the classroom. No wonder he put himself on a billboard to gain interest in his business. Who wouldn't want to spend time with him?

How noticeable would it be if I took a picture of his bicep and forearm as he lifts the slideshow clicker? For comparison purposes only. *Focus on boater safety, Avery. This is not the time. You may need this information one day.*

I drag myself out of my carnal musings as Sawyer begins telling a story about a friend named Mason.

"When Mason and I were probably eleven or twelve, we decided to take our inflatable sailboat down the coast. We had been sailing for probably an hour when a storm came out of nowhere. The wind whipped that little boat all over the place and ended up taking the sail with it. The storm pushed us down toward Twin Peaks. My mom had threatened us with everything, including death, if she ever found us or heard about us sailing down there. We had no way to sail home and couldn't call Mom because we weren't about to be picked up at Twin Peaks and face her wrath. Mason and I had no choice but to row the boat all the way back to where we were supposed to be.

"Luckily, a fisherman came by and helped us. We ate candy bars and drank Cokes while he towed our boat back to shore. My mom was furious when she found out we were out in the storm and lost the sail, but I don't think she ever found out we were by Twin Peaks. We lived to sail another day.

"So lesson learned here is to always check the weather before you go out. There won't always be a friendly fisherman to save your ass," he concludes, and everyone chuckles at his story.

"Let's take a little break before we begin the second half of today's class. See you guys in ten minutes," Sawyer dismisses us.

I don't need to go to the bathroom, and I brought my metal water jug with me, so I pull my phone out of my purse to scroll.

Just as I click on the social media icon, the air around me starts to sizzle, causing my nipples to take notice of the change in the atmosphere. I slowly raise my eyes from my phone to his lean hips, up his muscular torso, and over wide shoulders to meet his gaze as he stops in front of me.

"How are you doing? It seemed like you handled the safety talk pretty well. Was I too boring?"

"No, you did a great job! I learned a lot." *Like when you smile, you get little lines around your eyes, and your voice gets a happy timbre when you talk about your friends and family.*

"Good. Emily told me the slideshow brought back too many memories of suffering through high school, and I need to do something else. I'm glad I can prove her wrong," he gloats.

"I never said that. I said it was informative," I respond with a smile.

His face breaks into an answering grin, showing his straight, white teeth and dimples. My ovaries sigh simultaneously.

"You've got jokes," he banters as he leans his hip into the table across from me.

"Mostly just sarcasm that only resonates with a small set of elite people. Welcome to the group. We meet on Thursdays," I reply saucily.

"Thanks for the invite. I have been waiting on this membership opportunity for a while."

I have to look away from him before he sees my eyes bug out at the acceptance of the fake invitation. I meant it as a joke, since he is way out of my league. I am pretty and work out to keep up with four-year-olds, but he is panty-melting sexy. I don't know how to take his acceptance since we were joking around. Would he accept an offer for a real date? Would I have the lady balls to ask him?

He does me a favor and breaks the silence. "Well, Avery, I hope the rest of the class is as inspiringly educational as the first half. Send me a signal if I start sounding like Charlie Brown's teacher," he jokes as he stands back up.

I laugh and say, "Will do."

The rest of the class continues like the first half. Sawyer's voice puts me in a lust hypnosis, so I only catch the high points of what he is saying. I know most of this information already since I have always lived by the water, but some of it is new. Through his random stories about Mason and Savannah, I feel like I get to know him more than anyone I have met since Riley.

The slideshow goes black as Sawyer clicks off of the last screen.

"Okay, how was your first class? Everyone ready to get outside next Saturday?"

Everyone cheers.

"All right then. That's all the boring stuff, I promise. Next week we will bring the Portland Pudgies out to the beach to learn some basic sailing techniques and all the neat features these boats have. See you guys then," Sawyer dismisses us.

Everyone starts to chat as they scoot their chairs back and walk to the stairs. I feel weird not saying goodbye to Sawyer, but I don't want to make more out of our interaction than there was by staying behind to talk to him when no one else does.

I take my cue to leave when I see his back turned to me while he disconnects the laptop from the projector. I force my legs to walk away before I do anything to embarrass myself further.

"How was the class?" Riley asks as soon as she sits down at the high top I saved for us at Shipwrecked. The place is packed, and I can barely hear the juke box over the crowd.

"You are never going to believe this. Mr. Look at My Sculpted Chest Billboard Model owns Pirate's Life and is teaching the class. His name is Sawyer Davis," I spill in one breath.

"Shut the front door. First, is he as hot in person? Second, what kind of conceited asshole advertises for their business with their body? I would probably die of mortification if I had to see my tits and ass on a billboard every day when I drove in to work. Dead. No more breathing."

"Wouldn't your dad be the one on the billboard?" I ask.

"Oh, God. That might be even worse. Hairy chest and beer gut on display with oil-stained pants and a baseball hat that is older than me. We may never have another customer again." She shivers at her mental image.

I laugh at her reaction. I have met her dad many times in our six-year friendship. He is a wonderful guy, always ready with a smile, a joke, or an ear to listen.

"That's enough of that. Back to you. Answer my questions."

"Well, I was doing pretty good while I waited on the class to start. Then I overheard a conversation that put me into the beginning of a panic attack. I went to the bathroom to calm down. It didn't help. When I left the bathroom, I was in full-on panic mode and ran right into Sawyer.

"I grabbed his arm to keep from falling. He spoke to my soul with his melted chocolate eyes and audiobook narrator voice and calmed me down enough to stay for the rest of the class."

Riley just sits there and looks at me.

"What?" I ask.

"I don't even know where to start." She pauses for a few seconds. "Are you okay after the attack? The last one set you back for a little bit."

"Yes, I feel totally normal actually. I don't know if I didn't go as deep, or if Sawyer did something different to bring me out of it, but I have been fine the rest of the day."

"Good deal. So the actual class didn't bother you any?"

My mouth splits into a wide grin as I say, "I was bothered all right, but the material wasn't the cause. I spent the better part of the rest of the class fantasizing about him. Luckily, I know boater safety and the laws, so it's not a terrible problem. I'll be fine for the rest of the class," I tell her as I take a drink of my Wild Pirate, the cocktail special of the day.

"Jesus, Avery. At least you made it through the first day. Now I need to know the answers to my other questions."

"OMG, Riley. He is so much hotter in person than on the billboard, and he is so nice, not conceited at all. He was really concerned for me and even checked on me during the break. He was funny during the class and even laughed at my sarcasm." I sigh as I think about our encounters.

"Oh, no. Your face just got replaced with a heart eyes emoji."

"Shut up. You didn't feel his bicep or watch his tight ass as he walked back and forth all morning, or you would be in a puddle right next to me."

She bursts out into laughter. "Oh, girl. I can't wait to hear how the rest of this class goes."

The music changes to an iconic pop song, and a woman wearing a bright pink "Get Shipwrecked" crop top says into a mic, "That's right, people. It's Single Saturday! Where are all my single ladies? Get up here!"

One or two women walk up to the stage on unsteady legs. They have obviously had some liquid courage.

"That's not gonna do. I live here, too. I know what the dating pool looks like. There has to be a lot more single women in here tonight!"

She pauses to see if anyone else comes up to the makeshift stage in one corner.

"Everyone who participates gets a drink on the house!" she yells into the mic.

I look at Riley.

"I haven't had enough to drink for whatever she has planned."

"Well, this will get you one drink closer," I say as I stand up and grab her hand.

We make our way to the stage to cheers from the crowd.

"Okay, ladies. Tonight's competition is a dance-off. Who has been spending way too much time scrolling social media this week and knows all the dance trends?"

Riley glares at me. "What did you get us into?"

"I didn't know it was going to be a competition, but now my competitive side is kicking in. Let's do this!"

The woman's voice comes back out over the speakers. "Okay, ladies, line up on the front of the stage. I will play a song, and you will show us what you've got. The crowd will vote to see who goes to the next round."

After three rounds, Riley and I are the only ones left.

"Congratulations, ladies. We have one song left. Who is it going to be?" She pumps her hands palms up, and the crowd starts cheering so loudly I can barely hear myself think.

The music comes on, and I know I am going to win. I have done this dance hundreds of times in my kitchen. I start the moves, adding a little extra swing in my hips and pop to my chest. I'm killing it!

I happen to look over at Riley, and she is standing still with her fingers pointed in my direction.

I stop dancing and cover my face with my hands.

"I hate you," I mouth at her.

"This is your jam. You knew you were going to win."

"I think we have our winner! Thank you to everyone who played. See you all again next month for our next contest," the woman announces.

She comes close enough to say in my ear, "Congratulations, girl! All of your drinks are on the house tonight. If anyone asks, just tell them Sav said so." She walks off the stage, and the juke box turns back on.

"What did you win?" Riley asks as we walk off the stage.

"Free drinks tonight. We better get started on that! The Wild Pirate is on pointe, and I need another," I tell her as we walk toward the bar arm in arm.

CHAPTER 7
TWERKING GODDESS

Sawyer

I wipe the sweat off my brow as I unload the last Pudgy from the carrier onto the strip of beach between the office building and the dock. These things weigh less than 130 pounds, but their length makes them unwieldy out of the water.

The second beginner sailing class is tomorrow, and I need to check over the boats to make sure everything is accounted for. There is nothing worse than raising the sail and not having a corner tie or the grommet to tie it to.

My shirt flaps in the breeze as I finish the inventory. Everything is accounted for.

I look up when I hear the back door open. The person walking through makes me smile.

"Hey, Sav. I haven't seen you this week. Where have you been?"

"Oh, you know. Working my fingers to the bone to keep the family business alive while you frolic on the beach."

"It's not like you're out roofing houses or trimming trees. You pour beer and gossip," I say as she rises to her tiptoes to give me a hug. We both know there is a lot more that goes into our jobs than what meets the eye. We just like to razz each other about it.

"Speaking about my grueling job, you should have been at Shipwrecked on Saturday."

I shoot her a glare. "Do I look dumb? I know exactly what day that was. I have it circled and starred on my calendar as a day I have to find something, anything, to do other than go to

Shipwrecked. I don't need twenty single women getting drunk and handsy and throwing themselves at me."

"Well, it might help to change that attitude if they did. I was just telling you because this woman and her friend came last week, and I think you would be really interested in her."

"Why is that?" I challenge as I put my hands on my hips.

"They show up every month or so to have drinks on the deck. They are chill, just hanging out and not trolling. They aren't your average bar flies. I got the impression she and her friend didn't know it was Single Saturday. They just happened to come to the bar that night. She joked with her friend, didn't openly try to pick up any guys, and brushed the ones away who tried to pick her up. Her drinks were on the house, and she only had three. Oh, and she can drop it like it's hot and twerk like a pro."

"And why do you think this prime specimen is single?"

"It's just a vibe I got. We single women can spot each other in the wild."

A grin breaks out on my face at her answer. "How am I supposed to get in touch with this twerking goddess? You don't even know her name."

"Next time she comes in, can I give her your number?"

"I think I might have hit an all-time low with this one. My sister is picking up women for me at the bar."

"It's okay, big brother. It gets harder to meet people after you turn thirty."

"I'm not thirty yet!!! Did Mom put you up to this?" I ask incredulously.

Sav bends over, laughing. "No, but it's really funny that you think she would."

"I hate you," I say without meaning it. We have always been tight. She hung out with Mason and me a lot when we were

50

growing up. She called me once a week to catch up when I was a SEAL. Now we live in the same town again, and we normally see each other at least once a week and text a few times a week.

I feel kind of weird admitting this to my sister, even though we share pretty much everything. My hands slip off my hips and into the pockets of my shorts. I draw a line in the sand with the toe of my shoe. "I may not need that number. I might have met someone."

The look of shock on Savannah's face is priceless. She raises her hands in the air and shouts, "What? When? Why are you holding out on me? Does Mason know before me?"

"Wow. Calm down," I say as I put my hands palms down in front of me. "I haven't seen you to tell you about her, if there is anything to tell, and no, I haven't told Mason either. She is in my beginner sailing class. We met, she was working through some things, and I helped her with a situation."

Savannah crosses her arms and looks me up and down a few times. I am getting ready to ask her what she is doing, when she says, "I guess I'll start looking for a dress to wear to your wedding because you are a goner. You can't not fall for the damsel in distress. It's hard coded into your DNA to help people and make everything perfect," she says.

I have to stop myself from rolling my eyes like a teenager. "I only talked to her for a few minutes. No one is getting married."

"But this is a huge step for you. When was the last time you went out with anyone? Even a hookup?"

"I'm not telling my sister when the last time I got laid was."

"Been that long, huh? Kinda figured."

I give her an exasperated look.

"It's okay. You have been busy building a business and a house. Not everyone can handle a social life, too."

"Don't you have somewhere to be?"

"I'm actually meeting Mom for coffee at Rise and Dine in a few minutes. I just wanted to stop in and harass you since I had time and haven't seen you this week. I'll tell Mom to be on the lookout for a mother of the groom dress."

"Well, it's been less than fun, so I'll see you later," I tell her sarcastically.

"I'm glad you got to see me. I know you miss our bonding time," she says as she waves and walks back into the office.

I shake my head at her prattling and tie the boats to the makeshift dock I installed a few weeks ago just for this purpose.

My alarm goes off Saturday morning, and I practically hop out of bed to take a shower. I put a little more effort into getting ready this morning than I usually do. I don't want to think too hard about why that would be.

I trim my beard back to a respectable scruff and put some product in my hair before running my hands through it a few times. I apply moisturizer, sunblock, and a little cologne.

I pick out light gray golf shorts and a charcoal, short-sleeved Pirate's Life button-up. I leave the top three buttons undone like usual. I slip into my boat shoes and catch my reflection in the long mirror by the bathroom door. I look good, but not so good you can tell I spent a little bit of extra time getting ready this morning.

When I get to Pirate's Life, Emily is already at the front desk.

"Morning, Em. How's it going?"

"I got waitlisted for another Divemaster class. Will I ever get in? I just want to be able to add value to this place," she says sullenly.

"You are probably more valuable than me at this point, and yes, you will get in. You just have to be patient. It will happen when the time is right."

"Did you read that in your horoscope this morning?" she asks mockingly as I walk past her to my office.

"Are you wearing cologne? Wait, is your hair styled? Who is she?" she continues.

I keep walking and shut the door to my office. What is with the women in my life? Can't a guy just look nice without a reason?

"It's the blond one with the perky boobs, isn't it? Avery, right?" Emily yells through my door.

I put my head in my hands. Hopefully no one has shown up for the class yet. Not only is my employee yelling through the office, but she is discussing the assets of one of the women in the class, even if she does have a really fine *asset*.

I hear people start to come inside a few minutes later, so I take a deep breath. I can act normal around a woman I find attractive. I'm an adult, not a hormonal teenager.

I open the door to my office and see Avery in the lobby talking to Jill. I may need to make that a mantra today because my body is acting like a hormonal teenager at the sight of her.

Avery has on jeans shorts that are short enough that the front pockets hang out of the bottom, a brown tank top that dips low in the front, and boat shoes. Her blond hair is braided into two braids.

Holy mother of all fantasies. My cock takes notice and tries to get a better view through the zipper of my shorts. *I am not a hormonal teenager.*

I discreetly rearrange my semi-hard dick and walk the rest of the way to the lobby.

"Hey, guys. Looks like everyone is here, so let's get started." I try really hard not to stare at Avery as I make my opening comments. "Like I said last week, this week we are going to go over the basics of how to sail and the aspects of the boat. Any questions before we start?"

No one says anything.

"All right then. There are four Portland Pudgies outside on the beach. Pair up and pick your Pudgy. I will follow you out in a second."

They all file outside.

Emily says, "Definitely the blond with the perky boobs. You were practically peeing a circle around her. It looks like she is going to pair up with that middle-aged woman, so you don't have to worry about some dude getting close to her while you are working with everyone else."

"Don't you have something to do?"

"Nope. I already applied to every dive school in the country, and all the invoices are already printed for next week. I'm literally just here to look pretty and collect a paycheck today."

"Well, could you do that with less commentary?" I ask, and her laughter follows me out the back door.

Avery is indeed with another woman. I relax a little. Emily may have gotten under my skin with that comment.

Everyone is standing by their boats, so I begin the class. "We will start by going over the names for parts of this boat, learn how to tie a few important sailing knots, and raise the sail." We spend about an hour working through these steps.

As I finish unraveling a botched anchor hitch for a married couple, I glance down the line of boats to see if anyone else is struggling to get their sail up.

My eyes almost pop out of my head. Avery is bent over, tying a knot with that peach ass in the air. *I am not a hormonal teenager.* I look away before the rest of my body can take note of her position and raise its own sail.

"Is everyone comfortable with putting the sail together and tying all the knots?" I ask as I look down the line of Pudgies.

Everyone nods or gives affirmative answers.

"This sun is beating down pretty hard today, so let's take a short break. When you come back, we will move on to basic sailing maneuvers."

Everyone leaves to get their water bottles, and I take a few minutes to look out at the deep blue water. A small white fishing boat with a teal hull sails past, and the captain waves.

I love this community. Everyone is friendly, even if you have never met.

The class trickles back out to the makeshift dock, so I begin the next section of the class.

"There are seven basic maneuvers you need to be proficient in before heading out into the water. Tacking, jibing, heaving to, quick stop, safety position, and head to wind. We will finish up with performing the sailing clock. We will go over these one by one. Feel free to stop me and ask questions if you need to. I will not be on the boat with you to perform these maneuvers, so now is the time to get confident in your abilities."

We spend the next hour and a half working on how to steer the boat into the wind to avoid a knockdown or capsize, stalling the boat, setting the sail to take a break, boat control, and steering. Everyone is doing a really good job asking questions and giving their partner turns at the helm. I am really happy with how well this class is turning out.

"Did you guys understand the sailing clock?" I ask Avery and Jill as I walk over to their Pudgy. "That one is a little harder to master when you are sitting on the beach and nothing is moving."

Avery answers, "I'm not sure. Can you watch me while I talk you through it?"

She seems way more at ease today. Maybe she just needed to get over the initial reaction to trying something out of her comfort zone.

"Sure. Hop in and start close hauled. We will go from there."

"I'm going to go grab a drink. I will be right back," Jill says.

I nod in her direction and shift my focus back to Avery. From my position standing and her position sitting in the Pudgy, I can see all the way down her shirt to a magnificent display of cleavage and the lace cups of an emerald green bra.

I mentally groan. There is no way she knew that is my favorite color and wore it for me. *I am not a hormonal teenager.*

Avery flows through the steps with just a slight correction from me. She is a natural.

"How do you feel about this week?" I ask, checking to see if my assessment is correct.

"I am really glad I took this class. I don't feel any anxiety sitting in the Pudgy. I feel confident I can do these steps. I understand the reasoning behind the maneuvers and when to do them." She smiles, and I can feel warmth in my stomach.

Avery runs her gaze up my body from where she sits in the Pudgy on the ground. "You are an excellent teacher, Sawyer. I think everyone is having fun and learning. I am getting to know Jill, and we work well together." Was it wishful thinking, or did her voice get a little husky when she said my name?

"Thank you for the feedback. I wasn't sure how this would work out. It's kind of been my project baby that I have raised from conception."

Terrible choice of words. Now I can only think of what happens during conception. *I am not a hormonal teenager.*

"Well, you did an excellent job planning this."

"Thank you," I tell her, full of pride at her review.

I turn to look around at the class. Everyone seems ready to move on to the last part of the morning.

"Everyone looked really good going through the maneuvers. We need to go over safety precautions and emergency procedures before I let you go for the day.

"I chose these dinghies specifically for this class. These boats are practically unsinkable, and you can use them as lifeboats. They are very stable in the water and hard to capsize. They are also easy to row, but you can also add a motor or a sail kit like I did for the purpose of this class. We will start with where to find the safety gear and how to use it. Then we will go over what to do if you do happen to turn over."

The safety portion takes about an hour for everyone to have a chance to try the steps. I keep a close eye on Avery, watching for any signs of distress. I'm not sure what triggered her reaction last week, so I don't know if I should be watching for something this week.

I notice her tense up a few times, but she sits down and takes calming breaths to relax. I am beyond impressed with her resolve to continue this class.

I walk to the front of the line of Pudgies so everyone can see me.

"How does everyone feel about the emergency procedures?"

I hear cheers and see raised thumbs that I take to mean everyone feels comfortable with the boats.

"Since you guys did so good today, I am going to put these boats back in the water. Next week you are going to sail around this cove. There are rarely any waves, and the wind blows just enough to get these babies moving a tad slower than your grandma."

I get several laughs from the class. "Any questions?"

No one says anything.

"Then I guess we are done for this morning. If you think of anything, please call us. If Emily doesn't know, she will forward your questions to me. See you next week!"

Everyone starts walking to the parking lot, but Avery sticks behind.

CHAPTER 8
BARE-CHESTED GLORY

Avery

When Jill and I paired up, I told her I had water anxiety, so I might have to stop doing whatever we were doing if it got to be too much. She gave me a hug and told me she was proud of me for even trying to conquer my fear.

I did so well keeping it together through the first two parts of today's class. I thought I was overcoming my fear a little at a time.

We start going over safety procedures, and I consider faking diarrhea.

"If for some reason your Pudgy does capsize, it will likely turn back over by itself. If it does not, grab these handholds in the keel and turn it over." He demonstrates on a nearby Pudgy.

My heart starts beating faster at the thought of a wave big enough to turn the boat over.

"These boats are built with a double-walled hull, so they will pick up very little water when capsized. What other problems might make this a little tricky?" he asks the class.

Jill says, "There might be big waves, and you are bobbing in the water. You don't have anything to push against to get the boat to flip back over. It's going to take a lot of upper body strength."

The thought of being submerged in the ocean with waves around me has my vision starting to go in and out and my palms sweating.

Jill notices I am starting to have an issue and says softly, "Sit down on the dock and try to relax. I will finish up for us."

Through the anxiety fogging my brain, I can hear Sawyer's calming voice instructing the group on how to stow the sail and safety supplies.

My heart slows down closer to a normal pace, and my palms stop sweating.

I open my eyes, and I can focus on my surroundings again. Jill has everything put away, and Sawyer moves to the front of the group, facing the water.

I look at him with the building in the background as he asks some questions that the group answers.

"Then I guess we are done for this morning. If you think of anything, please call us. If Emily doesn't know, she will forward your questions to me. See you next week!"

Everyone starts walking to the parking lot as Sawyer kneels to check the boat he is standing in front of.

Without thinking about what I am doing, I stand up and walk over to him. He must hear me walking over because he stands up and looks at me.

I don't stop walking until our shoes almost touch, and I wrap my arms around his rock-hard chest in a tight embrace.

Sawyer tenses for the slightest of seconds before he relaxes and returns the hug, wrapping his muscular arms around my back.

The smell of his cologne encases me in a safety net. I just breathe him in for a few minutes as I cling to him. Safe. He makes me feel safe.

His stomach is hard and warm where it is pressed into mine. My face is touching the smooth tan skin above his pecs where his shirt is unbuttoned an indecent number of buttons.

"Do you need me to do anything else, Avery?" he asks quietly.

What a loaded question. I need so many things when it comes to this man. I just shake my head and keep hugging him rather than let my internal thoughts out.

"Let's breathe together. Deep breath in. Now slowly let it out. Keep doing this with me."

I listen to his calming voice giving me instructions for a few more minutes.

"There you go. You are coming back around," Sawyer says as our breathing synchronizes.

I can feel his nose resting in my hair as the embrace continues.

My body returns to normal, and I reluctantly remove my arms and step away from him.

His eyes move over my body from top to bottom and back up, checking to see if anything else is wrong with me.

He looks so handsome standing there in front of me. Like a savior sent to rescue me from myself.

"Thank you. I thought I was doing so good, but then I started to panic. Jill helped me a little bit, but it wouldn't go away totally. I'm sorry I just attacked you like that."

"Don't worry about it. I am always willing to help out however I can."

"Thank you. I better get going so you can finish up here and do whatever else you have going on today," I say as I reluctantly start walking to the parking lot.

"See you next week, Avery."

I raise my hand in farewell but keep walking. He felt so good pressed to me that I don't trust myself to turn back around.

When I get home, I lie down on the couch. I know I should get up and get some lunch, but I don't really feel like eating. I just want to relax and not think.

I wake up to loud pounding. I am a little groggy, so it takes me a few seconds to figure out where the sound is coming from.

I roll off the couch and walk to my front door. Looking through the peep hole, I see my mom on the other side. I open the door, and she bursts through, waving her arms in a frenzy.

"Avery Mae Sutton, where have you been? I have been calling you for the last hour, and you won't answer. My imagination finally got the best of me, so I had to come look for you."

"I had sailing lessons this morning and lay down on the couch when I got home. I must have passed out hard. I think my phone is in my purse."

I walk over to the coat rack and retrieve my phone. The screen is filled with notifications. Texts and calls from Mom.

MOM: Hey, honey. How was sailing today? Let's get lunch and talk about it.

MOM: What time does the class end? I thought it was a morning class.

MOM: Where are you? I called Pirate's Life to confirm it is a morning class.

MOM: ANSWER YOUR PHONE.

A few texts from Riley.

RILEY: Hey! How was class? Any arm candy groping today?

RILEY: I finished that book. Let's get together tonight or tomorrow morning to chat.

RILEY: Why aren't you answering me? Are you okay?

RILEY: Seriously, text me back.

The last two are sounding a little worried, so I text her back before she also shows up at my house.

ME: I'm fine. I just fell asleep after class. We can meet tomorrow morning if you want.

There is a group text from Wild Child.

GAIL: Hey, ladies! I know it's Saturday, but if I don't text you now I won't remember. We need to meet this week to start putting together the end of year Field Day. What days do you have available this week?

CANDACE: Tuesday works best for me. I can probably do Wednesday, but I will need to leave right at 3:45. Heathen #1 has a dentist appointment.

GAIL: I can do Tuesday.

CANDACE: Avery?

I text them back even though I have left them hanging for two hours.

ME: Yes, Tuesday is fine.

GAIL: <thumbs-up emoji>

CANDACE: <thumbs-up emoji>

I put my phone down on the kitchen counter when it dings again.

RILEY: Holey Moley at 9?

ME: Sounds good!

"Don't mind me, the mom who came over here in a panic because her daughter wouldn't answer her phone and thought something had happened to her. Just keep on texting your friends while I wait on the couch."

I put my phone down on the counter again. Now that I have responded to everyone, it should be silent for a while.

"Okay, Mom. I'm sorry. I had sailing class this morning. We worked with the boats on the beach behind the office, learning how to actually sail and tie knots. That was really interesting, and I enjoyed it. Then we talked about what to do if you have an emergency or your boat capsizes. We went through different scenarios, and I had a small panic attack. I calmed down enough to drive home. I guess the stress and emotions took more out of me than I thought. I fell asleep on the couch until you knocked on the door. I'm really sorry I worried you."

"Oh, honey. Come here," she says and wraps me in a lavender-scented motherly hug.

I can't help but compare this hug with the last one I received. Nothing beats a hug from your mother, but hugging Sawyer feels amazing in a different way.

When Mom has ensured I am safe, she releases me.

"It's a little late for lunch now, but do you want to go out for an early dinner? Your dad should be finishing up at Silver Seaside any time now. He had to go in for an issue with the computer system not saving bookings or something. Like he's an IT guy." Mom scoffs.

"I'm sure he figured it out even though he can barely use his cell phone. He knows that place like the back of his hand. Let me change my clothes and brush my hair, and I'll meet you there."

"Sounds good, honey. I will call your father to tell him to stay at Double S. See you in a bit!" she says as she walks out my front door, and I head to my bathroom to freshen up.

I love Sunday mornings in Wild Shore before the tourist season begins. Everything slows down, and people just relax. The weather is getting warmer, so I put on denim shorts and a white crop tank top. I pull my hair up into a messy bun and slip into some brown leather sandals.

I get in Chili to take the drive across town. There is one car driving up The Drop out of town. In a few weeks, it will be packed.

I drive by a few kids playing in a nicely landscaped yard. They run and shriek as a small dog chases them.

I get a pang in my chest. I want a family. I am ready to start building a life with someone. I am tired of waking up and going to bed alone. I want what my parents have.

The orange creamsicle-colored building with bright white trim and two red doors with a red awning-topped window between them comes into view as I turn onto Ocean Boulevard.

I find a parking spot relatively close. As soon as I open my car door, the smell of sugar and the layered doughnuts Holey Moley is famous for invades my car. I take a long inhale to enjoy the smell when a deep rumble gets closer to me.

A sleek motorcycle pulls in beside me. The woman rider takes off her helmet and long red curls fall down her slender back. My best friend is beautiful. Until she opens her mouth.

"I didn't come here to smell the air. I need some cream in my mouth stat. Let's get in there before the line gets any longer and I have to have a lame glazed donut," she says as she hangs her helmet on the handlebar and swings her jean-clad leg and biker boot over the seat.

"If you were that worried about eating lame donuts, you should have gotten up earlier."

"I know. It's a dangerous game I play, but I love sleeping in on Sunday. It's the only day my dad refuses to open the shop. Every other day, the doors slide open at seven. This girl needs a break," she says as we walk toward Holey Moley.

"I'll have a chocolate-covered strawberry layered donut," I tell the kid behind the counter when we finally make it up there.

"I'll take that key lime filled one with the white icing," Riley says.

He puts our donuts into a small box, and I hand another worker some cash. I put the change in the tip jar and keep walking out the opposite door. The line doesn't stop moving in here.

We walk along The Boardwalk until we find an empty table. The water is calm today, and I can see the gradual change from translucent to teal to dark blue as the water gets deeper. Everyone says the water is so clear you can see the sand until the water is well over your head. The thought makes me shudder internally.

"So how was sailing yesterday? Any more accidental bicep gropings?" she asks as we sit down.

I don't reply. I'm not sure how to reply.

"Spill. What happened? Did you fall down and grab his shirt to steady yourself and it ripped, leaving him in his bare-chested glory?"

"No, but I did get a pretty good feel of that gloriousness."

"What?" Riley asks as her eyes go round.

"Yep. I was freaking out a little after the safety portion of the class and just flung my arms around him and held on for dear life. Luckily, this happened after everyone else had left. That would have been a little embarrassing if he were still talking," I say as I take a bite of my donut. My taste buds explode and go to heaven.

"I'm not sure how to respond to that. Worry that you were having another attack so soon, ask how his chest felt against you, or check your forehead for a fever because my best friend

66

would never throw herself at a man. I'm just not sure where to start."

"I'll just tell you what you really want to know. It felt like I was hugging satin-covered steel. His skin is warm and smooth, and his pecs and abs are rock-solid. He hugged me back with those strong arms as tight as I was holding him. Oh, and he smells delicious. Manly with a hint of spice. Very outdoorsy. I wish I could tell you more, but as soon as I came back to myself, I backed away from him. It was like my body was possessed, like it knew he could help me."

"Oh, it knows all right. I bet he could help you all night long, in any way you needed him to."

"Why are we friends?" I say, laughing. We continue eating our doughnuts and chatting until we need to get back home to do our weekend chores.

CHAPTER 9
IT'S NOT A CRUSH

Sawyer

I stretch my arms and watch a gull fly overhead, dipping and soaring with the sea breeze. A navy blue truck with oversized tires and a lift kit pulls up beside my Jeep in the Pirate's Life parking lot.

Mason gets out and starts walking my way wearing an old UE School of Medicine T-shirt with the sleeves cut off and black athletic shorts.

"Nice of you to join me, Sunshine. I was going to give you five more minutes then leave you," I tell him as I switch to stretching my legs.

"Don't start with me. I haven't been to bed since yesterday morning. I just left the hospital and came straight here. Some dumbass tourist decided to BASE jump off The Wall last night. He didn't clear the platform and ended up rolling down the cliff. He must have hit every tree and pointy rock on the way down. Steep Creek SAR found him, and Cruze airlifted him out and brought him over. What a mess. Why do people do stupid shit like that?"

"Well, that was a little hurtful. I kind of enjoy doing things like that," I reply with fake chagrin.

"Your situation is different. You have years of training on this guy and way more gear," Mason says as he finishes stretching.

"You ready?"

"I guess. If I fall asleep running and lie down, don't let the gulls peck me."

We take off jogging at a medium pace back toward The Boardwalk. When Mason and I were in high school, we started meeting at the end of The Boardwalk at dawn three times a week to make the jog to the north bluff and back. When I got discharged and Mason moved home after medical school, we started meeting again. It is a little more than eight miles and just the right amount to keep us in shape.

Sometimes we talk. Sometimes we just keep each other silent company if one of us is working through something.

We jog past Salty Dog. Benny is cutting up peppers and onions to get ready for the day ahead. He waves the hand holding his knife, and we wave back.

I can smell Holey Moley before I can see it, and my stomach growls. There is already a line out one door.

Mason must be able to see my mind working.

"You don't need one of those. Just because it has strawberries on it doesn't make it healthy. I am not killing myself running with you so you can eat junk."

"Well, maybe I am. I haven't had one in a long time. Maybe today is the day to break my streak."

"Guess that was the first and last time you model for a billboard." Mason chuckles.

"Just for that I'm letting the gulls peck you."

We jog another mile, and the boardwalk ends at the pier. We skirt the entry steps and keep jogging.

We approach Shipwrecked, and Mason lets out a wolf whistle that can be heard on the other side of Magnolia Ridge. I look over, and Savannah is bent over, planting flowers in the barrels that line the large deck.

I punch him in the shoulder. "Knock it off. She's my sister."

"I know. I do it just to piss you off." He smirks.

Savannah looks up and waves as we jog past.

"Morning, guys!" she yells over the sound of the water crashing on the shore.

The resorts and vacation homes dotting the north bluff come into view as we round a bend. The Silver Seaside is by far the most ostentatious. More vacation homes seem to get built every year up here.

We round the sign indicating the end of the public beach and jog back down the beach.

"How are the weekend sailing lessons going? I keep forgetting to ask about them every time I see you."

"They are actually going better than I thought they would. Everyone seems to be learning and getting along as a group. Some of the partners are making friends. We are going to head out into the water this week. I think everyone will really like it."

Except for one person.

Mason must have been looking at me when that thought crossed my mind, because he asks, "But...?"

"There is something about the class that triggers a panic attack for one of the clients. I'm worried about how that will play out this week when we are on the water."

"How did the last two weeks go?"

"She keeps pushing through when most people would have already quit by now. I am amazed by her perseverance and ambition."

"And her body?"

"She is so damn sexy." I stop talking and glare at him. "Seriously? Why did you ask that?"

"You got this weird look on your face when you started talking about her. I knew something was up, and it wasn't hard to figure out. Oh, and I talked to Sav a couple days ago. She was gloating because she knew you had a crush before I did," he finishes with a laugh.

"It's not a crush," I deny.

"Have you had thoughts about this woman outside of when she is at sailing lessons?"

"She is in my beginner sailing class. I stress about that class all the time."

"Have you thought about her when it didn't involve sailing?"

I am thankful we have been jogging for almost six miles because I can feel my face heat. I'm hoping I can push it off as exertion and not what I am beginning to think is a blush.

I am almost thirty years old. Since when do I blush when asked about a woman?

"I'm going to take the silence as a yes and not ask any more questions down that line. I don't even want to know what happens in that bedroom that has never seen a woman."

"My mom and Savannah have been in there lots of times," I reply as we come up to Shipwrecked again.

"Nice comeback," he says with a shudder.

I rub my middle finger along the side of my nose. Mason laughs when he sees the gesture.

Savannah is nowhere to be seen when we pass the bar. I make a mental note to tell her the flowers look nice. The deck is lined with rum barrels turned into benches. Every third one has a bouquet of orange, red, and pink flowers and some kind of green vines.

We continue chatting as we finish the jog down The Boardwalk and back to Pirate's Life.

"Is it just me or does that run get longer every time?" Mason asks as he bends over, panting.

"You are getting a little too old to be running that far. You better pick up a cane on the way to the Early Bird Special tonight."

"We're the same age, asshole," he declares as he starts stretching.

"But I am in way better shape," I brag as I bend over to stretch out my calves.

Mason takes the opportunity to push me over into the sand.

"And better looking," I say as I roll over on my ass to look at him.

He takes off running to his truck and yells, "That's not what your sister says!"

"Keep your grubby hands away from my sister!" I bellow back.

"All the ladies say they are magical," he drawls as he gets into his truck. He sticks his head out the window and continues, "Your mom told me that just the other day. She also complimented my bedside manner."

"You are no longer my best friend," I deadpan.

He throws his head back and laughs then puts his truck in gear and leaves.

I slowly get up and wipe the sand from my legs and shorts.

I need to go to the lumber yard on the other side of Magnolia Ridge today. I am ready to start on the half bathroom down the hall from the kitchen. I need to get some fixtures so I know where to run the plumbing and maybe look at tile. My mom and sister would probably kill me if I bought tile without their approval, but I'm going to look just in case.

After heading home to shower, I get back in the Jeep and drive to The Drop. The trees on Magnolia Ridge are starting to come out of dormancy and sprout leaves. Just one more sign that summer and tourist season are right around the corner.

There is a car coming down The Climb from Steep Creek when I get to The Split. We both take The Pass to the bigger community of Magnolia.

I walk around the home improvement store, looking for sales or tools I might need one day.

I decide I have shopped long enough, so I walk back to the plumbing department. I am doing a thorough examination of the toilet aisle when an employee walks up to me.

This store promotes the hiring of servicemen, and I notice the patch on his vest proclaiming him an Army Veteran.

He takes in my Navy T-shirt and smiles. "You swabbies will look for water anywhere." He chortles as he slaps his knee and laughs at his own joke.

"Hey there, Ground Pounder," I say, returning the smile.

"Can I help you with something today?"

"I'm getting ready to finish a half bath, so I need to buy a toilet to get the measurements before I cut a hole in the floor."

"This one is our best seller. People like the buttons on top instead of the handle. I just want to know where they put the spray if the flusher is on top?"

"That is an excellent question." We stand there as I look over the specs of the models again. "I think I'm going to stick with the tank flusher. Just seems easier to work on if I need to replace something."

"That's what I think too. Bring your cart over here, and we can load one on there."

He is surprisingly strong for an older man, and we get the large box loaded quickly.

"Do you need any plumbing fittings or a water line?" he asks as he rubs his hands together to remove any dirt.

"Nope. I bought all the rough plumbing a while ago. I'm just now getting around to putting it in. Thanks for your help and thanks for your service," I say as I push the cart to the checkout.

CHAPTER 10
POSITIVE AFFIRMATIONS

Avery

"Come back, Aspen! You're out too far, sis!" I shout to my twin sister. The surf report for today said we were going to have three-to-four-foot waves, so my sister and I begged our mom to take us to the beach while Dad is at the resort. Aspen and I have been boogie boarding for hours. Mom has been splitting her time between reading a book with a shirtless man on the front and watching us.

"Aspen! Seriously, get back here! That's way too far out!" I yell, but she is not listening. She is so far away, and the waves are crashing really loudly on the beach. I yell as loud as I can with my hands cupping my mouth to project my voice, "Aspen! Aspen!"

A large wave, bigger than any we have seen all day, comes up behind Aspen. She is watching a man paddle board farther down the beach and doesn't see the wave coming.

"Aspen, look out for that wave!" I boom with the loudest scream I have ever made.

The sound of my voice must reach her this time, since she looks back at the same time the wave breaks over on top of her. The force of the water knocks her off the boogie board, and she goes under.

"Nooooo!" My deafening scream alerts Mom that something is wrong, and she comes running from her beach chair to where I am standing on the shoreline.

"Where is Aspen?" my mom shrieks. "Aspen! Aspen!"

I point to her hot pink boogie board bobbing in the water, but she is nowhere to be seen.

"Help! Someone help my daughter!" my mom howls as she starts running through the white foam and suspended sand to where Aspen's board is.

The man on the paddle board jumps off and starts swimming to Aspen's board. When he gets there, he starts diving and looking for her. Mom reaches him and starts doing the same thing. They search for several minutes. Their searching becomes more frantic as more people join in.

Mom stands up and lifts her head to the sky, and the worst sound I have ever heard leaves her mouth.

BEEP! BEEP! BEEP!

The sound of my phone alarm going off wakes me up from my nightmare and I drag in huge gulps of air. My heart is racing as I open my eyes. It takes a few seconds for me to realize I am in my bedroom hundreds of miles from that beach and not witnessing my twin sister drown.

I breathe in through my nose and slowly out through my mouth to try to slow my heart rate. I don't get this nightmare very often, but even fifteen years later, my body reacts like I am at that beach again.

After a few minutes, my breathing and heart rate have lowered enough that I can get out of bed. I walk across the hall to my bathroom. The tile is cold on my feet and helps to bring me back to the present.

I don't even glance at the mirror on my way to the shower. I know what I look like. I have seen the aftermath of that dream enough times to know it's not pretty. I reach into the shower stall and turn the knob all the way to hot.

Grabbing the bottom hem of my sleep shirt, I pull it over my head and toss it in the general direction of the dirty laundry hamper. I don't wait for the shower to warm up anymore. Instead, I step right under the shower head and let the lukewarm water fall down on me.

I let my residual emotion wash down the drain with the water that is now steaming. The recurrent nightmare sometimes happens on the anniversary of her death. Sometimes it happens on our birthday. Sometimes it comes out of nowhere.

This time it occurred because of what is on my agenda for today. Today is the day I have been dreading for three weeks. Jill and I will be taking our Pudgy into the cove at Pirate's Life.

Three weeks ago, it sounded like a sound plan. I am in the water, but the water isn't touching me. On the day I actually have to get in the water, I am not so sure.

I can't stall any longer, so I get out of the shower and wrap my body in a fluffy lavender towel. I wrap my hair in a sage striped towel to help it dry and keep it out of my face while I get ready.

I walk across the hallway to pick out my outfit. I put on my hot pink and bright blue striped bikini and cover it up with some matching hot pink athletic shorts and a white tank top. I slip into my Sperrys and walk back to the bathroom where I pull my mostly dry hair up into a messy bun and apply SPF moisturizer to my face.

Physically, I am ready for the day. Mentally, I'm not sure.

On the drive to Pirate's Life, I seriously question turning around and going home. I don't have to do this. I can try taking the class again in a few more months. Sawyer and Jill will understand. I decide to call my mom for some positive affirmations.

I press the handsfree button on my steering wheel and say, "Call Mom."

The male Aussie AI replies, "Calling Mom cell."

Mom picks up on the second ring. "Hey, honey. Are you on your way to sailing class?"

"Yes, but I woke up to the nightmare, and now I'm freaking out. I need some reassurance."

"Oh, Avery. I wondered if the big day would trigger the nightmare. I understand your fear, but you are stronger than your fear now. You are taking back your life. You have been putting this off for way too long. You live two miles from one of the best beaches in the world and should be able to take advantage of it without fear of something going wrong. Do you need me to come stand on the dock and cheer you on? You know I will!"

Mom's offer of support makes me crack the first smile I have had all day. "No, Mom. I am feeling better now. Thank you for the encouragement," I tell her with a slight giggle.

"Don't think I won't be there fist pumping and hollering about every stride you make. Just say the slightest word, and I will get in my car and burn rubber all the way to Pirate's Life," she says more lightheartedly than before.

My giggle turns more into a chuckle. "No, thanks, Mom. I think I would rather be nervous and anxious than suffer the supreme embarrassment of a Marie Sutton support rally," I tell her.

"Well, you just let me know if you change your mind. Your dad is trying to master the putting green in front of the house. Typical Saturday morning. How many times can you play the same hole and still not know how to sink the putt?" Mom asks with a laugh.

"You know it's not the putt he is working on. He's just keeping up on all the gossip with his cronies that are playing through. It's like having a rotating party without having to do any preparation." We both laugh as I pull into a parking spot.

"I'm here, so I'm going to get off here. I will talk to you later. Love you."

"Good luck, honey. Let me know how it goes. Love you!" Mom says as she ends the call.

I take a deep breath and get out of Chili. I grab my water jug and walk down the path toward the dock where the rest of the class is waiting on instructions from Sawyer.

"Everyone is here now, so are you guys ready to do some actual sailing today?" Sawyer asks.

A chorus of "Yeah" and "Yes" replies to his question.

"You guys looked good last week when we did the maneuvers on the beach. Does anyone have any questions before you head out today?" Sawyer asks, looking through the group. His gaze briefly lands on me, but I refuse to meet his eyes.

No one responds to his question, so he takes that as a negative and claps his hands together. "The conditions are perfect for a first outing. The wind is blowing enough to get you moving, but you shouldn't have to make any split-second decisions. Get your Pudgy away from the dock then work through the seven maneuvers we talked about. You have this whole cove, so spread out.

"Since everyone worked well together last weekend, we will keep the same pairs and Pudgy. I am taking out the small dive boat so I can check on you guys. Let's get some wind in our sails!"

Laughter and conversation float through the early morning summer air as the small group of students excitedly walk down to the dock.

I look out past the end of the long dock at the shiny blue water and small swells and hang back. I know I am perfectly safe in the small cove Pirate's Life uses for lessons, but my muscles won't move.

Even with Mom's pep talk, I don't think I am ready for this. The feeling of defeat is almost worse than the fear that keeps trying to wiggle its way up my spine.

Sawyer notices that I didn't walk down to the dock with everyone else and comes over to me.

"Avery, how are you today? Are you good with going out?" Sawyer asks.

I focus on the V where his light grey shirt opens up to display his pecs.

"I don't know if I can do this today. I'm not ready. I tried so hard to make myself do this, but I just can't yet," I tell him in an almost whisper as tears fill my eyes.

"Hey. That is perfectly fine. I don't want you to do anything you aren't comfortable with. You need to do this at your own pace. There is no timeline on how fast you have to conquer a fear. Everyone works at their own pace," Sawyer reassures me.

He puts one large, calloused hand on my shoulder and grips my wrist with the other one, checking my pulse.

"Avery, look at me. Look at my eyes."

I drag my gaze up from his chest and meet his concerned gaze. I start to get lost in the comfort the warm chocolate depths provide.

"If you are not ready, you are not ready. You are in control of how or when you overcome your fear. Do not beat yourself up over that day not being today. You have worked so hard to get to this point. I know you will continue to work hard to get to where you want to be."

His quietly spoken words of encouragement and calloused hand tracing circles around my wrist have my pulse jumping for reasons other than fear. The sounds of the other students getting their Pudgies set up filters through my lust haze. I remember where we are, and I step away from him.

CHAPTER 11
THOUGHT BUBBLES

Sawyer

With Avery's history of panic attacks triggered by this class, I immediately go into medic mode at the first sign she isn't feeling right. I'm glad she knows her boundaries and didn't let the pressure to succeed push her to do something she isn't ready for. I realize I am caressing the smooth skin of her dainty wrist where I was monitoring her pulse.

Since she slammed into me in the classroom, I have wanted to get closer to her, preferably naked. My imagination has been working overtime on what she looks like under those shorty shorts and tank tops. I have jerked off to visions of her long legs, peach-shaped ass, and breasts that try to spill out of her skimpy bikini so many times my cock is borderline raw.

I realize I am awkwardly holding her, so I drop my hands before they do something dumb like pull her to me and press my lips to hers.

"Thank you for that. I think I am getting better at controlling my panic reaction, but it always helps to have something or someone to coach me through it," she says, looking up at me with relief in her blue eyes.

"I need to get going to oversee the lesson. Feel free to sit on the dock and watch the class. That bench over there has a great view. It's where I do my best thinking. Or you can go home for the day and rest. The choice is yours," I say understandingly.

"I think I will sit on the bench and watch the rest of class sail," she ventures.

I start walking backward on the long dock and say, "That sounds like an excellent plan. If you are gone before I get back to shore, I hope today hasn't turned you off of sailing. Hopefully, you feel comfortable enough to try again next week." I raise my hand in a wave and turn to jog the rest of the way to the small dive boat I am going to use today.

Hopefully, she is still here when the lesson is done, and I can talk to her again. I need to make sure she is okay. At least that is what I tell myself.

Before I release the mooring on the dive boat, I look around the cove at the three Pudgies sailing from one side to the other. They are doing great. They made it out to the middle of the inlet and got their sails raised. They are working through tying the ropes and using the rudder to direct their small watercraft.

One couple is having a hard time getting away from the dock. I walk down to where they were moored and give them some one-on-one instruction. I can see their frustration turn to joy as what I told them works, and they are moving farther away from the dock. In no time they are raising their sail and whipping around the cove with everyone else.

With everyone away from the dock, I walk back to the dive boat and start maneuvering around and through the Pudgies, making sure everyone is getting a chance to be in charge of their watercraft.

I look up at the office and see Avery. She is sitting on the bench with her gaze trained on the cove.

I turn my attention back to the students. They are calling out to each other with encouragement and assistance.

This class is doing really well, so I am going to let them sail up the coast next week. Maybe Avery will join us. Would she be angry if I assigned her to my sailboat instead of letting her sail with Jill? Would that make my need to be around her too obvious? I can always tell anyone who asks that she is with me because she didn't participate this week, and I'm not sure of her ability on the open water. That sounds way more reasonable than I want to be her knight in shining armor if she would happen to need anything.

I watch the students for another hour and give instructions when asked or needed. It is time to finish this class. I give one long blast on my whistle to alert everyone it is time to head in. Pudgies start moving to the dock with way more ease than they left.

After everyone moors their Pudgies, we meet at the trail by the end of the dock.

"You guys did awesome today! Who wants to head up the coast next week?" I ask them.

My question is met with cheers and hands waving in the air.

"Sounds good. We will meet here at the same time and go on a little trip. Bring plenty of water and sunblock, since we will be out there for a few hours. See everyone next week!" I impart.

They say their goodbyes and walk back up the path to leave. I walk back down the dock to check that everyone moored their Pudgies and put everything away correctly.

With my checks done, I look back up at the bench. Avery is still sitting there. Has she been waiting there the whole time to talk to me, or is she just enjoying the beautiful weather? I hope she isn't going to tell me she isn't coming back, but if that is best for her, that is what needs to happen. I want to spend more time with her, even if it is just a few hours, but I don't want to chance another panic attack.

I walk to the bench and sit down beside her but far enough away that we aren't touching.

"So you're still here. I'm going to take that as a sign that you are still interested in the wonderful hobby of sailing," I insinuate as I turn to look at her with a smile.

Her hair is wind-blown, and her shoulders are a little pink from spending hours on this bench.

"I don't know if I'm ready to sail, but watching the Pudgies glide around the cove was very relaxing. There is something beautiful about the sails flapping and catching in the breeze. Everyone looked like they had a lot of fun out there," she offers.

"It is very calming. You forget all of your problems when you are out there. It is just you and the boat with the wind in your hair and sun on your face," I tell her.

"That sounds amazing. I could use some total relaxation. Too bad the thought of getting on a boat gives me the opposite reaction."

"Do you want to talk about it?" I ask.

"Not really. It's something I'm working through, and it's pretty personal," she replies.

"Well, if you ever want someone to confide in, I am usually here. This place has become my life," I tell her.

She turns to face me. "You mean someone like you doesn't have a wife or a girlfriend waiting at the door to kiss you when you come home?" As soon as the question leaves her mouth, her cheeks and neck turn bright red, and she looks away from me.

"Oh my God. Forget I asked that. Let's just blame that on being in the sun for a few hours," she insists quickly.

Her question and reaction make me laugh. "No, no one is waiting at the door to welcome me home after a long day here. Not even a dog," I confirm as I stare out at the crystal clear water. "What about you? Do you have anyone waiting on you to get home from your sailing lesson today?"

Avery turns back to look at me. Her eyes move over my face and down my chest as she decides how to answer. When her gaze returns to my face, her blush gets even darker. Yes, I totally caught her checking me out.

She must like what she sees because she replies, "No, no one is waiting on me today or any other day. Not even a cat."

"Well, in that case, would you like to grab some lunch? There is a little café a block from here. I eat there most Saturdays between excursions." I try to play off the invitation as casual, but I feel like I just asked her to HOCO. I want to get to know her and find out if this pull I have to her goes both ways.

"Sure. That sounds good. I was in a bit of a hurry this morning, so I missed breakfast. I'm getting pretty hungry," she replies as she stands up. "Lead the way, Sawyer."

I don't know whether her accepting my invitation to lunch or her saying my name in a slightly husky voice gives me the bigger rush. I am really glad I get to spend more time with her, but the way she said my name makes my lower abdomen clench. I want to hear her moan it while my face is between her thighs or I'm buried deep inside her.

Whoa, boy. Slow down. It has been a while, but this is only lunch between two people getting to know one another. No one is going to be between anyone's thighs or moaning anyone's name today. Except me in the shower later when I stroke my cock to fantasies of her again.

We are walking up the path to the office when I remember I don't have any money or my phone on me. "I need to grab a few things out of my office, and then we can walk over there. I will meet you out front," I tell her.

"Sounds good. I need to get my purse," she replies as she veers toward the parking lot, and I open the back door.

I grab my phone and wallet out of my office. On my way out, I happen to catch a glimpse of myself in the mirror. I look like a surfer and not a respectable business owner. My hair is wild from the last few hours spent on the water. My skin has a slightly salty sheen from the spray of the waves hitting my boat. My Pirate's Life shirt is unbuttoned to mid-chest, showing off my pecs. Too late to change anything now.

I walk to the lobby, and Emily is sitting at the desk, reading a diving pamphlet.

"I'll be back in a little bit, Em. I'm going to Rise and Dine for lunch."

"Alone? I saw Avery sitting on the bench while everyone else sailed. Did she stay to talk to you?"

"Yes, she stayed. She is just going through some stuff and decided not to sail today."

"So you are taking her out to lunch?"

"What is it with everyone thinking they can drag information out of me by asking questions at the right time? First Mase and now you."

"You're kind of an open book when it comes to her. I can practically see your tongue rolling out and a conversation bubble saying 'Hubba hubba' coming from your brain."

I give her a smirk. "I'll see you later. Hold down the fort."

"Got it, bossman. Go get the girl before you are too old to enjoy her."

I shake my head as I go out the front door.

Avery is walking around the corner of the building as she looks at something on her phone. I get a few seconds to stare at her without anyone noticing. She is so effortlessly sexy. Her lips shine with fresh pink lipgloss she must have applied while she was at her car. I want to sample it to see if her lips taste like berries or watermelon. The question is going to cloud my mind forever now.

"Rise and Dine is just on the next street over. Have you ever been there?" I ask her when she finishes with whatever she is doing on her phone.

"Actually, I have. My best friend Riley and I eat brunch there every once in a while. The lattes are amazing. Oh, and the sugar cookies. And those pumpkin streusel bar things they have in fall. Gah. My mouth is watering just thinking about it," she answers, waxing poetic about Pepper's baking skills.

Her best friend Riley? Has he ever been more than a friend? A best friend with the good benefits? What are the odds that I finally find someone I am interested in, and she isn't totally available?

Since I grew up in Wild Shore, I know pretty much everyone who lives here. There are some people who moved here while I was in the service whom I haven't met, but for the most part, this is a small community, and everyone knows everyone else.

I can't think of anyone named Riley. Is he older? Younger? Riley sounds like one of those rich guy names that only summer here. He comes in on Daddy's yacht, and they drink champagne out of crystal flutes and listen to jazz music. They get tipsy on the bubbles and have missionary sex then have brunch at Rise and Dine because he can't be bothered to cook her breakfast.

Reel it in, Saw. She said they were friends, and she doesn't have anyone waiting on her at home. Maybe you can replace him as her *best friend*.

I really hope Emily was joking about those thought bubbles above my head.

During my internal freak-out, we arrive at Rise and Dine. I open the glass door for Avery and follow her in, hoping I wasn't too awkward when I got in my head and stopped conversing during our short walk.

CHAPTER 12

I NEED YOUR SAUCE

Avery

Sawyer holds the door open to Rise and Dine, and I walk in before him. The sign at the entryway says to seat yourself, so I walk to the first empty booth I can find and sit down. Sawyer sits across from me. I take the menu out of the caddy at the end of the table and look at my options.

I better enjoy every moment of this lunch because he isn't very likely to ever invite me again. He stopped talking after I told him all the desserts I love to get here. He probably thinks I'm going to order everything on the menu and stick him with the bill.

A frazzled waitress walks up to our table and places a silverware roll down in front of each of us. "Hey, guys. Steph called in today, and I couldn't find anyone to cover for her, so you get me. I'm trying to run the back and serve, so it might be a bit slow," she rushes out with a slight New York accent.

"Hey, Pepper. That's no problem. I hope Steph is okay," Sawyer sympathizes.

"She said her daughter is sick. Let's hope she feels better by Monday."

"Poor kid and poor Steph. Having a sick kid is rough," Sawyer says.

"Do you know what you want, or do you need a minute?" Pepper asks as she looks my way and pulls a pen and notepad out of her apron. "He eats the same thing every Saturday," she imparts and points her pen at Sawyer.

"I'll take a Coke and the BLT on white with seasoned fries," I tell her.

Pepper lowers her arms and looks at Sawyer as she says, "So I guess I'll make that two."

A huge smile comes over Sawyer's face that shows both dimples and the crow's feet around his eyes. I melt into a puddle on the floor under the table.

"I guess so, Pep. We'll keep it easy for you," he replies, and she walks off, shaking her head.

Sawyer clears his throat. "So, uh, tell me about yourself. We haven't ever actually talked, and I just realized I don't know much about you."

"Well, I have lived here since I graduated college. My parents moved here my sophomore year of college when my dad got the GM position at the Silver Seaside. My mom is a stay-at-home mom, so I have always spent a lot of time with her, and I still do. I talk to her daily, sometimes more than once a day. I spent college breaks here and fell in love with the area. When I graduated, it felt right to move where they were. I packed up Chili and stayed with them until I found a place."

"Chili?"

"The red VW Beetle I got when I turned sixteen."

He chuckles at my answer. "Very fitting. Sounds like your family is pretty close," he says as he gets more comfortable in the booth and clasps his hands in front of him on the table. The move makes his forearms pop. My fingers tingle at the memory of exactly how those muscles feel.

He continues talking while I'm trying to keep from drooling. "I am really close to my family, too. My mom and dad have owned Shipwrecked since before I was born. My sister runs it now, since my parents semiretired last year. They decided to travel, and she was basically running the place anyway."

"I have been there several times. I love their cocktails, and the atmosphere is always fun and cheerful. It's a great place to grab a drink when you are at the beach or out with the girls," I say, getting a little more comfortable with him.

"So I know what your family does, but what do you do?" he asks.

"Oh my gosh. I totally forgot to tell you that. I got carried away with my family. I teach the four-year-old class at Wild Child Preschool. Some days they are definitely wild children, but for the most part they are great," I effuse as our Cokes are placed in front of us.

"I just realized I didn't introduce myself when I took your order, and I don't think we have met. I'm Pepper. I own Rise and Dine. I am usually stuck in the kitchen, so I don't meet very many of my customers." She sticks her hand out for me to shake.

"I'm Avery. It's nice to meet the woman behind the delicious desserts and coffee recipes. I love your brunch, so I am excited to try the lunch menu," I remark as we shake.

"Thank you! Baking is one of my favorite things to do, so I'm always happy when someone loves my creations. I better get back there before your lunch gets burnt. That would be an excellent way to introduce you to the food." Pepper chuckles as she walks off.

"She seems really nice," I think out loud as I watch her walk away and joke with some of the other customers before going through the swinging door to the kitchen.

"Oh, she is. We have had a lot of fun together, not to mention all the stupid shit we have tried," he says as he smiles with untold memories.

Have they ever been more than friends? Their easy camaraderie and the way he talks about her says they could have. The thought doesn't sit well with me.

"The answer is no."

"I'm sorry. Did I miss something?" I ask, confused about what he means.

"Your face says you want to know if we have ever been more than friends. We haven't. She moved to Wild Shore and opened Rise and Dine about the same time my enlistment was over. She was new in town, and I was trying to remember how to be a civilian and start a business as well. We just clicked and have been close ever since. She is one of my best friends," he clarifies, making my jealousy sink back inside me.

"That wasn't what I was thinking." Although it totally was.

"Okay," he says sarcastically, calling me out on my lie.

Pepper places our plates on the table in front of us and walks to the next table to drop off more plates. We both reach over to grab the mustard, and our hands touch. We jerk away and speak at the same time, "Go ahead."

We laugh, and Sawyer says, "Ladies first," and draws his hand back beside his plate. After I make a good size puddle on my plate, I pass the bottle across the table to him.

"Thanks," he says as he does the same and puts it back in the caddy.

I pick up my sandwich and take a bite. The smoky flavor of the crisp bacon hits my tongue mixed with the acidic taste of fresh tomato and the sweetness of a house spread. I moan embarrassingly loud.

My eyes widen as I look across the table at Sawyer. His sandwich is raised halfway between the table and his slack-jawed mouth, and he is looking straight at me, his pupils slightly dilated. I chew the rest of the bite and swallow before saying, "Please kill me now. I can't believe I just did that. I think I will just wrap this up and leave the country so I never have to see you again. I am so embarrassed."

He gives me another one of those big grins and says with laughter in his voice, "No need. I know how great these are. I prepared myself to keep my reaction internal."

"It's the sauce, isn't it? It's not as sweet as Miracle Whip but way better than plain mayonnaise. Maybe it's the bacon. It's perfectly done. This may be better than the desserts Pepper makes."

"Well, I'll take that as confirmation that everything tastes good," Pepper says as she walks up to our table.

"Oh my God, Pepper. This is amazing. I need your sauce on everything now. How do you make it?" I respond with absolute honesty.

"A chef never gives away their best recipes." She beams with a wink. She flips through her notepad and rips off a piece of paper. "I'm going to leave the bill here because I don't know when I'll have time to swing back by. No rush. Avery, it was great to meet you. I hope to see you again soon. Sawyer, I'll see you tomorrow afternoon."

That ugly green monster is back from out of nowhere. What is my problem? I barely know the man, and now my hormones think I'm the only one who can spend time with him. Sheesh.

"I told you. It's not like what your face is saying. A big group of us get together one Sunday a month and hang out on the beach. Tomorrow is the day. You are welcome to come. Bring a chair and a cooler. You can meet the rest of my friends and my sister. It's an afternoon to relax and catch up."

"I'm not sure what else I have planned for tomorrow. I will let you know," I tell him as I pick up my sandwich and continue eating.

We chat about things happening around the town in the next few weeks and people we both know. Before I know it, my sandwich and fries are all gone and so are Sawyer's. Neither of us is hinting we are ready to leave the café.

We chat for a little longer until my phone rings. It is my mom. I silence it. It immediately starts ringing again.

Sawyer says, "If you need to get that, it's not a big deal."

"It's my mom. She knows how I feel about water and that today we were supposed to take the Pudgies out. I told her I would call her when I was done, and I haven't yet. She's probably freaking out."

"You better answer then."

"Hey, Mom. I am at lunch with a friend. Can I call you back in a little while?"

Her voice comes through the phone, "Oh, sure, honey. I just wanted to check on you. Talk later. Love you!"

"Love you, Mom," I say before I press the red button and set my phone face down on the table.

"So a friend, eh?" Sawyer asks.

"Shut up. What was I supposed to tell her? I'm out eating lunch with my sailing instructor who also happens to be a hunky billboard model? She would likely show up to meet you, and no one wants that."

Can I facepalm myself in real life?

"That freaking billboard. What was Emily thinking putting that thing up there?"

"Probably what all the women and some of the men think every time they drive by it," I scoff with a laugh.

"Oh, yeah? What would that be?" he asks with a returning smile.

I really stepped into that one.

"That you have a really sturdy-looking boat and know how to use it, obviously."

We both lean back in raucous laughter.

"I knew it was the confidence in my sailing skills that had so many people calling. Emily keeps telling me it was my shirtless chest, but I knew she had to be wrong."

Sawyer looks down at his sturdy, black watch with a bunch of dials on it.

"I really hate to break this up, but I have an excursion leaving in a half an hour. Emily will kill me if I am late this early in the season. Don't worry about the check. I will get it," he says.

"Are you sure? I have some cash I can put down."

"Yep. My treat," he insists as he flashes that panty-melting smile. He places some bills on the table next to the stack of dishes, and we get up.

He motions for me to walk in front of him to the door. When we get to the bar, he yells, "Money is on the table, Pep. See you tomorrow!"

A yell comes from the back. "Thanks, Saw! Later!"

We walk out the door into the sunny afternoon. We get a few steps away from the building, and Sawyer reaches down to take my hand in his.

He squeezes lightly and asks, "Is this okay? I don't want to overstep, so tell me if I was reading your signals wrong."

"Nope, you are reading them just fine."

His large hand is warm and rough in mine. It feels strong and capable like the hand of a man that works for a living and makes me feel safe in his presence. We walk hand in hand back to Pirate's Life, commenting on the random things we see.

"I'm serious about tomorrow. We meet up after lunch a little way down the beach from Shipwrecked. You can't miss us."

"Okay. I will have to see how my morning goes. Thanks for lunch and the invite. I had a good time," I say as we stop in front of the building and face each other.

"Me too, Avery."

I hear something that sounds like "Fuck it" right before his lips land on mine.

It takes me less than a second to respond to his kiss. My eyes flutter closed as I run my hands up his chest and grab his shirt. I push up onto my tiptoes to make the angle a little better, and his hands find my hips to pull me flush with his hard body. His tongue traces the seam of my lips, and my mouth opens in a sigh. He takes the opportunity to tangle his tongue with mine. The feeling causes a shiver to shoot through my body and desire to pool low in my belly.

Just as the rest of my body starts to react to his kiss, the front door opens, and Emily yells, "Our clients pay you to sail them around not play hockey with someone's tonsils while they wait!"

He breaks the kiss and rests his forehead on mine as he lets out a little groan.

"*Okay, Mom.* Tell them I will meet them out back."

I hear the door shutting to let us know she went back inside.

"Well, that was embarrassing and not well planned," he says.

"We may have to try it again sometime when we are less likely to get interrupted."

"Anytime you want to, I'm game."

"You better go. I'll see you later," I say as I start walking to my car.

"Bye, Avery."

I unlock the door and sit in Chili for a few minutes before starting the engine. I can't believe that just happened. Sawyer just kissed me, and I kissed him back in one of the hottest kisses I have ever had.

CHAPTER 13
FIRST ONE IN GETS THE BALL

Sawyer

"Go long!" I yell to Mason as I throw the football down the beach. He takes off running for a few seconds before turning and catches the perfectly placed pass. It's like we are still seniors playing varsity under the Friday Night Lights and not two old guys reliving their glory days since our ten-year reunion has already come and gone. Some routes you never forget.

I see Pepper wearing a pink-and-white bikini with a skirt thing tied around her waist, walking down the beach behind Mason, carrying her chair and a cooler. Mason follows my gaze and walks over to her. They exchange some words, and Mason takes her chair and cooler, and she takes the football. Her eyes zero in on me, and I know I'm in for an inquisition.

When they make it to where I'm standing, Mason pops open her chair, places it by his, and puts her cooler beside it.

Without even saying hello, she starts in. "So how was your date yesterday? You're lucky I was drowning, or I would have spent more time at your table sizing her up."

Mason interrupts before I can respond. "Wait. What? Saw was on a date yesterday? With an actual woman?" He swings his gaze from Pepper to me. "Was it Sailing Class Woman? Did you get her number? Something more?" He finishes his barrage of questions by raising his eyebrows twice suggestively.

"No, you goon. I didn't get her number or 'something more,'" I deny, putting emphasis on the last two words.

He turns back to Pepper and raises his brow, silently asking for more details.

She doesn't keep him waiting. "Her name is Avery, and she is really pretty. Steph called in sick yesterday, so I was running Rise and Dine by myself, so I didn't get to spend very much time eavesdropping or asking questions. That's all I really know, other than she gushed with praise over my BLT and loves my desserts."

"That doesn't give me much to go on, Pep. Everyone loves your BLT. I would probably give up bachelorhood if you made them for me every day."

"I will make them for you every day, and you don't even have to put a ring on it. Just come to Rise and Dine and place your order like everyone else. Don't forget to leave a fat tip," she sasses with a wink in his direction.

We all laugh at their joking banter.

"Hey, guys!" Savannah squeals as she skips toward us from Shipwrecked. She has on a Shipwrecked button-up and short jean shorts. I don't miss the way Mason's eyes follow her as she sets down her chair and cooler by Pepper's and starts unbuttoning her shirt to reveal her lime green bikini top.

He must feel my gaze, since he looks over my way then immediately turns to the water. He says he flirts with her to mess with me, but I'm not sure I believe him.

"I'm ready to sit down and relax. This week has been busy. The tourist season seems to start earlier every year." She sighs before continuing, "I heard someone say all the hotels are booked solid. Looks like it's going to be a great year for business!" She flops down in her chair and opens her cooler. She pulls out a cocktail in a can and slides it into her "I Got Shipwrecked" can koozie from the merchandise counter at the bar.

Since we all have a stake in the tourism of Wild Shore, we chat for a while more about the upcoming tourist season.

Mason asks, "Did you bring your speaker, Saw? We need some music."

"Yeah. It's in the side pocket of my cooler. Let me get it out."

I set the speaker in the sand in the middle of the horseshoe our chairs form. I get out my phone to Bluetooth some music. We sit and catch up for a while longer. It's nice to have a group of close friends that do things like this together. I would only change one thing, and she might show up this afternoon.

The playlist ends, and I pick up my phone to start another one. My home screen informs me it is almost four o'clock. My spirits sink a tiny bit since Avery hasn't shown up yet. She did say she would have to check her schedule and didn't give me a definitive answer. I tune back into the conversation with my friends and try to let my disappointment flow away with the tide.

It is not working. I need a distraction.

"I'm going to take a dip. Anyone want to join me?" I ask.

I hear "Yeah," "Sure," and "Let's go," coming from the circle.

"Grab the ball, Pep, so we can play a little two-on-two," I say.

"That's not fair. You guys always team up against us," Pepper gripes as she grabs the ball and runs to the crystal clear water. "First one in gets to pick their partner and gets the ball!"

We all take off running after her. We play catch and splash each other, jumping on each other's backs to try to push each other under the water. We take it back to elementary school and do handstand contests. Laughter and trash talk fly as we enjoy the sunny afternoon and great company.

Pepper breaks up our fun when she says, "I hate to leave, but I have to get home. I have to be at Rise and Dine at four in the morning to start baking."

Savannah cringes. "Yeah, I have to get going, too. I need to do some inventory in the morning. I have to place alcohol and food orders, or we are going to run out before the end of the week. That would look real good for a beach bar at the beginning of the season."

Mason groans. "I need to go check on BASE jump guy before I go home. I really hope this isn't an omen to how the rest of the tourist season is going to go," Mason implores, looking at the sky.

We all laugh at his misery while silently agreeing.

"Well, I already did everything I needed to do to prepare for next week, like a responsible business owner, so I'm going to sit right here and have a drink, listen to my music, and watch the sunset," I chime in.

"You mean Emily has everything under control, and you just have to show up," Mason teases.

"Well, that too. See you guys later," I tell them as they walk back to their vehicles.

The sun should set in a little less than an hour. It looks like it is going to be amazing. It makes me think about the place I usually sit to watch sunsets and who was sitting on that bench yesterday.

I'm still pretty bummed Avery didn't show up. I was hoping to introduce her to Mason and my sister and see what they thought about her. She is obviously gorgeous, and I liked spending time with her yesterday as well. I hope that kiss didn't give her second thoughts about coming today.

I pick up my phone to put on a campfire country playlist and grab a beer from my cooler.

I love being here. The sound of the waves and gulls calling are a balm to my soul. The beach and the water are where I belong. Does that mean I don't belong with Avery since she has ocean-water-induced anxiety?

I don't like that train of thought. There has to be something I can do to help her since it is obvious she is trying to overcome her fear.

I hear someone walking up behind me, but I don't think anything about it. This is a public beach, and sunset is a pretty popular time.

The person gets closer to me, so I glance over. Avery is standing a few feet from my chair with an unsure look on her face.

"Hey, Sawyer. I wasn't sure if you would still be here. Do you care if I join you? You look like you are deep in thought, so I don't want to intrude."

"Avery! Hey! I'm glad you made it. Everyone left a little earlier, so I was just sitting out here relaxing, waiting on the sunset. Have a seat."

She takes a teal and pink chevron-patterned beach mat out of her tote bag and unrolls it on the ground beside my chair. She sits down on the mat and toes off her brown flip flops.

Even in my low beach chair, I am still sitting higher than her. I look over as she takes a metal water bottle out of her tote bag and arranges her things on the mat. She is wearing a flowy, mustard yellow sundress with white and brown flowers printed on it. The top is cut in a low V that gives me a great view of her cleavage. The bottom hit almost to her knees when she was standing, but now that she is sitting with her hands behind her and leaning back, the bottom is more mid-thigh. God, she has nice legs that would look even better wrapped around my waist as I sink inside her tight pussy. I shift to relieve the pressure on my cock.

She looks up at me and says, "Sorry I couldn't get out here sooner. Riley called this morning with an emergency, so I had to make a drive down the coast. By the time we got the situation taken care of, it was almost three. We decided to grab a late lunch, and I got stuck in the Sunday afternoon traffic and didn't get home until almost five. I am exhausted from the craziness of the day, but I decided to come out here in case you guys were still here. If not, I had planned to sit and enjoy a peaceful sunset before the chaos starts again."

My mind instantly goes into anti-Riley mode as jealousy replaces the desire in my gut. I understand she had a life before me. Doesn't mean I have to like it. Or him.

"Well, I'm glad you made it back safely and decided to take a chance on me being here. Maybe you can make it next time we get together. They are great people, and I think you would like them," I offer.

"I would like that. I don't have very many friends since I didn't move here until after college. It's hard to make friends when you hang out with preschoolers all day and just want to relax in the quiet when you get home," she muses with a small giggle as she looks back out at the water.

The sun is making a steady fall to the horizon. She gives a little shiver and leans forward to look in her bag, giving me a view of her slender back.

"Well, shoot. I must have forgotten my cardigan in my car. I could have sworn I put it in my tote. The breeze coming off the water is a little chilly."

"I don't have a jacket or a shirt with me, or I would let you borrow it. The sunset won't be much longer. I can move down there to block the wind if you think it will help."

"Sure. I'll move my stuff so you can sit on the mat." She nods.

I throw my empty beer can into the trash bag we all used today and tie it up. I put the bag by my cooler so it doesn't get lost in the dark. I look over at Avery, and she has her stuff pushed to one side of the mat.

She is sitting with her legs crossed and her hands in her lap, looking up at me with those deep blue eyes. My stomach clenches at her pose, and my mind comes up with its own ideas about what we should be doing on this beach mat waiting for the sun to set.

CHAPTER 14

INTERNATIONAL SIGN

Avery

Sawyer sits down beside me, but he's still too far away to block much wind. We sit in silence for a few minutes and watch the last of the families on the beach pack up their toys and blankets. I am starting to get cold chills.

"Uh, Sawyer, I hate to sound like a whiner, but I'm getting goosebumps. I think I may have to give in and head home."

"I hate for you to leave without seeing the sunset. It looks like it is going to be one of the best ones I have seen in a while. Do you want to share body heat?"

The look in his eyes is enough to get my blood pumping and warm me up from the inside out.

"We can try that and see how it goes. We will both be able to see the sunset, I can share your warmth, and you will be blocking all the wind," I say with a small smile on my lips. I feel like a middle schooler asking my crush to dance with me at the Winter Ball.

"Sure. Hop up, and I will shift."

I stand up and look around the beach. We are the only people left. The breeze must have driven even the most hardy of sunset watchers away.

Sawyer moves to the side of the blanket and faces the sun. He straightens his legs out in front of him and opens them wide enough that I can sit between them.

He looks over at me, signaling that he is ready for me to sit down in front of him. I walk back over to the mat and sit between his legs. I am far enough away that we aren't touching, but I can smell the sunscreen and seawater on his skin. I give a subtle sniff to see if I can catch a hint of his spicy cologne, but it is gone by this time of day.

We sit in silence for a few minutes, enjoying the view and the time spent together.

"Can I ask you about your panic attacks? You seem fine here on the beach, so it's not being around the water that is the problem," he says.

"Being around water isn't the problem. I love to swim in a pool. I love to sit on the beach and suntan or hang out with friends. I just can't get in ocean water."

"Have you always been afraid of the water and it grew into something you can't control, or did something happen?"

I pause before answering. The only person in Wild Shore who knows about Aspen besides my parents is Riley. Am I ready to let someone else in? I enjoy spending time with Sawyer, and he is undeniably attractive. That kiss tried to short circuit my brain, so I know the chemistry is there. I can see us taking this thing we have to another level. I would have to let him in one day. It is too big of a piece of me to never tell my partner.

"Something happened before my dad got transferred to Silver Seaside," I decide to tell him. I open my mouth to tell him more, but nothing comes out. My body gives a little shiver. I don't know if it is from the thought of sharing the most personal details about myself or the chill of the evening.

Sawyer notices the tremor and asks, "Do you need to scoot closer to get some heat?"

I try to scoot a little closer both to get warmer and to stall my answer. Every time I move, the mat just bunches between us. Sawyer sees my predicament and tries to help me out by moving forward.

We move at the same time, and his chest crashes into my back. My breath gets lodged in my throat from the sensation of having full contact with his warm skin. I go still as I wait to see if this new position is okay.

Warmth seeps into my body from his. This is wonderful. My neck is starting to get a crick from keeping my head away from him, so I give in and press the back of my head to his shoulder. I slowly sink back into him and use his muscular chest for support.

He takes a small breath in and holds it for a few seconds before slowly letting it out. I guess this position is okay with him. We settle in and wait the final minutes until the sun meets the horizon, neither of us pushing to continue our conversation.

The sky explodes into shades of blue, purple, pink, and orange. The display literally takes my breath away, and I gasp as I watch the patterns change. This is definitely the best sunset we have had in a while. Being pressed into Sawyer only makes it better.

It only takes a few short minutes for the sun to fully set. The playlist switches over to a love ballad. We sit there in silence as the music floats over us. This is perfect.

"How about I tell you about my worst day? If you feel comfortable when I'm done, you can share your worst day. Talking about it in my own time helped me come to terms with what happened."

I nod for him to continue. Maybe talking to someone who has experienced anxiety will help. Talking to a therapist did not help me.

He starts talking so quietly I can barely hear him over the sound of the waves crashing on the nearby shoreline. "I told you I was in the Navy and did two tours. That's not quite truthful. I was actually a SEAL. My team and I went on missions all over the world at a moment's notice, taking out the worst of the worst. We had been tracking this band of insurgents for a few months. We got intel that they were holed up in a remote location. My team was tapped to see if the intel was accurate. We loaded up in the bird and flew to a few klicks from where we knew they were hiding. When we started to land, we took enemy fire. The bird went down hard in the middle of the desert with barely any cover. Comms were sketchy, but we got through what had happened, and HQ said they would send evac. By the time evac arrived, there were only three of us left. I tried to save the rest of them, but they were too badly injured."

He pauses his story and takes a few breaths. My heart aches for him and what he lost that day.

"I took a bullet in the thigh. The pilot had some wounds from the landing and a couple bullet grazes. The other guy just had some scrapes. The pilot and I were transferred to a military hospital. We had been on several missions together, so we knew each other. We recuperated together and became pretty close. We both returned to active duty. He continued flying birds, and I came back to an entirely different team, since mine didn't exist anymore. We went out on a few training missions to see how we gelled as a team. Every time I got in the bird, it didn't feel right. I didn't feel like a part of the team like I did with my old team. Part of it was grief, and part of it was that we didn't have time to build trust. My enlistment was almost up, so I spent the last few weeks of my career helping new recruits and took an honorable discharge. I still talk to the pilot. He saw who knows how many missions after the one that changed my life. He loves to fly and says he will never stop. I just couldn't do it anymore."

I feel his chest expanding into me as he takes a few deep breaths after that story, and I let it soak in. I know he will show empathy if I share my story. By all accounts, he lost some people who were like brothers that day and almost lost his own life.

I take a deep breath and let it out slowly. I can do this. I need to do this to begin the next season of my life.

"When I was twelve, my mom took my twin sister Aspen and me to the beach to boogie board one afternoon. We lived pretty close to the beach, so we went all the time. We were both really strong swimmers and understood water safety and what to do if you got swept out to sea. I was tired of boogie boarding, but Aspen wanted to catch a few more waves. I put my board up and went back to the edge of the water to watch her. She got distracted watching a paddle boarder and started to drift farther out. I yelled for her, but she couldn't hear me."

My body starts to shake. His arms come around me to pull me closer to him. I can feel his warm breath on my neck from where he is resting his chin on my shoulder. I spend a few moments taking in the comfort his hold provides.

"A big wave came crashing down on Aspen, and she fell off her board. Several people tried to find her, but it was too late. The waves kept getting bigger and closer together. They found her a few hours later floating a little ways down the beach."

Huge tears fall from my eyes, and I can't control my racking breaths and heaving gulps for air. I haven't told that story in a lot of years. Sawyer doesn't try to fill the silence with words that can't come close to expressing his feelings. He just holds me tighter in his comforting embrace and lets me cry. I didn't know I was still holding this much emotion inside me.

I cry for several more minutes. The sky is totally black now, with only the moon reflecting off the water to give us any light. The stars shine down on us, adding to the beauty of the night.

My emotions start to level out, but Sawyer does not loosen his hold. He turns his head to me, and I feel his lips pressing small kisses on the side of my neck, making my heart rush for an entirely different reason.

I turn on the mat so I sit sideways between his legs. I wrap my arms around his neck and pull him to me. Our lips meet in a tentative kiss since neither of us is sure what the other wants or how far to take this.

His tongue licks the seam of my lips, and I open for him. He explores my mouth, and his rough hand lands on my upper thigh, right below the hem of my dress. He grips my thigh and slowly starts rubbing a trail back and forth, barely slipping under my dress before retreating down to my knee and repeating the movement. Fire burns my skin from his touch.

My hands leave his neck to slowly roam down his body. I glide over his shoulders and press my nails into the ropey muscles. His pecs are well-defined from the physical strength it takes to sail. I find his nipples, and they turn into tiny, hard peaks when my fingers brush over them.

We continue kissing as my hands make their way down his stomach. I trace the ridges of his abdominal muscles with the pad of one finger. One, two, three on each side. A full six-pack on top of a prominent Adonis belt. The billboard was not photoshopped.

When I get to the band of his swim trunks, I chicken out before going any further and run my hands back up his chest and into his wind-blown hair.

I get a little more brazen and break the kiss while I turn to face him, one leg on each side of his hips.

I place a few kisses on the side of his mouth, his short beard tickling my lips. I use the grip I have on his hair to tilt his head back, giving me better access to continue my exploration. I keep moving down his chin to his neck where I place little nips that I follow up with a touch of my tongue.

He moans deep in his throat and grabs my ass under my dress, one lace covered cheek in each of his rough palms. He gives me a tight squeeze and rocks me toward him so my pussy brushes what is undoubtedly a massive erection with only a scrap of underwear and his swim trunks between us. Wetness floods my core, and I moan.

The sound startles me, and I open my eyes to look at him. He is looking right back at me. He smirks, and I bury my face in the crook of his shoulder, embarrassed that I am straddling his hips, desperate to take what I have wanted for so long.

When I calm down, I pull away from him and look away. I can only imagine what I look like right now. Tears falling down my cheeks, mascara running everywhere, eyes poofy from crying and bright with desire. What a seductive picture I make.

He takes my chin between his thumb and finger and tilts my face back to his. His thumbs move up my cheeks before swiping under my eyes.

"Thank you," I snivel in a voice raw from crying earlier. I'm not sure if I mean for providing a listening ear, a safe place to cry, cleaning my face, or one of the best make-out sessions I have had in a while.

"I should probably say the same thing. Thank you for sharing something so personal with me." He leans forward and places a kiss on my forehead.

"You make me feel safe enough to let you in. I haven't told anyone that story in a really long time. I keep it bundled up inside me. I am glad I found someone who understands my emotions when they hit," I say.

A massive cold chill wracks my entire body.

"We better get you home before you get sick," Sawyer says as he removes his arms from around me.

"You aren't even wearing a shirt! How are you not an ice cube?"

"I was sharing body heat with a woman I'm trying to get to know. I'm not going to wuss out on a romantic evening watching the sunset and then holding her under the stars because I chose not to wear a shirt today. I'm made of sterner stuff than that," he says, laughing. "And if Pepper, Savannah, or Mason ever heard I did, I would never live it down."

We stand up and shake the sand out of the mat before folding it. I put it back in my tote bag while he folds his beach chair and puts it on his back like a backpack.

"Where did you park? I will walk you back."

"In the lot right behind here. It's not too far," I say.

He picks up the trash bag and cooler in one hand and reaches out to me with the other.

It feels natural and right to put my hand in his as we walk to the lot.

When we get to Chili, I take the keys out of my tote and unlock the doors. I put my tote in the trunk so I don't get sand in my interior. Even living my entire life by the beach, having sand in my car drives me crazy.

I walk back to the driver's door, and Sawyer opens it for me.

"I had a really nice evening. I like spending time with you, Avery."

"I did, too. I'm glad you were still here when I got here."

I look up at him, and his eyes are filled with something I can't decipher.

I lick my lips in the international sign for Kiss Me Now. He takes the signal and runs his palm up the side of my face. He leans in and presses a tender kiss to my lips. He pulls away slowly and drops his hand.

"I'll see you later, Avery. Drive safely on your way home," he says quietly.

"You too," I practically whisper.

He steps away from me, and I get in my car. I close the door, put my seatbelt on, and turn the ignition. I back out of the parking space and drive to the exit. I glance in the rearview mirror when I get to the stop sign at the end of the lot. He is still staring at me. I give a little wave and turn onto Ocean Boulevard to make the short drive home.

CHAPTER 15
SEALED LIPS

Sawyer

It is finally Saturday. This week has been crazy. My days have been filled with tourist excursions and guided sailing trips, and my nights have been filled with thoughts of Avery.

I can't imagine watching your twin sister drown. I don't know what I would do if Sav died, let alone if I watched it happen as a kid.

I can't get the memory of our evening out of my mind. The way she opened up about her twin sister. The way she felt in my arms. The way she took what she wanted from that kiss. The way she straddled my lap and how her hot pussy felt against my hard cock.

Every night when I lay down in my bed, I wanted to contact Avery so badly. I almost looked in her sailing class contract for a phone number. I had to talk myself out of that so many times. Not only is that borderline illegal, if she wanted me to have her number, she would have given it to me. My number is plastered around town and on the internet, so if she wanted to get ahold of me, she could have.

Instead of stalking her on the internet, I researched how to overcome water phobia. I found several techniques that I think might work. If she comes to class today, I will ask her if she would like to try some.

That's IF she comes. I can totally understand why she wouldn't. Going from not even being able to get on a boat to taking a three-to-four hour trip on the water is a huge jump.

I continue walking down the dock, checking the Pudgies. Taking someone out for the first time on the coast is a pretty big undertaking. Multiply that by four, and I may have bit off more than I can chew. I will be sailing The Emerald in front of them, so if something goes way wrong, I can swing around and help. But for the most part, they will have to rely on each other and their knowledge to make the right decisions.

People start pulling into the lot beside the office building and getting out of their cars. They chat amongst themselves as they spray on sunscreen and get what they need for the trip.

I'm ready to get this day started. Once tourist season is in full swing, I don't have time to sail for pleasure. After the trip this morning, I plan on taking The Emerald out by myself. It may be my last pleasure trip for a few months.

Someone sees me at the dock, so they all start walking down the path to meet me down here. I scan the parking lot for a red Bug but don't see it yet.

When they all make it to the dock, I start my spiel. "Morning, guys! Are you ready for today?" I get a boisterous mix of yells and claps. "Well, then I won't make you wait forever before we start. We are going to keep the same pairs and Pudgy assignment from the last two weeks. Before we head out on the open sea, we will sail around the cove for a while so you get the hang of it again.

"While you are out there, try to think about what to do if something goes wrong. Do you know how to handle a wind change? Do you know what to do if you get a big wave and capsize? Do you know how to flip the Pudgy back over? Today is a beautiful day to sail, so I don't really expect that to happen, but it is something you need to know how to do. Any questions?"

No one responds.

"All right then. You all did great last week, so I'm excited to see what you can do this week. I will give two whistle blasts when I think you all are ready to leave the cove and head to the coast. Let's go!"

They all cheer and yell as they walk around me to get to their assigned vessels. I look up at the parking lot. Still no Avery.

I walk up to Jill while she is getting her stuff stored in her Pudgy. "Hey, I don't see Avery this morning, so you will not have a partner again. Are you okay with that, or do you want to go with me or another group?"

"Can we play it by ear? I'll sail around the cove again and see how I do. If I feel confident, I would like to try to sail the coast. If I struggle, will I be able to tender to your boat?"

"Yes. I will check your Pudgy over to make sure it has a hook and that I have the ropes I need in The Emerald. Let me know how you are feeling before we leave, so I know if I need to keep a close eye on you."

"Sure thing, Sawyer."

The class has been sailing for about twenty minutes. They are doing excellent. I can't hold off leaving any more. Avery isn't coming. I blow my whistle twice and look for Jill. She gives me a thumbs-up, so I head for the mouth of the cove. A line of Pudgies starts to form behind me like baby ducks following their mom.

The sun is shining beautifully. The wind is blowing enough to give us about two to three knots of speed. Perfect for beginners.

We sail up the coast past Shipwrecked. Savannah is standing on the large deck that faces the water, opening umbrellas on several tables. I wave, and she cups her hands around her mouth and gives a whoop of support to all the beginner sailors.

We sail up to the line of hotels on the north end of Wild Shore. It took us about an hour and a half to get here. I blow the whistle one time so everyone knows to gather.

When everyone is close enough to hear me, I yell, "How was the trip? Anyone have any issues? It looked like you all knew what you were doing."

They are all smiles, and no one says anything about any issues.

"Well, okay then. Let's head back. The sailing should be easier since the tide should pull us in that direction. Who wants to stop by Shipwrecked and have a drink on me for completing the course?"

Everyone cheers, so I set sail back down the coast. The Pudgies fall in line.

We reach Shipwrecked in a little under an hour. Savannah is standing on the deck, changing the sign to open when we float up to the dock.

She greets us by saying, "Hey, guys! You look good out there! And a little thirsty. I just mixed up a few pitchers of Wild Pirate. Come on up here and get a drink for finishing the class!"

The class whoops and hollers with their excitement for making the sail up the coast and back down and the free drink. My sister is known for her signature cocktails, so they know they are in for a treat.

Savannah walks into the bar and starts pouring and handing out drinks. The class disperses around the bar and the deck to relax and have their drinks.

I walk up to the bar and take a seat in front of Savannah. She pours a drink and sits it in front of me.

"Thanks, Sav."

Her eyes light up with curiosity, and she scans the bar. "You're welcome. So which one is she?"

"Who?" I ask, confused.

"The girl you took to Rise and Dine that is in your sailing class," she says with exasperation evident in her voice.

"She didn't show up today."

"What? She didn't come to the last class? Is she okay?"

"She wasn't feeling up to it this morning."

"That's too bad that she put in all the work and then missed the fun stuff. Do you have time to let her have a make-up session? I know your spots start to fill up really quickly when tourists start coming in."

"This doesn't go any further than us. I am only telling you because I'm starting to have real feelings for her, and I need to talk to someone about this."

"Yeah, no problem. These lips are sealed."

"Avery has anxiety associated with water due to a past trauma. She decided to try sailing to work on conquering her fear, but she had a panic attack the first week before class started and had some issues at the end of the second class. She showed up last week but decided not to go out. She sat on the bench behind the office and watched us in the cove. She must have decided she couldn't handle going up the coast today and didn't show up."

"Oh, wow. That's terrible. I can't imagine not being in the water. It is a huge part of who we are and what we do. Would that cause an issue with you guys if you become a couple?"

"I don't think so. She is actively trying to work through her anxiety. She was fine sitting with me on the beach the other night," I tell her.

"Wait. When did you guys hang out on the beach? Why are you withholding information from me, Saw? I'm your sister!"

"Well, Sister, we have both been busy this week, and I haven't even seen you until now. I'm telling you now, so that counts in my book."

"You didn't answer the real question," she reminds me.

"After lunch on Saturday, I invited her to come hang out with us at the beach. She said maybe. She ended up having to go help her friend Riley with something and didn't get back until late in the day. She decided to come to the beach to see if we were still there. It was only me, so we watched the sunset together."

"Ooooo. How romantic. Did you guys have heart eyes for each other?" she harasses me.

"Wouldn't you like to know?" I finish my drink and slide the empty glass toward her.

"Excellent as always, Sav. Put the drinks on my tab. I'll be through to pay it later," I tell her as I get up to round up the class.

"I wasn't done talking to you! Don't think you can hide from this conversation forever!" she yells at my back.

I shake my head and walk through the bar, motioning to the class that it is time to go. When we get to the deck, the rest of the class is standing up and getting ready to leave.

We walk down to the Pudgies and The Emerald tied to Shipwrecked's dock. Everyone makes it back under sail and headed in the right direction in very little time. They are doing really well. I hope they decide to do the more advanced sailing classes or want to learn the tricks of sailboat racing.

We make it back to the cove at Pirate's Life and moor the Pudgies. The group congregates at the end of the dock for my post-class words.

"Well, you all made it back. How does it feel?"

Everyone cheers. I hear several people say, "Great" and "Awesome."

"That's good to know. You all did excellent. I would love to have you guys back for some one-on-one lessons sailing that rig." I point at The Emerald.

I see the looks of excitement and wonder on their faces.

Jill asks, "You'd really let me sail that?

"Of course I would. It's not like I would just send you out by yourself. I'll be there teaching you how to handle a larger vessel and how to run more than one sail. It's a good time, and I think you guys would really enjoy it. When you are ready, just come by the office, and we'll see when I can fit you in for some lessons. Any questions?"

No one says anything, so I assume they are happy with what they learned.

"Then I'm glad you guys tried the beginner sailing class with Pirate's Life and hope to see you back here or out on the water one day."

They say their goodbyes and thanks and head up the path to the parking lot.

I walk down the dock, checking the mooring on the Pudgies and that everything is stored securely since I only use the Pudgies for this class. They are really only good for one or two people and not made for day sailing.

I walk over to The Emerald to do a pre-sail check. Everything looks ready to go. I look up at the parking lot to make sure everyone left and see a red Bug.

My heart rate speeds up with excitement and nervousness to see Avery again.

CHAPTER 16
LISTENING TO YOURSELF

Avery

Since I didn't sail in the cove last week, I knew there was no way I could manage going up the coast today. I also didn't want to risk having a panic attack and causing a big scene that would distract the rest of the class, so I decided to skip the last lesson.

I felt bad about not telling Sawyer I wasn't going to be there. We haven't exchanged numbers, and it didn't feel right calling the Pirate's Life office to leave a message for him, so I decided to talk to him in person when they got back.

This approach also gives me the added bonus of seeing if the chemistry we had on the beach was from our heightened emotions or if we are building a deeper connection.

Riley and I made plans to meet at the Silver Seaside pool this afternoon to discuss the book we are reading together, but I should have enough time to talk to Sawyer before I need to be there. After I get out of the shower, I pick out one of my favorite bikinis, hot pink bottoms with a hot pink and grey top. I put on my white coverup and gray flip flops and twist my wet hair into a messy bun.

I catch a glimpse of myself in the mirror on my way out of my room. My cheeks are flushed and my eyes are sparkling. I look happy and excited at the thought of spending even the smallest amount of time with Sawyer. This is definitely more than just physical attraction on my part.

I pull a beach towel out of the hall closet and toss it in my tote bag. I grab my Kindle, sunglasses, phone, metal water jug, and the bottle of sunscreen I put on the counter earlier and put them in my tote as well. I can't think of anything else I will need, so I swipe my keys off the table by the door and head out.

The drive to Pirate's Life is beautiful today. I bet they are having a blast sailing up the coast. The wind is blowing through my hair and the sun is shining on me since I put the convertible top down before I left home. It's one of those days that just makes anything feel possible.

I pull into the parking lot of Pirate's Life and find a place to park. The class must still be out sailing since there are only two boats at the dock. *Perfect.*

I'm not sure how long I will need to wait, so I grab my tote and start walking across the parking lot.

The office manager stands up from where she was sitting on an Adirondack chair in front of the building and waves.

"Morning! How can I help you today?"

When I get close enough for her to see me, she says, "Oh, hey, Avery. You're a little late to sail up the coast with the beginner class. They should be close to being back by now."

"I know. I decided not to go this morning. I was hoping to talk to Sawyer when he got back."

She makes a face that I can't figure out. Why does she care if I talk to Sawyer?

"Well, I know Sawyer won't want to miss seeing you. Have a seat, and we can wait for them in the sunshine. Sawyer said they were going to stop at Shipwrecked for a celebratory drink on the way back."

She looks at her watch. "They should be here within the next thirty minutes. I'm Emily, by the way. I don't know if I introduced myself when you signed up for the class."

I walk to the front of the store and sit in the green chair that matches the one she is sitting in. This is the most comfortable

Adirondack chair I have ever sat in. They aren't all made the same, and this one is perfect.

"So, Avery—" Emily begins as the phone rings from inside the building. "Duty calls. I'll be right back."

I lean my head back and close my eyes to wait for her to return. The ocean breeze counteracts the heat from the sun shining on my bare skin to create the perfect atmosphere for relaxation. I can hear some birds calling each other and the recently budded leaves rustling. A car drives by every few minutes to add to the soundtrack.

This is wonderful. I wonder if Sawyer would let me sit here after work and decompress.

I can hear the phone ringing again, and Emily discussing catamaran rates and availability. This place is busy. I let my mind wander until I hear people laughing and chatting. The class must be back.

I stand up and pick up my tote. I wave at Emily through the open door. She waves back from the front desk where she has the phone cradled between her neck and shoulder as she scrolls through whatever is on the computer screen in front of her.

I walk around the back of the building to the bench at the mouth of the path. Everyone but Sawyer has made it up from the dock. He is walking down the line of boats, checking each Pudgy, and doesn't even know I am here. I feel a little like a creeper just staring at him, but I can't help myself.

His light blue Pirate's Life button-up is blowing in the breeze, giving me glimpses of the bronze skin and hard muscles below. His hair is windblown and messy, making me want to run my fingers through it. He is hands down the best-looking man I have ever seen. My insides warm and melt in agreement.

He decides the Pudgies are secure and goes to the beautiful sailboat for a few minutes. He looks up toward the parking lot then over at the bench. Our eyes lock, and he smiles. My breath leaves me for a few seconds. I could see that look a million times and never get used to the effect it has on me.

He starts walking up the path, and my heart picks up speed for an entirely different reason than the last time I was on this path. How should I react after our evening spent on the beach?

He takes the problem out of my hands as he walks up to me and gives me a tight hug. My breasts smash into his hard chest and my face into his shoulder.

He says into my ear, "You're late for the sail up the coast. Did you want to discuss a private sailing? I'm sure that can be arranged."

His beard rubs my skin, eliciting memories that cause my nipples to pebble.

He runs his nose up the side of my ear before releasing me from the hug.

"Well, uh, no. That's not actually why I am here. I want to apologize for not showing up this morning and not calling beforehand. That was inconsiderate. You are trying to run a business and can't be waiting around for people to show up," I blurt.

"Hey, Avery, calm down. It's fine," he reassures me as he takes my hand. "I had hoped to see you today, but I wasn't totally sure you would show up. That's a huge step that I don't know if you are ready for. I kept checking for you, but we left on time as planned. No problem."

That puts me at ease, and I look down at my small hand nestled in his large, tan one. He gives it a squeeze.

He starts walking to the bench and tugs me along. He sits and pulls me down so we can stare out at the blue water. He manspreads and places his arm along the back of the bench but doesn't touch me.

I have to break the silence. "How was the trip today?"

"It was great! The wind was perfect for beginners, and everyone did really well. I am confident in their skills to navigate small dinghies, and I'm pretty sure a few are going to come back to learn how to run more than one sail and bigger vessels. It was a great start to the beginner sailing program. Everyone really excelled," he gushes.

"Everyone except for me," I say with a mixture of embarrassment and chagrin.

Sawyer bumps his shoulder into mine and brings his arm down around me, tucking me close to him.

"Hey, you did excellent on the dry section. You knew exactly what direction to turn the sail and what to do in an emergency. You also knew the answer to every one of the first week questions. But most of all, you listened to yourself and knew when to tap out. I'm proud of you, Avery."

I look up at him and see him looking down at me.

"Really?" I gasp as I search his face.

"Yes, really. That shows true self-awareness to know when you are ready to move on to the next step. Not everyone has to move at the same pace. Some of the beginner classes may not get to take the trip up the coast, and we stay in the cove for two weeks. If you did show up today, I was going to have you sail with me so I could keep an eye on you and let you do the things you felt comfortable with."

"The rest of the class would have been giving me the side eye, wondering why I was getting preferential treatment. They would likely think we are sleeping together or something." As soon as the words leave my mouth, I feel my face explode in heat, and I look down.

Sawyer puts his finger under my chin and tips my face back towards him. "Only in my dreams," he confides as he leans forward and kisses me. The arm that was around my shoulders moves to the base of my head so he can position me how he wants me.

The kiss starts out slow as he presses his lips to mine. My lips open on a gasp, and he takes the opportunity to pull my bottom lip between his teeth as his other hand drifts up to cup my face. He slides his tongue across my lip before exploring my mouth. Withdrawing, he places small kisses around my mouth before diving back in with his tongue.

I break out of my shock enough to actively participate. My tongue rubs along his as my hand rises up his chest to the open neck of his shirt.

The kiss slows as we lean back and open our eyes to stare at each other. I am slightly dazed. I have always doubted that your lips can tingle after a kiss but not anymore.

CHAPTER 17
MAYBE YOU'RE A BAD KISSER

Sawyer

I want to devour her. The way she responds when I kiss her makes me want to see her face when I kiss her everywhere. She is gripping my shirt and hanging on for dear life. She is as into the kiss as I am. Her pupils are dilated, and I can see her chest rising and falling.

Damn that coverup for keeping me from seeing what the swimsuit holds underneath. A cleavage peek a day keeps the doctor away, or something like that.

I look back at her eyes and smile a little sheepishly as I drop my hand from her face. She must realize she is still gripping my shirt since she lets go quickly and puts her hands on her thighs and looks down.

"Wow, I wasn't expecting that, but I'm glad it happened," I tell her.

She whips her head back in my direction. "Me too."

We smile at each other, and she rocks away from me, giggling.

From behind us, Emily yells, "Saw, are you taking Emy out today for pleasure? There is a family here that wants to take a trip up the coast. The afternoon calendar is clear, but I didn't know if you made plans."

I take a deep breath and sit back against the bench as Avery stiffens beside me. I can't tell if she is embarrassed about being caught again or if she thinks I am getting ready to take another woman out for an afternoon of debauchery.

Thanks, Emily, for interrupting us with a double entendre and ruining my mojo. She must have a whole wall of gold medals in cockblocking displayed at home.

"I was planning to go out by myself, but I can take them. Give me fifteen minutes to get everything ready."

"All right, boss man. I will let them know," Emily confirms, and I hear her footsteps walking back inside.

"No rest for the wicked, I guess," Avery observes.

I turn my head toward her, open one eye, and with a grin full of mischief say, "You haven't even seen wicked yet, babe."

Her cheeks flush as expected, and we both laugh.

"I have to get The Emerald ready to sail, so I better go. Can't make customers mad this early in the season."

"Yeah, I told Riley I would be at the Silver Seaside pool at one, so I better get going." She stands up and turns to walk back to the parking lot.

The mention of her spending the afternoon with Riley at a luxury resort pool makes my jealousy fly to the surface. I want to be the one she spends an afternoon with in a swimsuit followed by time out of a swimsuit.

I stand up and grab her wrist, causing her to turn and bump into my chest. When she makes an "oh" sound, I grip the back of her head with my other hand and pull her lips to mine, then my tongue dives in for a deep, possessive kiss.

As she lets out a little, breathy moan, I release her. "I hope you think about that kiss this afternoon as much as I will be."

I give her ass a smack and leave her standing awestruck as I walk back down the dock to The Emerald. I need to get below deck to adjust the semi I have before I meet the family at the office. I go through the pre-sail checklist in hopes of calming my body down.

The refrigerator has drinks, and the cabinets have plenty of snacks. We will sail for a couple hours, have a snack, then sail back. We will be back in plenty of time before dark.

Everything is ready, my body included, so I walk back up the path to the office. The family is standing outside the building. A man and a woman in their late thirties and two middle-school-aged girls.

The sight of them immediately makes me think of Avery and her twin sister. They are excitedly pointing at a couple of sailboats racing in front of the cove. One is barely pulling ahead of the other, and one girl starts to cheer louder and jumps up and down.

"I won! Orange is my favorite color, so I knew that one was going to win!" she crows.

Their mom tries to calm them down by saying, "Okay, girls. Our captain is here. Let's pay attention to him, so we can get out on the water too."

I give her a thankful look and clap my hands in front of me. "I see you girls like racing. Do you want to see how fast we can go?"

They raise their hands in the air and jump up and down and scream. I love it when kids get excited about sailing. If they catch the bug young, they will continue to come back and generate more business.

"Well then, let's get to it." Emily got them outfitted with life vests while I readied the boat, so we are ready to set sail.

We board The Emerald, and one girl and a parent sit on the benches on both sides of the large steering wheel. I steer us to the mouth of the cove under the power of the electric motor.

"Since you guys are new to sailing, I will captain and crew this vessel. You guys just sit back, relax, and have fun." I set the emerald green mainsail and let the mainsheet ease. The mainsail catches a small breeze and luffs. The boom tugs on the preventer, and we are ready to raise the charcoal jib.

The sails catch wind, and I pull rigging. A glance at the digital gauges shows we are at about eight knots. Everyone is smiling as we cut through the crystal-clear blue water. The beautiful weather of this morning is continuing this afternoon. This is why I love my job.

We head up the coast, looking at all the large houses that dot the rocky shore. We pass the Silver Seaside, and I can't help but look for a hot pink bikini. The pool is dotted with people, but at this distance I can't make anyone out.

We continue up the coast for another hour. I have been chatting with the adults about sailing and the myriad of services Pirate's Life has while the girls sunbathe on the emerald green cushions they pulled out of storage. I decide it is time for a little swim and snack.

"You girls ready to jump in?"

They both squeal, "Yes!" and scramble to sit up.

I lower the sails so we come to a standstill. "Do you girls like to snorkel? There's usually a school of fish that swims through here."

They nod, and I get out the snorkel masks I keep on board.

They put on their masks and jump off the stern. They find the school of fish and exclaim about the colors and different kinds. After about a half hour, they get back on board, and I store their gear.

We all head below deck to rummage through the drinks and snacks. We take our findings to the deck and lie out in the sun.

When we are done with our snack, I collect the trash and stow it below deck. I raise the mainsail and jib, and we head back down the coast.

I trim the jib and the mainsail to pick up more speed.

"You guys ready to race?" I yell over the wind.

"Yes!" the girls yell back.

I trim the sails a couple more inches, and they fill with air, propelling the boat through the water. We are up to fifteen knots and really flying through the surf. I might be able to get a few more if I trimmed the sail a little more, but this is plenty fast for first-time sailors.

We are almost back to Pirate's Life when I ask the girls if they want to drive. I heave to so the boat slows to an easily manageable pace.

They take turns manning the wheel and acting like pirates. Their joy in the water reaffirms why I work so hard to keep my business alive.

I drop sail and use the electric motor to bring the boat back to its place at the dock.

The family gets off the boat and stands on the dock.

"Thank you, Sawyer, for fitting us into your schedule. I know you probably had other plans, but I'm glad you shared your afternoon with us," the woman says. "The girls will talk about this for weeks."

"I'm always happy to introduce people to the sailing life," I reply. "I'm glad you guys had fun."

"I'm sure we will be back," the man says as they wave and walk up the path to the parking lot.

I get busy stowing the sails and rigging. I am starving since I have been on the water since breakfast with only the snack to eat after the girls snorkeled.

The only time I had to eat lunch today I spent with Avery, and I wouldn't even trade that time for one of Pepper's BLTs and seasoned fries.

I walk in the back door of Pirate's Life, and Emily greets me with a slip of paper in one hand and a smile on her face.

"I can't call anyone back right now, Em. I could eat the south end of a northbound tiger," I bluster as I try to walk past her.

"First, eww. Second, I'd say you've got time to call this person back."

"Who is it? My mom can wait."

"Well, it's a woman but definitely not your mom," she jokes.

I grab the paper out of her hand and read the name. Avery. She left her number! My face splits into a huge smile as my hunger pangs dissipate slightly.

Emily wags her finger at me. "Don't think I didn't see you two out there on the bench sucking on each other's faces. Thank God I noticed you before I sent that family out there to meet you. What a wonderful advertisement that would be for your business."

"I think it fits right in with the pirate's life theme. Sailing, wenching, shirtless billboards. Now if only I had a bottle of rum. I think I'll do that right now, actually. I'm sure Sav will set me right up," I say as I stuff the number in my pocket and back out the door.

"I can't deal with you anymore," Emily declares.

"You love me," I shout through the closing door.

I get in my Jeep and drive up Ocean Boulevard to Shipwrecked. I have to stop twice for traffic, and there is a small crowd on The Boardwalk. It seems tourist season is upon us.

The crowd doesn't diminish when I get to Shipwrecked. The gravel parking lot is full, and all the tables are occupied. There is a band playing on the deck, and people are up dancing. I look around until I find a single seat at the bar. When the waitress comes over, I order a burger, fries, and a beer.

I pull the slip of paper out of my pocket and run it between my fingers. Is it too early to contact her? Don't you have to wait so long before you make contact after a date these days? Does the evening at the beach count as a date? Does today?

It has been so long since I have done anything like this I don't know the rules anymore. Actually, I have never done anything like this. I want more than just a quick fuck. The way I feel about Avery is way deeper than anything I have ever felt for anyone before, so I don't want to screw this up.

Savannah comes strolling by, sets my beer down, and pulls the paper out of my fingers. She stretches it out between her fingers and reads.

"Ooohhhhhh, somebody got Avery's number! Is this a 'Call me to schedule a class' or a 'Call me for a good time' number?" she asks.

I don't know how to answer her. "Give me that back, you ass. She showed up when I got back to Pirate's Life with the beginner sailing class earlier. We sat on the bench for a little while. Then a family showed up, and I had to take an excursion and she went to spend the afternoon at Silver Seaside with Riley."

She looks at me for a minute then asks, "What aren't you telling me? There is something going on in that mind of yours."

"I don't know how she is feeling. We watched the sunset together and shared some deeply personal stories. She came to Pirate's Life today and left her number. We have kissed a few times, and now she is spending the afternoon with Riley. Is she into me or not?"

"Maybe you're a bad kisser." Sav snickers.

"You're not helping. And I know she likes kissing me from her reactions."

"Okay, you can stop right there," she declares.

I laugh at her response as the waitress sets down my burger and fries.

"I guess you won't know unless you use the number. I gotta get going. I'll talk to you later," she says and walks down the bar to another customer.

I replay her words over and over in my mind while I eat my dinner.

There was never a doubt in my mind if I would use the number. The question is when.

CHAPTER 18
BABY-MAKING PRACTICE

Avery

It has been two days since I gave Emily my number to give to Sawyer. That was one of the most embarrassing things I have ever done. When I walked to the parking lot, I decided to do something bold. I searched through my purse until I found a scrap piece of paper that didn't have someone's masterpiece drawn on it. I wrote my name and cell number and walked back inside the office.

Emily was standing behind the desk and smiled when I walked in. It felt like middle school when you call a landline and your crush's parent answers. When she asked me if I wanted to schedule a make-up lesson I was mortified when I said no and asked her to give my number to Sawyer.

She raised her eyebrow and put the slip of paper on the desk. I can probably never go back there now. She likely put it in the stack with the other women drooling over his shirtless billboard.

The sound of little feet walking down the hallway brings me out of my reverie.

"We're back, Miss Sutton! Did you miss us?" Desiree asks in her little girl voice. She is the sweetest little girl I have ever met.

"Always, Des. It is lonely in here without all of you guys," I say.

"You should come with us next time!"

"I have to stay in here and think about the fun things we are going to be doing after lunch so you guys get so smart you go right to high school after this year!" I joke.

"I can't skip kindergarten!" she says with horror. "My mom says it's going to be soooo much fun!"

"I bet it will be. We only have a couple weeks left of school, then you will take a few months off. Then off to kindergarten! You guys are going to do so great, but first, you have to make it through the rest of preschool. Go take your seat, and we will get started."

I pick up my crazy words board, and they sound out nonsense CVC words. Some of these kids are still having letter-sound recognition issues, but for the most part, they all have a strong foundation for reading.

We do a few more activities and have a snack before they go outside to burn off some energy before packing their bags for pickup.

Today was long. I don't know if it is the end of the year excitement or my lack of sleep catching up with me, but I need a nap. My phone dings in my purse. I have it on Do Not Disturb during school hours, so it usually goes off with whatever texts, emails, and social media tags I have gotten as soon as the day is over.

I glance over and see a text from my mom amid all the socials and scam calls.

MOM: Do you want to come to SS for dinner? Your dad has a late meeting with some department managers, and we are going to eat after.

ME: Sounds good. It's been a long week already, and I don't want to cook.

MOM: It's Monday, Avery.

ME: Yep, and it's already been a long week <laughing emoji>

MOM: SMH. Anyway, we will meet you in the dining room at 7:30. That should give you plenty of time to take a nap and rejuvenate.

ME: <eye roll emoji>

Mom dislikes a message.

I laugh at my mom's use of technology. She accidentally sent me a reaction to a text one day, and now she uses them all the time.

I pull out the stack of papers the class did today and start putting stickers on them. We did a lowercase letter test today, and they all did so well I break out the smelly stickers. The life of a preschool teacher.

I finish up and pack my things to leave. I glance at my phone one more time just in case I missed a notification from an unknown number from around here. No dice.

I walk out to Chili and put the top down to enjoy the drive home. When I walk in the door I still have about two hours until I need to meet my parents, so I set my phone alarm and lie down on the couch with my Kindle.

The blaring of my alarm brings me out of the fairytale world Riley has us reading about. When I remember why I set an alarm, I walk to my bathroom and change clothes and brush my hair. I add a little mascara since the Silver Seaside restaurant is one of the more upscale in the area, and my mom will disown me if I show up looking like a hobo.

The sun is about to set when I walk outside to get in Chili. My mind wanders back to the last sunset I watched. *Why hasn't Sawyer messaged me?* I thought after that parting kiss, he would want to see where the attraction led. Guess I was wrong. *Uggghhh.*

I back out of my driveway and drive through my neighborhood as it prepares for the end of another day. I drive along the base of the ridge past Balls Deep Sea, the golf course my parents live on. The lavishly landscaped entrance is adorned with water features on both sides. I can tell my mom helped pick out the plants.

I drive up the gentle incline to the entrance of Silver Seaside and park in the valet area. This place awes me every time I see it. The resort is a grand structure with various rooflines spanning up the cliff side. Several of the windows are illuminated with a warm, inviting glow.

I get out of my car and walk up to the large, opulent entrance flanked by white columns. The doorman opens the oversized door, and I walk into the large open lobby. The main desk is straight ahead. A huge stone fireplace dominates the wall to the left with seating placed sporadically throughout the area.

The grand staircase, elevator, and restaurant entrance are to the right. I walk to the restaurant and see the Front Desk Manager, Shelby, walking my way. She is a few years younger than me, a little shorter and thinner than me, and has long dark brown hair.

"Hey, Shelby! Is the meeting over? I was supposed to meet Mom and Dad when he is done," I say.

"Hey, Avery! We just finished. I need to take care of something, so I'll catch you later," she says as she quickly walks away.

I wonder what major issue she is dealing with. I'm sure Dad will have some scoop.

I keep walking to the restaurant entrance and see Mom sitting by the wall of windows that faces the water. The sun set on the way over here, so all she can see outside is the torches and fireplaces lit across the expansive deck and the Edison lights that encircle the area. It makes for a pretty scene. Perfect for a wedding.

Where did that thought come from?

"Hey, Mom. Thanks for the invite," I say when I get close to her table. She stands up and gives me a hug.

"I'm so glad you could make it, Avery. Your dad texted that he had to put some stuff in his office, and he would be right out. You are just in time."

"Awesome," I say as I sit in the chair across from Mom and closest to the window. "Do you know what you are having? What's the special tonight?"

"I'm actually not sure. You know I just get whatever the chef fixes me. I'm not a pole parker like your dad."

"This place has the best salmon," my dad and I chorus, me mocking him and him defending his choice as he walks up behind me.

We all laugh as he leans over and kisses me on the forehead and Mom on the lips before sitting down beside her. My family has always been demonstrative of our love, but it increased after Aspen's death.

The waitress sees Dad sit down and shows up immediately to take our orders. We all get water with lemon. No surprise to anyone, Dad gets the salmon, rice, and broccoli, Mom gets the Chef's Choice, and I go with a medium ribeye, baked potato with butter and sour cream, and salad with house ranch. I go all out when we eat here. I can't help myself. My stomach will hurt so bad when I leave, but it is worth it.

"So what's going on here? I saw Shelby leave the meeting in a rush to get somewhere. She looked a little flustered," I pry.

"The shareholders decided to do their quarterly meeting here next quarter, so we have to figure out where to put everybody without moving guests around. Their meeting will be during peak time, which is smart for them to see how we operate at max capacity, but bad timing for us on such short notice. Shelby needs to figure out where everyone is going to stay, get a conference room reserved, and get dinner tables reserved. She's going to be busy getting that sorted before we book any more people," Dad answers.

"That poor girl. You run her ragged," Mom says.

"Marie, you know I'm going to retire one day, and it's very likely she will be running this place. She has to learn how to handle the stress and make things work. I am very impressed with how well she does her job and won't worry one bit when that day comes. I am going to leave this place in competent hands," Dad replies.

I didn't know he was planning to retire soon, but my parents are getting to be that age. Next thing you know, they will be asking for grandbabies to spoil in their retirement.

"Avery, have you decided what you are going to do this summer when school lets out? I'm sure Shelby can find something for you to do if you don't find anything," Dad says.

"You know you don't have to work year-around. That's one of the perks of being a teacher. You get breaks. You can take the summer off, and we can lie by the pool and read scandalous novels until it's time for you to go back to inspiring the next generation," Mom tries to persuade me.

"I will do something, but I haven't really decided what just yet. I like to stay a little busy during the summer, or my mind goes to mush. Everyone in Wild Shore hires for summer help, so it won't be that hard to find something once I decide."

"Speaking of scandalous, I finally saw that billboard people have been talking about. Sheewwweeee. They really shouldn't put that along the road if they want people to focus on driving. The only thing I was focused on was how many abs that model had. That thing is a worse distraction than any phone. I don't know where they find those men, but you need to go there and bring one home. I bet he would make beautiful babies."

I almost choke on my own saliva. "Mom! You can't say things like that. Dad is sitting right here, and you are old enough to be that man's mom!"

"I didn't mean babies with me, sweetheart. I meant with you. It's about time for you to be getting serious in that department."

What am I supposed to tell her? He is even better in person? I'm closer to baby-making practice with him than anyone else? His kisses make me hotter than any man ever has?

Luckily, I am saved from having to respond by our waitress stopping in front of our table with a large tray of food. She passes out our plates and says she will be back in a few minutes with fresh waters and to check on our food.

As always, the food is delicious. My steak is cooked to perfection, tender and juicy. We finish the meal making small talk and catching up on our lives between bites. Before I know it, it is almost nine, and I need to be getting home.

We say our goodbyes, and I get in Chili to drive home. My parents will likely stay in the room my dad keeps just for our use.

When I get home, I put all my stuff on the kitchen counter and walk to my bathroom. I strip out of the sundress and into a sleep shirt. I wash my face and brush my teeth and fall into bed.

I check to make sure my alarm is set on my phone. I swipe over to the text and call logs to see if I happened to miss anything from Sawyer. Nothing. I place my phone on the nightstand charging pad and look up at the ceiling in the dark.

I could have sworn he was into me. I could feel an impressive bulge in his shorts while we kissed. I have seen desire in his eyes. Could it just be a physical response, and he doesn't want more?

I slam my fists into the mattress to let out some frustration. I reach down to grab the comforter to pull the covers over my head and let out a groan.

How many days should I wait before giving up hope?

CHAPTER 19
FLYING AT THE SPEED OF A SNAIL

Sawyer

I finally concede I know nothing about dating and pull up my web browser. I type *How many days should I wait after a date before texting the person?*

Most of the sites say three days. That means tonight after I get through with another busy day, I can contact her.

What am I going to say? Hopefully, something comes to me today while I'm doing a private excursion this morning and a catamaran snorkel this afternoon. I can't believe how fast the sail slots booked this year, and the phone still rings off the hook. Thank God for Emily keeping everything up here running smoothly.

"Hey, guys! I've got The Emerald all ready to go, so as soon as you get your life jackets on, we can embark," I tell an older couple. They requested a three-hour sunrise sail to the south around the Twin Peaks since they are staying on the north end.

The south end is lined with a large rock wall except for one small inlet where an older man works on boats. He works mostly on diesel engines and sport boats, so I have only been in there a handful of times for minor repairs or to pick up parts I fix myself.

We make a leisurely sail down the coast in the dark, using the electric motor to propel us. The older couple cuddles together under a blanket on the bow and chats between themselves. They aren't looking for my company, but every once in a while, they point to something and ask about it, giving me plenty of time to think about Avery.

We get to the south end a few minutes before the sky starts to pinken. The views are beautiful this morning with the sun coming up over the Twin Peaks. I may have to start doing this more often when the days get shorter. No one wants to leave at 5:00 am to catch a sunrise, but 7:00 seems to be fine with the early birds.

It is only about thirty minutes to the back side of the Twin Peaks to catch the sunrise above them, so we don't have to leave too early to be in place before it comes up. The view was definitely worth it. It is something I would love to be able to share with Avery one day. When and if she is ever ready to make that move.

"We will hang out here until the sun is up a little higher. Would you guys like some coffee and bagels? I packed an assortment this morning just in case," I offer.

"That sounds wonderful. I was just thinking I wish I had eaten something before we left this morning," the woman replies.

We go below deck and pick out our breakfast and return to the bow to eat.

"What brings you to Wild Shore?"

Their hands move together, and the man says, "This beautiful lady has blessed me with forty years of her life. That's a milestone not many people meet, so we are celebrating."

"Congratulations. I'm honored you chose to sail with me. I can only hope to be doing the same thing one day."

But first I have to figure out how to use a phone number. Baby steps.

When the sun fully rises, I hoist the sail and take them a little farther south to look at the impressive cliffs and a few small waterfalls. We circle back around so they can see the coast we passed in the dark.

When we get back to the dock the woman clasps my arm and says, "Thank you, Sawyer. That trip was beautiful. I am so glad we found you. If we come back this way, you will be the first person we call."

"Thank you, ma'am. I hope you enjoy the rest of your trip."

I watch as the man takes the woman's elbow to help her walk up the path back to their vehicle. I look away and return to The Emerald to clean up our mess, secure the sails, and prepare for the afternoon excursion.

The afternoon catamaran was wild, to say the least. I love bachelorette parties. Everyone is so happy, carefree, and out to have a good time. The music was catchy, and they kept razzing the bride for marrying her best friend's older brother that she had known since she was in diapers. Their friend group reminds me of my friends.

Avery said she doesn't have a lot of friends. I'm hoping to add a few more.

I put away the last of the washed and rinsed snorkel masks and stand up to stretch my back. Today was a long one, and the next few months look to be more of the same. I have to work hard during the summer months, since not many people want to sail when it gets colder during the winter.

I walk around the Jolly Rodger and collect the last of the trash bags. I throw the bags in the large dumpster on my way to the office. My stomach is growling, so I raid the small kitchen area where we store drinks and snacks for some dinner.

Turkey, pepper jack, and mustard and a bag of chips for the win. I grab a cold drink and walk back out to the bench to have my dinner and wait for the sun to set.

I wonder if Avery is busy. I finish my dinner while I think about calling her. Maybe a text is better to open the conversation in case she is busy. I saved her number in my phone after Savannah tried to steal it. I didn't want it to get lost before I worked up the nerve to contact her.

ME: Hey, Avery. This is Sawyer. I'm glad you stopped by on Saturday.

There. That doesn't sound desperate or needy.

After a few minutes, my phone dings.

AVERY: Hey, Sawyer. I felt it was the least I could do since I flaked on half of my course. You needed to know it was nothing you did.

ME: I appreciate that.

This feels kind of awkward. Should I ask her about her day? What she is doing now?

AVERY: I am trying to finish some landscaping before it gets dark. Can I call you?

Her message brings a vivid image to my mind of Avery bent over a planter, her perfect ass in the air, wearing short shorts. My mind continues down that path with her on her hands and knees pulling weeds. I groan as I feel my cock twitch in my shorts. *Do I have a gardener kink now?*

I text her back before my mind can come up with more images of Avery getting dirty.

ME: Sure

My phone immediately rings with Avery's number.

"Hello?" I answer.

"Hey, my mom dropped off some plants today and told me I had to get them in the ground before tonight's rain shower. I figured talking into my earbud is easier than me taking my gloves off and on to text you back. I got them planted, but now I have to spread the mulch I bought on the way home from work because Lord knows when Marie Sutton says to do something today she will drive by your house tomorrow to make sure it is done."

Her voice makes happiness unfurl inside my chest. She is what I need after a rough day. Just talking to her makes me feel more energized.

"She sounds a lot like my mom. It doesn't matter how old you get or how long you have been on your own, your mom will always tell you what to do," I sympathize, and we both laugh.

"What are you doing?"

"Sitting on the bench behind Pirate's Life, waiting for the sunset. The same thing I do pretty much every evening." Wishing you were here with me.

"I see how it is. You're having a relaxing evening while I'm sweating and lugging bags of mulch around my backyard," she chastises laughingly.

"Yeah, pretty much. I deserve this after spending the afternoon hanging out with a bunch of drunk bachelorettes on the Jolly Rodger. Those girls were wild."

The line goes silent when she doesn't respond.

"You still there? Did I lose ya?" I ask.

"No, I'm here."

Then it hits me like a ten-foot wave. "Those girls were just out having fun together. I had my hands full keeping the rum punch filled and making sure no one fell overboard. I don't take part in the craziness that happens on my excursions. I have to walk a fine line between fun captain and responsible business owner and make sure everyone has fun but stays safe. It's like herding cats after they all start drinking."

She chuckles softly. "I can see how your job would be rough, having to look at all those drunk women in skimpy bikinis all day and just drive them around."

"There's only been one woman I want to see in a skimpy bikini, and she always has it covered up every time I see her wearing one," I hint.

"Well, maybe you should see about working on that," she challenges saucily.

"I just finally got the nerve to contact her after she left me her number. I'm flying at the speed of a snail here."

Her laughter rings clear and joyful through my phone speaker.

"You can probably speed it up to turtle now that you have texted her."

"I don't know. Don't want to scare her off."

"She's not going to run scared. She's ready for more," Avery flirts.

I can hear thunder through the phone, followed by a small shriek.

"Hey, I hate to cut this conversation short, but I gotta get this stuff picked up before the storm gets here and the bags blow away. I will talk to you later," she tells me as I hear another rumble of thunder.

"Be careful in this storm," I warn.

"Bye, Sawyer," she says and the line goes dead.

I guess I better head home before the storm gets here.

I throw my trash in the dumpster and get in my Jeep for the ride to the base of the mountains. The rain starts falling enough to need wipers but not enough to make driving difficult.

I round the final bend on Ridge View Terrace before making my way down the winding driveway to the two-story house with a three-car attached garage I am slowly finishing. The rain is coming down a little harder, and thunder crashes around me, followed by streaks of lightning as I park the Jeep in its bay.

I walk through the barely functioning kitchen and unfinished living room to one of the few rooms I have finished, the four season room. There is a slight chill in the air, so I turn the gas fireplace in the corner to low and relax on the sectional to watch Mother Nature's display.

I hope Avery got inside before the rain started. It is making quite the soundtrack on the charcoal metal roof. As I sit there by myself, I think about my life and future. My life is a constant rotation of customers, parents, Sav, and friends, so I am very rarely alone. I must be getting old because having someone to snuggle with on nights like these is looking pretty appealing. Maybe I just finally found the right person to make me want to settle down.

The storm slowly moves through, and I turn off the fireplace and walk upstairs to the only other finished area, the master suite. I walk through the bedroom to the large bathroom and walk-in closet.

I turn on the water from the controls on the white tiled wall and walk to the closet to take off my shoes. I strip out of my clothes and toss them into the laundry basket as I wait for the water to warm up.

I step into the shower that is designed for two and settle under the waterfall shower head. I rinse the salt spray off my body and lather with soap.

The warm spray feels wonderful on my muscles. I sail year-round, so I stay in shape, but the first couple weeks of two a day sailings remind me that I slacked off all winter.

When I am clean, I step out and grab a towel off the warmer. I dry off and wrap it around my waist as I walk to the white sink with square bowls. I brush my teeth and apply the moisturizer that sits on the counter by a tube of sunscreen. My skin products cost more than my grocery bill, but I don't want to be one of those old weathered sailors with skin cancer when I'm fourty.

I toss the towel in the basket and walk to the closet for some black boxer briefs before slipping into bed.

I need to get to Pirate's Life early tomorrow to check for storm damage and ready the boats, so I set my alarm for an hour early. That should give me plenty of time to drain boats and fix anything before the first excursion. If there isn't any damage, I will just have breakfast at Rise and Dine.

The next morning dawns sunny and brisk. I grab a red, white, and blue flannel to put on over my red Pirate's Life button-up and drive the Jeep across town.

Looks like there are some small limbs down but nothing major. Pirate's Life doesn't have any damage, so I walk down the path to the dock. I start the bilge pumps on all the Pudgies and the dive boat and check to see that the auto pump is working on The Emerald. The water runs off the Jolly Rodger, so I don't have to worry about that.

Everything looks fine, so I turn off the pumps and take the short walk to Rise and Dine.

The bell twinkles when I open the door, and Pepper looks up at me from the counter where she is refilling pastries.

"Hey, stranger! You too good to come see me now, or does that new girlfriend have you on a short leash?"

"First off, I'm busy this time of year and can't spend all my time sitting around here gabbing with you like old ladies. Secondly, she's not my girlfriend," I say as I take a seat at the counter.

"Yet," Pepper protests, and I smile.

"Oh, I see that grin. She is toast when you go pulling out those dimples. You'll get whatever you want," she says as she points her finger at my face. "Lethal weapons for any girl's panties."

"They never worked on yours," I reply.

"That's because I don't wear any," she says cheekily over her shoulder as she walks back through the swinging door to the kitchen.

I screw up my face in a grimace. "Jesus, Pep. I didn't need that knowledge about your hedonistic New York ways."

I hear her laughter from the kitchen.

Stephanie walks over to take my order.

"How do you deal with her every day?" I joke.

"Well, she pays me and normally stays in her cave," Steph replies with the same humor. "What can I get you today?"

"Give me a large black coffee to go and a bacon, egg, and cheese biscuit."

"Can do. Give me a few minutes and that will be right up," she says as she walks away to punch my order into the computer system.

The door chime rings again, and I glance over my shoulder to see who came in.

The sight makes me draw in a deep breath. I'm glad Pep takes care of this place because my tongue is on the floor. Standing there looking through her purse is the girl of my dreams, mostly the dirty ones. Her dirty-blond hair is curled loosely down her back and held away from her face by her large sunglasses. She is wearing a cream sundress with burgundy and brown flowers and lace around the top, showing a hint of cleavage. She has on a cream cardigan with large brown buttons that is a little shorter than her dress and tan ankle boots.

I think I need to become a four-year-old, because I want to spend all day looking at her.

She finds what she is looking for and glances up, making eye contact with me. Her eyes light up, and her lips covered in something shiny curve into a huge smile.

"Morning, Sawyer!"

I get enough blood back to my brain to reply to her. "Hey, Avery. Did you get your stuff put away before the storm?"

She laughs as she walks over to me. "Nope. I got totally drenched, but when Mom drives by later, she can see what a wonderful job I did."

My image of her from last night instantly changes to her in a tight white shirt with nothing underneath. The chill of the rain soaking her shirt does its magic to show off her pebbled nipples. Avery walks to the counter and stands beside me. I take a breath and inhale her perfume. The scent of vanilla and wildflowers and the mental image make my cock start to twitch.

I can't get hard at Pepper's diner at seven thirty in the morning. *Think of something else.*

Steph walks up to us and sets my coffee down before I can respond.

"Pepper just set your sandwich on the window, so I'll get it as soon as I take her order," she tells me and turns to Avery. "What can I get you this morning?"

"I'll take a large chai latte to go," she answers.

"No problem. Just give me a couple minutes, and it will be right out." Steph grabs my sandwich off the counter and puts it by my coffee. She walks over to the complicated machine at the back of the counter and starts turning knobs and opening compartments. This is why I drink black coffee.

I turn back to Avery and continue our conversation. "I'm glad Marie isn't going to have to ground you. That would make it hard to call you after work tonight."

Avery scoffs. "My mom hasn't grounded me a day in my life. She gives one of her patented mom stares, and everyone within a mile radius starts acting right."

"They must teach that at birthing class because my mom has the same one," I say, and we both laugh.

Stephanie comes back with Avery's drink and sits it on the counter.

"Thank you." She smiles and places some cash on the bar. She looks at me and says, "I'd like to stay and chat, but four-year-olds don't wait for anyone!"

I get out my wallet and pay for my breakfast. "I'll walk you to your car," I say as I pick up my coffee and sandwich.

We walk out the door and over to Chili. She opens the door and bends over to put her purse in the passenger seat and her drink in the cup holder under the radio.

I would be lying if I said I didn't look. Her dress rises up her toned thighs, and I have to hold myself back from stepping into her, grabbing her hips, and pulling her ass against my hardening cock. Her little boots give her the perfect amount of lift to line up just right.

She stands back up and wipes the hair that is stuck to her lip gloss out of her face.

"I think you smudged it. Let me help." I step forward and put my drink and sandwich on the hood of her car. I cradle the back of her head with my hand and slant my mouth over hers.

She startles at the onslaught but immediately begins kissing me back. She tastes like minty toothpaste and everything I have ever wanted in a woman. My tongue explores her mouth, and she gives it a small suck, making my cock harden a little more.

I groan and break away from the kiss. I still have my hand in her hair as I nuzzle her ear.

"What are you doing to me, Avery?" I breathe deeply, the smell of her shampoo filling my nostrils.

"I don't know, but I hope it's the same thing you are doing to me," she purrs as she turns her head back to my lips for a small peck.

"I don't think I fixed your lip gloss." I smirk as I pull away from her.

She laughs. "That's okay. I have the tube with me. I will fix it when I get to work."

"You better get going, and I need to get to Pirate's Life. I have an excursion leaving soon, and Em will kill me if I am late." I pick up my breakfast from her car.

She steps forward and gives me a quick kiss before getting in and shutting the door. She puts on her seatbelt, starts her car, and drives away with a wave.

I make the trek back to Pirate's Life, eating my breakfast on the way. Emily is walking across the parking lot when I walk up to the front door. I unlock the deadbolt and hold the door open for her to walk in.

"I'm glad you got some breakfast today because it looks like another busy day," she warns as she walks past me.

I finish off my coffee and throw the cup and sandwich wrapper in the trash.

"I couldn't do it without you, Emily," I say as I point at her while walking out the back door to do pre-sail checks on The Emerald.

"And don't you forget it," she fires back.

CHAPTER 20
CHAIR ARM QUARTERBACK

Avery

My hot latte does nothing to help me cool down from the kiss Sawyer gave me in the parking lot. Talk about toe-curling. That man knows how to kiss.

When I park at Wild Child, I flip down the visor and fix my lip gloss. I would gladly do this every day if my send-off was like that.

It is time to focus on the four-year-olds. No more morning fantasies.

They get rowdier every day leading up to the end of school. The weather is getting nicer, so we try to incorporate more outdoor work into the schedule. Today we are going on an alphabet walk around the playground. We will start with A and continue through the alphabet, naming things we see.

I have several other things planned for the rest of this week and next week. The last day of school is just a full day of outdoor activities, including water games and a picnic. I have a meeting after school today with Candace and Gail to finish up our plan. I have a feeling this is going to be an epic year.

After an afternoon of working on CVC words and number recognition, the kids are dismissed. The pickup line is chaos with kids hanging out of car windows, yelling at each other before buckling in.

When the last car leaves, Candace looks at me and sighs. "Only seven more times, not that I'm counting. I have to go get a can of Coke and a glass of ice before we start this meeting.

I'm hanging on by a thread. I'll see you in a little bit in Gail's office."

I laugh with her, and we walk back inside the building. I go to my room and see Gail walking down the hallway.

"Candace needed a Coke. I'm going to grab my water, and we will be there."

"Sounds good," Gail replies as she opens the door to the multipurpose room. Her office is in the back behind the stage.

"Okay, ladies," Gail starts when we all get settled. "We got a lot planned the last time we met. We just need to think of two more games then go through what we have and what we need to buy. We have Water Cooties where they will carry one piece of a Cootie at a time down the grass and build it on the other end, Water Hula Hoop Relay where they hold hands and weave a wet hula hoop through themselves, Sponge Relay where they fill a sponge with water and take it to the other end and squeeze the water out, Scooter Driving where they will weave through cones and back on scooters, and just a relay race where we will call different things for them to do down and back like hopping or skipping. Any ideas for the last two?"

"I don't think it's really a field day without a Tug of War into a pool of water," Candace proposes.

"Agreed. When I was in elementary school, we did this over and under relay with a wet sponge, but the water came out of a toilet at the front of the line. The last person squeezed the water into a bowl and ran to the front to dunk the sponge in the toilet. That's something we can buy one time and use for a lot of years in different types of relays," I add.

"I like that. It's funny enough to make the kids enjoy it and easy enough for them to do," Gail agrees.

"So that's settled. What supplies do we need?" I ask.

Gail looks down at her list of activities and answers, "I have hula hoops, a rope, cones, and scooters. We will need sponges, a couple boxes of Cooties, four plastic kiddie pools, a blowup pool, two two-gallon buckets, and a toilet. Anything else?"

"I think that's all. If we need to run to the store after we get set up, we can. The kids are going to love it," Candace gushes.

"I think so too, but they are going to love anything that gets them outside and starts summer break. It's a fun way for the four-year-olds to remember preschool." I smile. "Who is going to get what?"

"I have to go to the Dollar Store this weekend, so I can pick up sponges, kiddie pools, and the blowup pool," Candace volunteers.

"I have to go to Walmart, so I can get the Cooties and buckets," Gail adds.

"I guess that leaves me with the toilet!" I chuckle. "I may have to leave the top down on Chili!"

"Oh my gosh! I didn't even think about that! I can take my husband's truck and pick one up this weekend," Gail says.

"I'll be fine. I'm sure it will fit. I have put larger things than a toilet in there before," I reply.

"I think we are good to go. I contacted the shaved ice school bus, and they said they will be here at one thirty. I'm sure we can get through the games and picnic before then," Gail says.

"I think it is going to work out fabulous! I've gotta run, so I will see you ladies tomorrow," Candace agrees.

"Bye," Gail and I say.

"I need to look over some papers before I go home," I groan as I get up and walk toward her door.

"See you tomorrow."

I walk back to my classroom to look at today's counting and number recognition quiz. These kids are doing so well. I hope they don't forget everything over the summer. I add smelly stickers and put them in their mailboxes to put in folders tomorrow.

I get my purse out of my desk and see that my phone has several notifications. There is a text from my mom.

MOM: The hostas look good! I can't wait until the iris blooms! <flower emoji>

I reply to her message even though it has been a few hours.

ME: Thanks! I finished the mulch right before the storm hit.

She replies immediately.

MOM: I'm glad you got them in the ground. They needed that rain.

I look back at my text app and see a text from Sawyer. Just seeing his name makes my heart pick up speed.

Sawyer: I hope you have a lot of extra lipgloss because I can't wait to mess it up again. Sorry, not sorry.

I also can't wait for him to mess up my lipgloss again. Maybe even my clothes. I reply to his message.

ME: Tons. Do your worst.

I figure he is out on an excursion right now and will text me back later.

I pack up the rest of my things and head home for the night.

I check on Riley, since I haven't heard from her in a couple days.

ME: Hey, girl. You hanging in there? I'm trying to give you space, but just know I would be up your ass deeper than a too small thong if I thought you wanted me there with you.

RILEY: I'm doing okay. It's just a lot to wrap my head around. You will be the first person I call when I'm ready.

ME: I better be. Nobody better be moving in on my BFF territory. I locked that shit down a long time ago.

RILEY: You're stuck with me forever.

ME: Let me know if you need anything. I mean ANYTHING. Tequila, food, book with good arm porn. LMK and I will be there in 2.5.

ME: Well maybe longer since summer tourism seems to have started <laughing emoji>

Riley: Thank you. Just reading your nonsense makes me feel better.

I walk to Chili and drive through the residential areas of Wild Shore to avoid the traffic closer to the shore. When I get home, I reheat some leftover chicken I baked last night in the air fryer and microwave a macaroni and cheese cup. I toss together a salad and take my meal to the back porch.

I love the view of Magnolia Ridge I have from back here. I can barely see The Split, but I can see where The Drop meanders down through the trees that are almost in full bloom now.

After I finish eating, I curl up on the wicker furniture and unlock my Kindle. The book about the catcher and the late spring weather put me in a sports romance kick. My current read features a hunky quarterback with trust issues.

I am just getting to the good part when my phone rings. Sawyer.

"Hello?" I answer like I didn't just read his name on my phone screen.

"Hey, Avery. Is this a bad time? You sound a little weird."

"Nope, I'm fine. Just spending the evening on my back porch with a hunky quarterback. What are you up to?"

The line goes silent.

"Sawyer?"

"I can call you back another time if you are with someone," he murmurs quietly, maybe a little sad.

"With someone? The only people who ever come over here are my parents and Riley. My parents are spending the evening listening to some live music on The Boardwalk, and Riley is at home."

I can hear him rub his hand up and down his scratchy beard. He exhales, "Fuck it. I'm just gonna put it out there," then draws in a deep breath.

"I'm going to be totally honest with you right now, Avery. I really like you, but if we take this any further, I don't want to share you with other guys. No porch cuddling with a quarterback. No friends with benefits with Riley, and I want to meet him. You met Pepper, so I feel like that is only fair. I want you to be mine only."

I am speechless. Did he just assume I'm sleeping with numerous guys and ask for monogamy in the same breath?

"You think I'm sleeping with other guys?"

"Yes. No. I don't know. You spend a lot of time with Riley and go see him whenever he calls. You just said you were spending the evening with some quarterback. I know you don't have any brothers. Oh, fuck. You met a quarterback while I was pussy-footing around deciding how to contact you. I don't know how I can compete with him, but I want to try. I was a quarterback in high school and can still throw a pretty good spiral if that sways your decision."

I start laughing and place my Kindle on the arm of the lounge chair I am sitting on so I can give this conversation all the focus it deserves.

"Oh my God. This is hilarious. The first guy I have been interested in for a long time thinks I'm some sort of sex vixen who can pull an NFL quarterback and simultaneously sleeping with my best friend who doesn't even have a penis." It is getting hard to breathe because I'm laughing so hard.

"Riley is my best friend and has been since I moved here. *She* owns Peak Mechanic on the south end of town and works on boats. The quarterback is the main character in a romance novel I am currently reading, and frankly, your billboard has way better arm porn than his book cover, so you would win anyway. I'm flattered you think that many guys would want me, but I haven't slept with anyone in longer than I care to admit."

"So all this time I have been jealous of the amount of time you spend with Riley thinking you are going to a booty call, and it's just you hanging out with another woman?"

"Jealous?" That's the only word I focus on.

He exhales deeply. "If you haven't noticed, I'm pretty hung up on you. At first, I decided I would take you any way I could get you, even if I had to share you with Riley. Now I want you all to myself. I don't want to wonder where you are at night because I want you by my side."

I am speechless.

"Avery?"

"Um, I-I'm still here," I stutter.

"Are you okay?"

"I think so. Just trying to wrap my head around this. So you want to be monogamous? Does that mean we are dating?"

"It means whatever you want it to mean as long as I'm the man in your life."

"I have to have book boyfriends. I can't give them up."

"I can do a lot of things those guys can't." I can hear his smile through the phone.

"I've read a lot of spicy books. Those guys set some pretty high standards and have a lot of ideas," I parry. "They seem pretty talented. In all areas. Not just throwing a football."

"You come over to my house, and I will show you some of my talents."

"Not all of them?"

"Nope. Gotta keep you guessing what else I can do," he tempts me.

"And when will you be showing me these talents?" I flirt.

Kill. Me. Now. I just solicited sex. From a guy I like and am on the road to more than liking.

CHAPTER 21
SUSPICION CONFIRMED

Sawyer

"And when will you be showing me these talents?" she flirts.

According to the dick that just tried to jump out of my pants, right now.

"Well, that all depends," I reply, acting like I'm cool with any time.

"On what?"

"When you are free this week."

Then I remember I own a business that is currently entering the busy season and add, "And when I'm not sailing. Which is pretty much never since the tourism floodgates seem to have opened overnight."

"I have noticed quite a bit more traffic in the last few days. School isn't even out yet. Guess some people decided to get a jump start on summer this year."

"Pirate's Life went from maybe five excursions a week to more than double. My body wasn't ready for a jump like that. We usually ease into the busy season."

"From what I could tell, you are in pretty good shape," she offers.

I can practically see her face palming as she admits to me that she was enjoying tracing my abs and shoulders that night on the beach.

"And every one of those muscles is sore right now." I laugh, and she joins in.

"Well, I guess the ball is in your court for when you show off your talents then. I only have the rest of this week and part of next, and I'll be able to join the ranks of the summer tourists. Lying by the pool drinking mixed drinks, reading a book on the beach. Just lounging around, working on my tan."

The mental images alone have me groaning. When I add in the thinly veiled offer of sex with Avery, I am three seconds away from calling everyone on the schedule and canceling.

It's been a while for me, and the memory of Avery rocking her hot pussy against me as she held on to my hair has fueled more than one shower session with my hand.

I am glad I waited to get home to call Avery from the comfort of my second story porch because I am tempted to take my dick in my hand and give it a few tugs.

"What are you up to tonight?" she asks.

Probably just shy of eight inches.

"Sitting on my upstairs porch, watching the ridge go to sleep."

"My back porch faces the ridge, too. Can you see The Split?

I would love to see your split right before I fill it with my cock.

"Barely. I can see The Climb where it turns back to wind up the ridge to Steep Creek. I can't see The Drop at all."

"I can see The Split if I stand at the very back of my yard. I can watch the cars drive along The Drop from my porch, though," she says.

"So you must live over by Balls."

"Yep. My parents live on the ninth hole actually. You would think my dad would be better at playing that one, but he's equally bad at them all. I will deny ever saying that." She giggles. "I live a few blocks to the west of the entrance. Since you can only see The Climb, you must live pretty far on the west side of Wild Shore."

"I bought a few acres on Ridge View Terrace when I got home from overseas and started building a house. I work on it

164

when I'm not sailing, so it will be at a standstill until fall. One day, I will get it done. I have the areas I use the most finished, my master suite, and the four season room. I finished the hardwood in the living room a few weeks ago, but it still needs trim. I think Mom and Sav are going to pick out the curtains and blinds now that the floor is finished. They said they needed the full picture to get the right aesthetic or something. They took over the finishes since I don't know and don't care all that much as long as it looks nice."

"I'm with them. It does help make final decisions when all the colors and textures are in place. When I moved into my house, I repainted and had new floors installed. I agonized for weeks about what couch to buy and what window treatments would go with it. My neighbors were probably glad I finally made a decision so they didn't have to see me walk around in my night shirt anymore."

"If they didn't want to see you, they shouldn't have been looking in your windows. That's why I ended up buying this place. If I want to sit on the porch in my boxers, that's what I do. No one can see me or say anything."

"You'd probably have a line of women halfway down the road staring at you if you could," she jokes.

"Would you be one of those women?"

"I might have gone out of my way to drive by your billboard once or twice. Just to make sure I had the right phone number to Pirate's Life of course."

"Of course," I agree, smiling at her joke.

We both get quiet as we enjoy the company, even if it is over the phone.

She breaks the silence first. "Sawyer?"

"Yeah, Avery."

"I don't want to end our conversation, but it's getting kind of late. I know you have to get up early tomorrow for an excursion. I want you to be well rested so you will be safe."

Realization hits me in the chest of what her life will be like if we do take this to the next step. Will she be in a constant state of worry over me while I'm sailing? I spend a good half of my waking hours with my feet on a boat deck. Will the constant worry take a toll on her? On a relationship? I hadn't thought about her fear like that before, that she would be scared *for* me. I just thought about it in relation to what activities we would be able to do together. Would I want someone I care about to live in constant fear every time I go to work?

"I've got a sunrise sail and an afternoon snorkel tomorrow, so it's going to be a long day. I enjoyed talking to you tonight. Sorry I took you away from your quarterback."

"He'll hold on until tomorrow night. He's not pushy."

I crack a smile. "Good to know he won't be mad when I cockblock him when I want to spend a little time with my woman."

"Your woman?"

I knew that would get a rise out of her.

"Don't you remember the part of this conversation where I claimed you for my own and no one else's?"

"Just seems a little archaic when you say those words out loud," she mocks, but I can tell she secretly likes it.

"Well, next time you see me, don't mind me if I rip my shirt off and beat my chest."

"Okay, Tarzan. I will talk to you later. Good night."

"Good night, Avery."

I may have a permanent grin on my face after that conversation.

I park on the road in front of my parents' house and walk around to the backyard. My parents are getting ready to go on a two-week trip, so they invited Sav and me for dinner before they left.

My mom sees me coming and stands up to give me a hug. My dad squeezes my shoulder when I sit down next to him in the wrought iron patio chair.

"How's Pirate's Life? Are you getting a lot of this early tourist traffic?" Mom asks.

"We have already doubled the number of excursions if not more. It's going to be a hell of a year if this keeps up. I might need you to take an excursion here and there when you get back to give me a little bit of a rest," I say, looking at my dad.

"I can probably fit that into my busy schedule. You gonna let me take The Emerald out?"

"Unless you would rather hang out with a bunch of drunk bachelorettes for a few hours."

"I think I'll take my chances pulling lines." He chuckles. "My afternoons on a boat with drunken women are far behind me."

My mom scoffs. "Like you ever had drunken women out on your boat."

"I got you on there, and that's all that matters," he counters, leaning over to kiss her.

Savannah walks up to us and smiles at Mom and Dad.

"You guys about ready to blow this popsicle stand?" she asks.

"In the morning," Mom replies.

She turns toward me and asks, "Where's your girlfriend? Did she already realize she can do better?"

"You are dead to me," I mouth.

Mom questions, "What new girlfriend? Why didn't you bring her?"

"See what you started?" I accuse Sav. I turn back to Mom and say, "It's still really new. I'm not sure when I will bring her to meet you guys. I don't want this asshole asking questions and scaring her off."

"Who? Me? I'd be on my best behavior," Sav huffs.

"And that's what I'm afraid of. If we do get serious, I will invite her over for dinner," I say, hoping to mollify my mom.

My dad gets up to go check on the grill, excusing himself from the conversation. He puts cheese on the burgers and closes the lid to let it melt.

Mom stands up and demands, "I want to meet her. It's about time you settle down and have some kids. Come help me bring out the sides and drinks."

Savannah and I follow her through the French door into the kitchen. She loads my arms with potato salad, a veggie tray, and a pitcher of sweet tea. She hands Savannah condiments, a bag of buns, and a stack of glasses, and we walk back out to the porch.

Mom follows with a pan of her famous baked macaroni and cheese and a plate for dad to put the burgers on.

"Saw, can you go get that stack of plates and silverware on the counter? Does anyone want ice? The tea is cold."

Everyone declines ice, and I head back inside. My phone dings with a text. The name on the screen instantly brings a smile to my face.

AVERY: <picture of legs under a pink fuzzy blanket and a hand holding a Kindle with a basketball player on the screen> Just so you know who I'm spending the night with.

The message makes my smile widen.

ME: He may be taller than me, but I've got better moves.

I put my phone back in my pocket and grab the plates to take outside.

I pass out the silverware and plates and sit down. My phone dings again, and I fish it out of my pocket.

AVERY: That has yet to be confirmed.

"Oh shit. Look at that smile. It's either his girlfriend, or Mason just sent you a dad joke," Savannah speculates.

"It's definitely her. Mason's jokes aren't anywhere near as funny as mine," Dad verifies as he scoops mac and cheese.

"Invite her over. We can hold dinner until she gets here," Mom tells me.

I slip my phone back in my pocket without replying. "She's busy tonight."

"I'm glad you found someone who doesn't fawn all over you and follow you around like a lost puppy. That's not good for you," Sav advises.

I ignore her and start eating.

Mom says, "So while we are gone, I need one of you to water the flowers, get the mail, and cut the grass. Who is available?"

"You act like you are leaving for a month and not like you do this every month," I reply.

"We want to get this traveling out of the way so when you give us grandbabies we can stay home and spend time with them."

"Didn't we already have this conversation? I'm not having a baby anytime soon."

"Oh, but I bet you are practicing with your new girlfriend," Savannah taunts as she dips a bell pepper into homemade ranch.

"We aren't practicing anything, and this is why I won't bring her here. I don't want you asking questions about grandbabies and scaring her off."

"So that's why you're still so grouchy. Still not getting any."

I glare at her. I'm not discussing my nonexistent sex life with any of them.

"This burger is grilled to perfection, Dad. The new cook at Shipwrecked doesn't have anything on you," I say, changing the subject.

"Suspicion confirmed with subject change," Savannah chimes in.

Dad talks over her like she didn't just butt into our conversation. "I flipped burgers for over thirty years to get this good. Give the kid at least a few months to figure it out."

"He had to learn how to manage the stress of the amount of orders too. He hasn't ever done anything that fast-paced before. He gets better every time we go in there," Mom defends. "He'll be fine."

We continue talking about the tourists and where Mom and Dad are going on vacation this month.

By the time I leave, it is after dark. I use the light of the moon to light the way to my Jeep.

I drive home thinking about when I'm going to have time to see Avery again.

CHAPTER 22

PIZZA, MUSCLE RUB, AND SMOOTH SKIN

Avery

I can't believe I'm doing this. In the mother of all desperate acts, I call Pirate's Life after dismissal.

"Pirate's Life, this is Emily."

"Hey, Emily. This is Avery. I took the beginner sailing class last month."

"Of course. I remember you. What's up?"

"I forgot to ask Sawyer when he would be done today, and he isn't answering his phone. Do you happen to know what time his last excursion will be back?"

"He just left on a sightseeing catamaran cruise. They will probably be out for two hours, so maybe around five?" she guesses.

"Okay. Thank you, Emily. I appreciate it."

"Just be good to him. He's an amazing person." The line goes dead before I can respond.

I start searching the web for homemade muscle rubs. I find one I like, and I have most of the ingredients.

After a quick trip to the store to get what I don't have, I head home to make this concoction.

The scents of eucalyptus, clove, peppermint, and rosemary fill my small kitchen as I add the essential oils to the melted coconut oil and shea butter.

Even if this doesn't help his sore muscles, it's going to smell wonderful.

I send him a text so I can get the timing right for the rest of my plan.

ME: Can you call me when you get back? I have a random question about boats.

With that taken care of, I go to my bathroom to shave and exfoliate every inch of my skin. A girl can never be too prepared.

I walk back to my bedroom and put on a light green plunge bra with emerald lace trim and matching underwear. I slip on a sage green sleeveless boho sundress that has a deep V and shows off all the cleavage the plunge bra creates. I leave my hair in beach waves and touch up my eye makeup and lip gloss.

I look at the time and see that Sawyer should be back from the excursion anytime.

A few minutes later, my phone rings.

"Hey!" I answer.

"Hey, yourself. What's up?"

His deep voice makes my insides go mushy, but there is an underlying tiredness that almost makes me rethink my plan. Almost.

"So today one of the boys in my class drew a boat, and I was asking him about it. He pointed to the back and said it was the poop deck. I thought he was joking with me, but he seemed serious when he was explaining the parts of the boat. Is that an actual thing, or did he misunderstand something?"

He chuckles before answering. "Sounds like you've got a future seaman on your hands. I haven't heard that term in a while. A poop deck is the small deck on the back of a bigger ship. None of my boats have one, but I have been on several that do. It's kind of a joke between sailors, but it does exist."

"Thank God I didn't look like an ass for doubting him. I just tried to steer the conversation away from it." I laugh.

"Probably a smart decision in a room full of four-year-olds."

"How were your excursions today?" I ask. I can hear the waves and seagulls in the background, so I know he's still at Pirate's Life.

"Pretty good. This afternoon was rough. The waves were coming in a little bigger, so I had to put more effort in. My arms aren't happy about that. As soon as I get the trash cleaned up, I'm headed home and going to bed."

"Sounds like you need it. I can't imagine being that physical every day."

"I'll get used to it soon. It just takes a few weeks to get back in the groove."

"I guess I better not keep you any longer so you can get home. I'll talk to you later, Sawyer."

"Oh, okay. Later, Avery."

The dejection in his voice for not talking to him longer is what pushes me to make the final decision to go through with my plan.

I call Pizza Pirate and order a large Wild Special. It will be ready in twenty minutes, so I grab the rest of what I need, slip on a pair of tan platform sandals, and drive over to pick it up.

Thankfully, the traffic gods are on my side, and I drive down Ocean Boulevard without stopping. I pick up the pizza and drive to where I think Sawyer lives.

Riley and I drive down Ridge View Terrace when we just want to cruise. I remember seeing a For Sale sign then a bunch of construction signs a couple years ago. I'm hoping that is where he lives, and I won't look like a psycho showing up to someone's house with pizza, muscle rub, and smooth skin.

I think I'm in luck. When I pull up and park in front of one of the three garage doors, no one comes out asking me what I'm doing.

This house is beautiful. The sage green siding complements the gray and brown stone wainscoting. The walnut-stained front door has sidelights and a top light making it appear larger under the covered porch held up by large circular columns. This is a house I probably daydreamed about living in when I was little.

I get out of my car and grab the pizza and my tote bag. I take a seat on the stained concrete porch and wait for Sawyer to get home.

I wait less than five minutes and a Jeep pulls up beside Chili. Sawyer looks at her like he's seeing things then looks over at his front door.

He cracks a smile, but I can see the weariness around his eyes. I made the right decision. He needs to relax and sleep.

I stand up as he gets out of his Jeep and walks up to me.

When he gets to the porch, he grabs my waist and pulls me to him for a scorching hot kiss. I don't waste any time opening my mouth for his tongue to explore. My hands rub over his shoulders and into his hair as his slide around to my ass.

After a few minutes, we end the kiss, but he starts running his nose up and down my neck. This man. I don't stand a chance.

Like I ever did anyway.

"Welcome home," I half moan, half whisper.

"It's never felt so good to be here."

"I brought you some things."

"I hope they are under this sexy as fuck dress, and I get to look for them."

That makes me laugh, and I tell him, "Maybe later. First things first. I brought a Wild Special from Pizza Pirate."

Sawyer groans. "Will you marry me?"

The question makes a little gasp come out of my mouth.

He laughs. "Guess I'll need to work on my approach." With a little sucking kiss to my neck, he pulls away from me, picks up the pizza box, and walks to the door. "Let's go eat this pizza before it gets any colder. Fair warning. This is a house under construction and a bachelor one at that. It's paper plates and beer and a lot of unfinished rooms on the other side of this door."

"That's fine by me."

He pokes some numbers into the keypad and the deadbolt unlocks. I'm not prepared for what is inside. Straight ahead the wall is just a huge bank of two-story windows with an amazing view of Magnolia Ridge under full bloom.

The bones of a kitchen and dining area are to the left, and a four season room with a massive fireplace is to the right off of the living area.

"This is beautiful, Sawyer. It is right out of a magazine."

"You must read the same magazines as Mom and Sav because they picked out most of this. I just wanted a lot of windows and a place to relax and enjoy the view."

"I think you succeeded," I say in awe as I walk around the large room.

"I'll get some plates and drinks and meet you out there." He points to the room with the large fireplace. "I have water and beer. Like I said, bachelor living." He smiles.

"How about one of each?"

He nods and walks to the huge kitchen. My hands itch to cook in a space like that as my husband hugs me from behind and the kids yell from their seats at the bar. The fantasy tugs at my chest with the possibility of that never being my reality.

I walk out to the four season room and sit down in the middle of the brown leather sectional. Sawyer comes back out with everything balanced on the pizza box.

He sits it down on the coffee table and opens the lid. The smell of Italian spices, melted cheese, and pizza dough fills my nostrils.

Sawyer puts a couple slices on each plate, and we start eating.

"I think I might have died on the way home, and this is heaven," he says as he leans his head back against the couch and closes his eyes when he finishes his pizza and beer.

"You just wait 'til you see what I have planned next."

He opens one eye and looks my way. "You set the bar pretty high already."

"Nah, that was baby hurdles. I'm shooting for Olympic level high jump."

"At least I'll die happy."

I shove his shoulder as I walk over to the light switch and dim the lights. I get the muscle rub out of my tote and take a stab in the dark. "Alexa, play a campfire country playlist at level three."

A female AI voice responds, "Now playing campfire country playlist."

"Did you break in here and scope the place out before I got home?"

"Nope, I just figured you wouldn't be the only person in the country not to have one."

I walk in front of him and put the tub on the coffee table.

"If I try something, will you let me know if you want me to stop?"

"I doubt you could do anything I wouldn't want you to do," he says as he lifts his head up and looks me in the eyes.

"Okay. Just let me know." I walk forward until my shins touch the couch between his manspread legs. I bend at the waist so he has a good view of my cleavage and start unbuttoning the few buttons he actually uses on his shirt. I keep my eyes on his face so I can gauge his reaction.

"I'm good so far. Continue on," he says as his lips pull up into a smirk.

I reach up to his shoulders and rub my hands down his warm skin as I take off his shirt. I toss it on the floor beside the sectional as I stand back up. I put my hands on my hips, looking around the room for the best way to proceed.

"I think this will work better on the lounge with your feet closest to the back."

"I like where this is going," he says lightly. I step back, and he gets up. He saunters over to the lounge and lies down on his back with his hands cupped behind his head.

I stand there slack-jawed, looking at him. Lord, the man is built. His biceps are like boulders on his upper arms. His skin is pulled tight across his torso, showing off abs, obliques, and that V. My eyes follow a dark happy trail to the black band of his underwear that sticks out above his shorts a tiny bit. I almost lose track of the plan. I quickly tear my gaze away and look back up his body.

What I see on his left pec gives me pause. I noticed he had a tattoo when we watched the sunset on the beach, but I was trying not to stare at his bare chest. Now I have no such qualms.

Tattooed in black ink is an eagle gripping a trident and a gun in his talons above a boat anchor. The words SEAL TEAM are above it, and THREE below it. THE ONLY EASY DAY WAS YESTERDAY is tattooed in a circle around the eagle.

The sight of the tattoo brings his story back to me, and I get a little emotional at what he has been through. I release a breath to slow the blood pulsing through my veins. "Actually, I think I'll have you start on your stomach and pull your shorts down a little."

"That's a bit kinky, but I'm up for it," he flirts as he unbuckles his belt and takes his shorts all the way off before turning over.

I open the little tub and take a large enough scoop to coat my hands and his back. The essential oil smell diffuses through the air around me, adding to the seductive atmosphere. I walk in front of him, and he looks up at me. I could get lost in those deep brown depths overflowing with desire. I gently push his head back down into the cushion. *Later, Avery.*

His back is dotted with old wounds and as muscular as the front. He has wide shoulders and well-defined traps that taper down to a small waist complete with sexy dimples.

I take a deep breath and rub my open palms down the center of his back several times to cover it in the muscle rub. He groans loudly when I push my thumbs deep into solid muscle and rub them down his spine from his neck to his underwear.

"Fuck, that feels so good. My back has been killing me," he moans into the couch cushion. "This may be better than what I had in mind."

"The night is young," I reply. I start massaging his back with my forearms. When I feel a particularly tight muscle, I dig my elbows in to relieve the tension. I get more muscle rub and push my fists into his shoulder blades where I feel a lot of knots. I keep working on those until I feel them loosen, and he groans at the release. I fight against an answering moan as the sound makes my nipples harden and rub against the silky cups of my bra when I move, exciting them even more.

I continue rubbing my hands along his back and sides more for my pleasure than his muscles' benefit. I can feel my wetness seeping out of my pussy and pooling in my underwear. It won't be long until it is running down my thigh.

"Can you turn over?" I ask in a husky voice.

"Yeah, but ignore what you see."

He turns over, and there is no way in hell I'm ignoring the massive tent in his underwear. Where was he hiding that thing? Is there a divot in the couch now?

I look a little closer, and there is a small wet spot on the gray material that tells me he was enjoying the massage for more than muscle relief also.

I walk to his side and lightly trace my fingertips over his tattoo.

"How long have you had this?"

"About two years. Most SEALs get them when they get discharged."

"Why isn't it on your billboard picture?"

"I'm not sure. It's pretty personal for me, so Emily must have had the photographer edit it out. I'm not sure how you missed it at the beach."

I continue running my fingers over the tattoo, and his hand comes up to grip my upper thigh. He catches my gaze, and I nod so he knows I am okay with the touch.

I get more muscle rub and smear it over his chest and shoulders. I go to work, finding the bunches of tight muscles. When I find a particularly tight one, he grips my thigh. When I smooth it out, he goes back to running his hand up and down, getting a little higher with every pass.

"How long have you been giving massages? This is amazing."

"You're actually my only client. I read a blog after work about the basics, and I'm making the rest up as I go," I admit.

His eyes catch mine before he says, "Let's keep it that way."

The possession in his statement sends electricity spiraling through my belly, and I look away.

Standing beside him is putting me at a weird angle and making my back sore. This would be so much easier from above him.

I decide to pull up my lace bikini panties and go for it. He's obviously into this. His erection hasn't gone down. If anything, it has grown along with the dark spot of precum.

I set the muscle rub on the cushion by his side and turn to face him. I take a fortifying breath and swing my leg over him so I am straddling him right below his erection.

He groans, and his hips jerk a little. Thinking I hurt him somehow, I move to get off the couch. He grips my thighs with both hands to stop my movement.

"Don't move, or I might embarrass myself."

CHAPTER 23
STRONG GAME

Sawyer

For the love of all that's holy, don't blow your load in your underwear while she's sitting on your lap.

My cock is nestled in the juncture of her thighs. I can feel her heat through the thin layers of our clothes and smell the heady scent of her arousal. My cock jumps with the realization and presses against her clit.

A breathy moan comes from her lips at the contact. I look into her eyes, and her pupils are blown wide with desire. She ignores my warning not to move and resumes running her hands over my chest and shoulders, down the muscles of my biceps.

Her hands are magical. They are finding all the muscles that have been abused in the last couple weeks and soothing the aches. I'm really hoping she decides to soothe the ache in some other places with those magical hands. Maybe even with her pussy if I'm lucky.

I let her continue setting the pace and resume rubbing her thighs with both hands now. I inch a little closer to that hot pussy with every stroke, almost touching the edge of her underwear with my thumbs. The thought of slipping my finger into her wet folds as she rubs my chest has precum dripping down my cock.

She rubs her knuckles over my tattoo and leans forward to kiss me. The position puts the tip of my cock right on her clit. She starts rocking back and forth, grinding her pussy on my cock, our underwear the only barrier.

My hand leaves her thigh and travels up her side to cup her breast. I find her hard nipple through her dress and bra and give it a light pinch. She groans into my mouth at the mixture of pleasure and pain.

She starts grinding harder on my cock, and I know I can't handle much more. It has been too long since I have had my dick in a sexy as fuck woman.

With the hand that is still on her thigh, I slip between her legs and underneath her lace underwear. She raises her hips to give me better access.

Fuck me. She's soft and bare. I trace her seam, giving her plenty of time to stop me before I go any further. She starts placing kisses along the underside of my jaw and rocking against my finger.

I slide my finger through her wetness to her clit. I stop to give it a swirl, and she moans. The sound makes my cock strain even harder.

I trail it back down and barely slip inside her tight channel. Her breathing increases as I push in a little deeper. She coats my finger in her wetness, making it easier to slide in and out.

She returns her lips to my mouth and slides her tongue in to duel with mine. I take the opportunity to add another finger. She starts pressing down to get them deeper into her needy pussy.

"You like that, baby?"

She replies with a moan and sucks on my lower lip. I almost come on the spot. The idea of where else she can use that skill has my balls tightening.

I keep fucking her with my fingers and use my thumb to circle her clit. She starts moaning louder, and her pussy gets so tight I can barely move. I can't wait to feel that around my cock.

"Oh, fuck yes. Just like that. I'm going to come," she pants as she throws her head back, her hands resting on my chest.

"Give it to me. Ride my fingers like you would ride my hard cock."

She speeds up and grinds down on my thumb to increase the pressure on her clit. With a few more strokes, she stills, and wetness coats my hand as she shouts her release to the ceiling. I continue stroking her pussy to lengthen her orgasm until her breathing slows.

My cock is straining under her, wanting some attention. She rises up on her knees, dislodging my fingers, and strokes the thick column of my erection through my underwear.

My dick has no shame. The tip peeks out of the top of my underwear leaving a shiny spot on my stomach.

"You don't have to…"

She silences me with a finger to my lips, and I stick my tongue out to lick the pad. The juvenile move makes her smile.

She pulls out my straining erection and strokes it. A steady stream drips from the head and down the shaft to lubricate her movements. She takes the finger she had pressed to my lips and runs it through the precum and around the engorged head. She sucks her finger between her lips to clean it, finishing with a little pop.

My eyes cross at the sight, and my cock grows impossibly thicker. She reaches for the hem of her dress and pulls it over her head uncovering a sight better than any I have ever witnessed.

Her tits jiggle in her green bra with emerald lace trim as she tosses the dress down. I can't help myself. I sit up and take them in my hands and run my tongue through the valley they create. I nip and kiss her cleavage, and she arches her back, giving me better access to the large globes.

"Even though this sight will star in all my fantasies, I'm going to take this off," I promise as I reach around behind her to the clasp.

The band loosens, causing the bra to ride up slightly. Her underboob game is strong. She shrugs out of the straps and tosses her bra to the side. My mouth practically waters at the sight of her hard, pink nipples pointing back at me without shame and begging for my mouth.

I cup her tits in my hands and pinch one nipple while I lick and suck the other. I lick my way across her chest and down to her other nipple as I start rolling the wet one between my fingers.

Avery's breaths start to come out in pants as her arousal begins to build again. She reaches between us to slide her panties to the side and notch my cock between her folds. My entire body spasms at the heat that scorches me. Her hips rock, sliding my cock through her wetness. My balls start to tingle, and I know I can't handle much more.

"Babe, I can't believe I'm saying this, but you need to stop. I'm about to come, and I don't want to yet."

She doesn't listen, but she does do what I ask. Sort of. Instead of sliding my dick through her folds, she starts tapping the head on her clit. It is almost worse.

"Avery," I moan as I throw my head back.

Her slick pussy lips hug my cock as she rubs herself from top to bottom. When she gets to her hole, she dips only the tip in and repeats the movement.

"Babe, what are you doing?" I pant.

"If you have to ask, I guess I'm not doing a very good job of showing you," she says saucily. My tip brushes her clit, and she groans.

"If this is going where I hope it is, we need to take a timeout so I can figure out if I have any condoms. If I do, they are probably expired, so this may have to be continued at another time."

She continues rubbing my cock through her pussy. "I'm on the pill and clean. I am okay with going bare if you are."

My dick must have understood her words way before the rest of me because it presses a little deeper into her wet hole.

"Fuck, you're so tight. I was tested for everything before I got discharged and haven't slept with anyone since. If you are sure, I am too."

She stands up on the couch and pushes her underwear down her legs. I grab her thighs to help steady her. Her pussy is even with my face, and I can smell the juices coating her. I can't stop myself from leaning forward and swiping my tongue through her. I make another pass and stop to suck her clit as her musk explodes on my tastebuds.

"Although that feels amazing and is something I want to revisit, I need your cock inside me. Now."

I don't think I have ever pulled my underwear off faster. When we are both naked, Avery sits back down on my lap, facing me. I lean back on my arms and take in the sexy seductress that has starred in every one of my fantasies since she slammed into my life. She gives my dick a pump, and I thrust up into her hand.

She presses against my shoulder, and I lie back on the couch. She leans forward and lines my cock up with her entrance. She lowers herself down, stretching to accommodate my width. I watch as her greedy hole swallows my hard cock in one long, slow movement.

I could come from the heat and tightness alone. I start mentally listing sailing knots to get my concentration off of how perfect she feels. *Bowline, stopper knot, clove hitch, sheet bend, rolling hitch.*

Her pussy bottoms out on my cock, and she groans. She flips her head to the side to get her hair out of the way and arches her back, pushing me in just a little deeper. She stays seated as we adjust to the new feeling, both of us breathing deeply.

She slowly leans forward and places her hands on the couch beside my face. Her hips rise until only the tip of my dick is still inside her. I put one hand on her shoulder and the other on her hip, feeling her soft skin under my fingertips. She kisses me then lowers herself back down, making me moan loudly with the tight grip on my cock. When she rises up again and sways forward, I take her hard nipple in my mouth, sucking on it until she moans.

She repeats the move a few more times before she sits up and places her hands on my chest. She slowly starts rocking her hips forward and backward making her body roll with the movement and her tits sway. I place my palm on her ass and squeeze the firm globe.

She speeds up, and I smack her ass cheek. The sensitive skin turns pink, making my possessiveness increase at the sight of my mark on her. The sensation of my cock being so deep inside her has her tilting her head back and a breathless moan coming out of her open mouth. I reach up and rub my thumb along the slender column, waiting for the day my cock is filling it.

She changes rhythm and starts to bounce slowly. I grab a handful of her ass in each hand and spread her cheeks to help her move. She bounces faster, and I moan at the different angle and the view of her large tits bouncing on her chest.

She leans over me as she breathes hard with exertion, and I try to make myself last until she comes again. She starts to rock back and forth, sliding her pussy up and down my entire cock. I stick my tongue out so her nipple brushes it every time she moves.

I grab her hips and guide her in her thrusts. One hand smacks her ass then grabs her muscular cheek. She moans loudly and pushes her hips deeper onto my cock, so I smack her other cheek, leaving matching prints.

I need a little more speed and a deeper thrust, so I plant my feet on the couch and bend my knees. I move both hands back to her hips to hold her still as I thrust up inside her with the force of my thighs.

The sound of her ass cheeks smacking my thighs makes my cock even harder. I push her down on my hips when I thrust upward so my cock can go even deeper into her tight pussy. I speed up my thrusts and fuck her hard, bottoming out in her tight pussy. She bites down on my shoulder with the sensation.

She gets out between pants, "Yeah, baby. Yeah. Oooo."

I stop thrusting and lay my legs back on the couch. I place my hands behind my head, and she takes over her pleasure. She grabs my forearms for balance and rolls her hips with my cock deep inside her, hitting her G-spot. She speeds up, and I know she is getting close.

"Oh fuck, baby. Your pussy feels so good," I groan deeply.

I grab her ass again, and she switches from rolling her hips to long, fast glides up and down my thick length, doing a few strokes of one then going back to the other.

I reach between us and gather some of her wetness on my finger. I start circling her clit, adding more pressure every few rounds.

"Oh, God. Yes. Yes," she yells as I feel her start to come.

Her pussy squeezes my cock, causing me to follow her over the edge, my dick shooting streams of hot cum deep into her pussy. She keeps rocking slowly as we breathe hard from our exertions and bask in the post-orgasm high.

Avery slumps forward, and her bare chest meets mine. We lie there, breathing hard for a few minutes as my cock slowly goes limp and slides out of her.

I sit up on the lounge and swing my legs to the ground. She hangs onto me like a koala bear, and I walk upstairs to my bedroom. I lay her down on my bed and go to the bathroom to get a warm wash cloth.

When I return, she follows me across the room with her eyes, but when I get close, she lowers them.

"No need to be shy now. That was hotter than my best fantasy. Sexy woman wearing matching underwear shows up with a pizza, gives me an amazing massage, and rides me until I see stars. This will be in the highlight reel for the rest of my life."

She laughs and covers her face with both hands.

"Oh my God. I'm a preschool teacher, for crying out loud. I can't be showing up at guys' houses and throwing myself at them like a porn star."

"Damn right you can't. You're mine. That just sealed the deal. This better be the only house you are showing up at, and you can repeat any part of what just happened at any time, and I will die a happy man."

"What if I don't want to be yours? You didn't exactly deliver on the *more talent than a book boyfriend* part of our deal."

I reach over and smack the side of her ass. "You wanna go again? I'm game for round two."

"I'm pretty sure my legs are jelly. I'm going to need a little bit," she says as she stretches her arms above her head and raises her back off my bed.

My dick instantly takes notice of her heavy breasts pushed in the air, her nipples still hard and swollen. I walk to her and run the wash cloth up her inner thigh where our mixed juices have leaked out and left a trail. Fuck, that's hot. I easily find her clit and rub a few circles under the guise of cleaning her up. She pushes against me, and I stop cleaning her.

"You said you needed a minute, greedy girl."

"You're making me change my mind," she moans.

I continue cleaning her as she gets more relaxed and sleepy in my bed. I toss the wash cloth in the direction of the bathroom and climb into bed beside her. I throw the covers over us and spoon her from behind.

How could I not guess how perfectly she would fit there. I wrap my arm over her side and cup her breast as my leg tangles with hers. I place a light kiss on the column of her exposed neck before laying my head down and passing out from exhaustion, fully sated.

CHAPTER 24
LIKE RIDING A BIKE

Avery

The beeping of my cellphone alarm from somewhere far away draws me out of the deepest sleep I have had in a long time. I tense when I realize I'm not in my bed in my small cape cod. My surroundings start to bombard my senses.

The smell of sandalwood and cloves permeates the pillowcase. The covers are pushed down to my waist where I must have shoved them after being heated from the furnace at my back. There is a suntanned, masculine hand cupping my breast. My pale legs are entangled with long, muscular ones tanned several shades darker by the sun.

My heart begins to slow as I realize I must have passed out after giving Sawyer his happy ending massage.

The hand cupping my breast tightens, and a hard cock pushes into my ass cheek.

Sawyer's gravely morning voice practically rumbles, "Morning, beautiful," before he places a kiss on my shoulder.

I scoot to my back so I can look at him.

"Morning. I hope this was okay. This wasn't really part of the plan. Sleeping over is kind of a big step."

"This is just the cherry on top of one of the best nights of my life," he says as he takes the opportunity presented and kisses down my chest to my exposed nipple. He sucks the small bud into a tight peak while his other hand trails down my stomach to my center.

My alarm goes off again, alerting me that I need to get going or I will be late for work.

I moan as he slowly slides a finger through my folds and finds me wet and ready. His hard cock juts out to my hip where a small pearl is forming on the tip.

My *Get Your Ass Out Of Bed Now* alarm goes off, and I groan.

"Even though this is rapidly becoming a very good morning, that was my messy bun alarm. I have to get ready for work. I'm already going to be late from the drive from your house to mine to get ready."

"Did you pack anything besides massage oil in that tote? You can use my bathroom and leave from here. It might even be closer," he says as he pushes his finger deeper into my pussy. He brings the digit back out and slides it up to circle my clit.

"Okay, we really need to table this for now. I have to get ready." He removes his finger and places it on my hip. "I brought a change of clothes but not much else."

"You can use whatever you need to from my bathroom. There is an extra toothbrush in one of the drawers under the sink. Help yourself."

I throw my legs over the bed and stand up. He smacks my ass, and I glower over my shoulder at him.

"I couldn't help myself. I like the way my handprint looks on that ass."

I roll my eyes as I walk across his room naked as the day I was born.

This bathroom was definitely not designed by a man, at least not the one who owns this house.

When I walk in the room, the first thing I notice is the huge white tiled shower with two rainfall shower heads with long built-in shelves to store your shower supplies under each one.

There is only shampoo and soap under one shower head, so I turn on the knob for that one.

A large soaker tub sits to the side of the shower. The toilet is in the corner with a privacy wall so two people can be in here at one time.

I turn to take in the rest of the room as the shower heats. The door I came in through is flanked with large white square sinks on each side, one side larger than the other. The larger side has another mirror above a makeup vanity complete with metal holders to store hair styling tools while they are hot. This entire side is clear. All the products are on the sink on the opposite side of the door.

A door to the side leads into a huge walk-in closet with clothes only on one side. This whole place was designed for two people to use and is just waiting for a woman to move in. She is going to be one lucky bitch to have all this and the man who goes with it.

I walk back over to the shower and climb in. The water is just the right temperature. I let it run down my body and soothe muscles I haven't used in a while as I lather my hair with Sawyer's shampoo.

I rub body wash over myself and get hints of sandalwood. I get a little thrill that I am going to smell like him all day today. I quickly rinse and turn the water off. I don't have time to luxuriate in the shower today.

I grab a towel off the warmer and dry off. I squeeze as much water from my hair as I can and wrap the towel around myself.

Sawyer must have slipped in here while I was showering since my tote is sitting on the makeup table beside my clothes from last night, and there is an unopened toothbrush and toothpaste on the sink.

I open the toothbrush and start brushing while I run my fingers through my hair. When I am done, I set the toothbrush and paste on the side of the sink, get the fresh set of clothes and small toiletry bag out of my tote, and put the dirty clothes in.

I find a hair elastic in the small bag and flip my head over to pull my damp hair into a messy bun. I put on the matching peach bra and panty set and below the knee tan flowy skirt and sleeveless blue blouse with a ruffled V-neck. Sawyer left my sandals by the vanity, so I slide those on as well.

I grab my toiletry bag from the sink and decide to use the bathroom to the fullest extent. I pull the small stool out from under the vanity and flip the switch for the vanity lights. I sit down and pull out eyeliner and mascara from the small pouch. I quickly apply them and turn the lights back off. I toss the pouch in the tote and give one last glance around this Mecca of bathrooms. *Goodbye, vanity table.*

I walk out of the bathroom, and the bedroom is empty. I head out the door and down the stairs. I can see Sawyer standing in the haphazard kitchen wearing gray sweats and looking out the window.

With a brazenness I usually don't have, I walk up behind him and wrap my arms around his stomach, my hands finding his hard pecs. He turns in my embrace and kisses me. The kiss quickly turns sensual, and he places his coffee cup down on the counter to grab my ass and pull me to him.

I end the kiss and back away. "I have to get to work."

He pulls me back and says, "Call in," before kissing me again.

"You have to go to work too," I say as I step back again.

"I'll call in."

"You can't call in. Emily sort of knows I was coming over here last night."

That gets his attention, and he drops his hands and leans away from me. "What?" he asks with a little rise to his voice.

"I didn't know what time to expect you to get home last night, so I called her to ask what your schedule was for yesterday. She told me what time you would be back, and I started planning from there."

His forehead comes to rest on mine.

"Great. She is going to give me so much shit today no matter how I play this off. Ugh."

His frustration makes me laugh. I put my hands on either side of his face and tilt his head so I can place a quick kiss on his lips. "I guess you will just have to take her punishment since she was instrumental in last night playing out the way it did."

"It was definitely worth whatever she has to say," he replies as he leans down to kiss me.

"I really have to go now."

"I'll walk you to your car."

I unlock the doors and place my tote on the passenger seat. Sawyer is standing behind me when I stand back up. He steps forward and gives me a fiery kiss before stepping back.

"Have a good day, Avery. I'll talk to you later. I should be done around five tonight, so you don't have to call Emily today to check," he says as he smiles. "You know. In case you wanted to hang out with me tonight. I'm sure my muscles will need some attention, especially the one between my legs."

I smack him on the bare shoulder with a laugh. "You are terrible. That's the last time I show up here bearing gifts."

"Bare gifts are the best kind. I'll be thinking about them all day. Maybe even a few minutes from now when I get in the shower."

I just shake my head and put my car in reverse. "Bye, Sawyer. Be careful today."

"I will be. Just for you, baby."

I back up and turn my car around to head down the twisty lane. I look in my rearview mirror, and Sawyer is still standing there. He lifts his hand in a wave, and I do the same.

ME: I have hot goss, and I can't hold it in much longer. Can you get away around 3:30?

RILEY: Probably. I could go for some ice cream. Scoop?

ME: You read my mind. I'll drive over right after school to try to get us a table on The Boardwalk.

RILEY: <thumbs-up emoji>

I navigate tourist traffic and park Chili in one of the lots near The Boardwalk. I see a family getting up from a table, so I hustle to it before someone else takes it.

I sit down and let the warm sun replenish my Vitamin D. The breeze off the water is relatively calm today, so hopefully Sawyer wasn't trying to get anywhere fast. I can barely hear the waves crashing over the sounds of kids laughing and yelling and gulls screeching.

I people watch for a few minutes to pass the time until Riley shows up. I hear her motorcycle before I can see her driving down Ocean Boulevard.

She parks beside me and takes off her helmet. Her face looks a little pale, and she might have lost a few pounds she didn't need to. I feel like a shit friend for abandoning her to spend time with a guy.

She walks down to the table, and I stand up to give her a tight hug.

"I have missed you so much. I feel like such an asshole for not making time to come see you. Are you sure you are doing okay?"

I can feel tears running down her face and onto my shoulder. My strong, unbreakable best friend might be breaking right before my eyes, and I don't know how to fix it.

"Some days are worse than others. Seeing you and feeling your sympathy just pulled out a deep well of emotion. I'll be okay in a few minutes."

She gives me one last tight squeeze and steps back, wiping her eyes.

"I know you didn't send me a teaser text to make me come up here and cry on a public beach. What's up?"

"I feel like an even bigger asshole now."

"I'm fine, or I will be. What's going on in Tourist Central? I have been actively staying away from all this. Are you trying the beginner sailing class again? Doesn't it start tomorrow?"

"No, I'm not doing another sailing class yet. I'm actually doing the instructor."

Riley's eyes get round as the meaning of my words kicks in.

"Shut the front door. You slept with Sawyer? Mr. Billboard Model?" Riley practically screams.

"Sssshhhh," I plead, looking around. "Not so loud, please. I would rather the whole world didn't know I just broke out of my chastity belt."

"When did this happen? How long have you been holding out on me?"

I look at my watch. "Well, you carry the one, and…about twenty hours ago."

"No way. Where? How?"

I open my mouth to respond, and she says, "Actually, skip those until later. Just give me a rating on a one to ten scale."

"If this is a scale of inches, I'm going with eight. I was kind of surprised it fit in me. I may choke to death when I give him head."

Riley snorts at that admission. "Do you even remember how to blow a guy?"

"Well, let's just hope it's like riding a bike, and I will get on that bitch and go to town because it's been a while."

We both laugh at my outlandish comparison.

"You have seen the billboard of his body. It doesn't lie and probably undersells him, to be honest. His dick is proportionate to the rest of him, thick and long. The dentist will definitely know what I have been up to. Just saying."

Riley smiles and shakes her head. I am happy to see she does remember how to smile and enjoy life.

I continue my assessment of Sawyer. "Now for the rest of the ratings. I was on top, and he let me do my thing. He knew exactly how to blow my mind, so I'll rate that a ten plus."

Riley raises one perfectly manicured eyebrow.

"No joke. He knew exactly where to put his hands and lips and how to use both."

I fan my face. "I'm getting a little hot just telling you about it."

"Okay. That rating sounds reasonable then. How did this life-altering event come to be?"

"You will never believe this. I got a Wild Special, drove to his house, gave him a massage to work the kinks out of all those muscles, then rode him until the cows came home."

"What a hussy. I have trained you so well. So was this a one-time thing, or are you a thing now?"

"The night before last, he laid it all out there. He wants to be monogamous and build a relationship with me. I want that too. He is everything I have ever wanted in a partner. He lets me be my quirky self, book boyfriends and all. He wants me to reach my goals and knows when to push me and when to back off. My mind knows he will provide comfort and safety and automatically turns to him when I need it."

"Sounds like you are falling for him."

"I totally am. He's perfect for me," I gush.

"What about his job? Does that give you any anxiety?"

"Surprisingly, no. If it did, I would walk away before I let him change anything about the way he lives. I have seen the way he interacts with the beginner sailing class and how he looks when he's standing on the deck of a boat. It's his happy place. I would never want him to give that up for me."

"Let's just hope it never comes to that," Riley says as she looks over at our favorite ice cream stand. "You lured me here with the promise of ice cream, so you better deliver. Let's go get our cones then walk down The Boardwalk while we eat them. I could use the exercise."

"Sounds good. My treat."

CHAPTER 25
IMPERTINENT FEMALE

Sawyer

"We are all booked for that day. Will another day work?" Emily asks whoever is on the telephone.

"I'm sorry. You can stop by that morning and check to see if there is a cancellation, but that's the best I can do."

I walk up to her desk to look for the box of folders for tomorrow's beginner sailing course. I start moving things around, and she puts her finger up and gives me a mean mug.

"I'm sorry that it's not going to work out this trip. Keep us in mind for next time!" Emily says.

She hangs up and looks over at me. "Why do people think that just because they want to do something we can move things around and make it happen for them? We. Are. Booked. How hard is that to comprehend? I'm not going to cancel another client who booked weeks ago just because you want to go on a sail and didn't decide until five minutes ago? Errrrgggghhh."

"I'm just here to get the folders for tomorrow's beginner sailing class so I can get them set out," I say in a peaceful voice.

"I already did that earlier today while you were out having fun in the sun," she snaps as she shoves some papers around on the desk.

"Hey, what's really wrong?" I ask.

"I got waitlisted for dive school again, and I am just annoyed."

I walk over to her and give her a hug. "It's fine. It will happen for you when the time is right. Just give it more time."

"I just feel bad because I told you my plans, and you bought that dive boat and now I can't follow through on my side of the bargain." Her emotions are really close to the surface. Luckily, living with Sav through her teenage years prepared me for this.

"Hey, don't worry about the boat. I have actually used it several times. It came in really handy with the beginner class, and I take it if I just need to make a quick trip somewhere and don't want to get the other boats out. It was a good purchase."

I can feel her shoulders drop as she releases some tension. I drop my arms, and she steps away.

"If you haven't noticed, we are booked completely solid for weeks. You know how much money this place makes. There is no need to worry about me buying a small dive boat. A schooner? Yes. Dive boat? No. It will be fine. I just bought four boats that see maybe six hours a month. Those are the ones I'm worried about paying for themselves. Who wants to sail around in a rubber duck?"

Emily laughs and wipes her eyes. "I think they looked cute when they lined up behind The Emerald last week. I should have had the photographer take a picture of that. A mom and her little ducks."

"You can't replace me with something called a Pudgy! I won't ever be able to live that down."

"Ooooo! Great idea for a tagline. *You called. Pudgy is calling you back!*"

"You aren't in charge of marketing anymore." I laugh as I walk back to my office.

"I'm literally in charge of everything but chauffeuring people around."

"Was that a thinly veiled ask for a raise?"

"No, but now that you mention it…HR did say something about raises and fat bonuses this year."

"I'll look through my email in case I missed it," I yell as I sit down at my desk to finish some paperwork and reply to messages.

My computer dings with an incoming email from Emily.

Mr. Davis,

It is with utmost certainty that I implore you to increase employee wages and bestow large bonuses on said employees.

Regards,

Emily, HR Manager

The message brings a smile to my face. This place wouldn't be the same without her. I click reply and type.

Indubitably.

I hit send and shut down my computer. I grab my phone off my desk and look for any messages since the last time I was in here. Nothing.

Emily yells, "Night, Sawyer. I'll lock the front door. See you tomorrow morning."

"Later, Em."

I make a lunchmeat sandwich and sort through the bags of chips until I find my favorite. I get a cold Coke out of the industrial refrigerator and walk outside to the bench. The sun should set in about a half hour.

I eat my sandwich and watch the boats bob in the water. A million thoughts fly through my mind, clogging my ability to focus on any one thing. I pick up my phone and put my elbows on my knees. I unlock my phone to look for any notifications. Nothing still. My finger hovers over Avery's contact information. Should I call her? Why is this so hard?

A shadow falls over me, and I look up. Avery is standing in front of me. I must have been really in my head not to hear her walk up.

"Excuse me, ma'am. I am trying to watch the sunset, and you are blocking the view."

She pushes my shoulders so I lean back against the bench and she steps between my knees. She leans forward and places her hands on the bench beside my shoulders. She continues moving forward as she quietly asks, "How about a better view?" and presses her lips to mine.

Our tongues mingle, and I reach up to grab two handfuls of her jean-shorts-covered ass.

We continue kissing, and I pull her forward onto my lap so she is straddling me. My cock appreciates this new position and comes out to investigate the warmth between her legs.

Avery grabs ahold of the longer hair on the top of my head and tilts my head back, breaking our kiss. She presses a hard kiss to my closed lips and moves to get off my lap. I hold her still until she gets the idea that I want her where she is.

"I took a chance I would find you here. How was your day?"

"Way better now," I say as I run my hands up her back. My thumbs come around to slide under the band of her bra over the loose material of her T-shirt.

"Mine too," she says as she starts to rock a little against my stiffening cock.

I groan, and the sound makes her nipples pebble. I move my hands from under her breasts to her nipples. I roll the hard peaks between my finger and thumb until she bows her back, trying to get her tits closer to me.

I take the opportunity and place my face in her cleavage and push her tits together with my hands. As a professional sailor, I can motorboat with the best of them.

Her nipples are straining through her shirt now, and I turn my head to gently bite down on one.

Avery hisses air through her lips, so I let off the pressure.

My cock is getting harder with every undulation of her hips.

"Babe, I'm going to embarrass myself on this bench if you don't stop. My cock is going to explode in my underwear in about three seconds."

"Well, we can't have that," she purrs as she stops rocking and sits up straight on my lap, bringing her eyes twinkling with humor even with mine.

"Can I get off your lap now, or are you going to pull me back down?"

"Just give me a few minutes."

"Can you hurry? Someone said the sun was getting ready to set, and I don't want to miss it."

I throw my head back and groan. "Why am I surrounded by impertinent females?"

"Because someone needs to keep your ego in check." She presses a quick kiss to my lips and slides off my lap to sit beside me.

She grabs my wrist and tosses my arm around her shoulder as she snuggles into my side and leans her head against my pec.

The move makes me smile. "Why, yes. By all means, burrow into my armpit. I can't guarantee the smell at this time of day, but suit yourself."

She makes a gagging noise and says in a choked voice, "I can't breathe."

I pull my arm in toward my chest, trapping her head even closer to my armpit for a few seconds as she giggles and struggles to get away from me. I let her back up, and she settles back in. I lean over to kiss her hair as we watch the sun bring another day to a close.

This is what I have been missing in my life.

"I really like the ones with purple in them, but any one I can stop and just watch happen around me is a good one."

"Agreed. I love sitting here to watch them. They make me appreciate the things I have."

She tilts her head up, and I brush her lips with mine in a kiss laden with something that feels a lot like love.

Darkness has fallen, and the only light this far from The Boardwalk is the moon and stars. We cuddle for a few more minutes before she stands up and grabs my hands.

"You better get home and get your beauty sleep. You never know when you will have to save a damsel in distress in the morning."

I let her pull me up and enclose her in a hug. I can't stop touching her. I love the way she feels against me.

"You blew into my life like a Cat 5, and I wouldn't change one bit of it."

"You saved me from myself and then kept saving me."

"Always, Avery."

We walk hand in hand to the parking lot. When we get to her car, she turns to me and asks, "When do you have excursions this weekend?"

"Why? Are you trying to plan a pizza party?"

"Nope. I need to go buy a toilet, and I'm not sure it will fit in the back of Chili. I was hoping to barter for a trip over Magnolia Ridge."

"Does this trip include installation when we get back? I'm pretty handy, so there's no need to pay someone when we can just *barter*."

"Thanks for the offer, but it's for Field Day at school. I just have to pick it up and drop it off."

"I have the beginner sailing class tomorrow morning, a snorkel excursion after lunch, and a sunset sail tomorrow evening. I probably won't be back home in time to go tomorrow night. I have a morning sail tour on Sunday. That will take a few hours, but I should be back by lunch. I'm meeting my friends at the beach that afternoon unless something changes tomorrow. We can meet here around noon on Sunday, grab some lunch, get your toilet, and spend the afternoon at the beach if you want to."

"I don't have any plans all weekend, so Sunday will work fine."

"Okay. I will see you Sunday," I say as I lean forward to give her a goodbye kiss. "Be careful on the drive home."

"You too. And tomorrow."

She gets in Chili and drives off with a wave.

I let out a huge breath and walk over to my Jeep. I wish we were going to the same place.

CHAPTER 26
PORCH BEER

Avery

"Hello?"

"Does it scream horny and desperate if I show up at Sawyer's house again without being invited?" I ask Riley as I sort through my underwear drawer for my long-forgotten lingerie.

"A little."

I can visualize her cringing.

"Do you think he would care if I showed up again? Can I pull off an *I was just in the neighborhood and thought I'd stop by*?"

"I—"

I cut her off. "Before you answer, I'm going to tell you the answer I want you to tell me so I feel validated in my decision to go over there tonight no matter what you were going to say. Tell me he has been thinking about me all day, and he's going home to an empty house to think about me all night. I might as well be there to keep him company and slob on his knob if he needs that too."

"Please never say that phrase again. I have secondhand embarrassment from all the way across town. I was one hundred percent on board until you said the words *slob on his knob.* You should probably stay home and read some erotica to brush up on current slang before you say something like that ever again."

"I don't think he will care what I call it if I'm doing it."

"Fair. You know I was going to tell you to go for it. Knock the cobwebs out of the lingerie drawer and pack a bag to spend the night. Get some, girl!"

"I like that answer much more than the first one you gave me. Stay home and read erotica when I have an actual billboard model pining for me alone in his beautiful house with a master bathroom begging for a woman to fill the other half with her clothes and makeup. Phuf."

"One of us has to be the voice of reason every once in a while," she says with a laugh. "It's just weird that it's me this time."

"I know. That's what scares me."

"Well, you know what they say. Don't do anything I wouldn't do, and that isn't much!"

I laugh at her joke. "Bye, Riley!"

As I'm lowering the phone from my ear, I hear her say, "If he's a dumbass and turns down a hot, willing woman, call me and we can go toilet paper his house or something!"

I click the end button and start going through my drawers with a huge smile on my face.

I take a guess on what time Sawyer will be home and drive to his house a little after nine. Hopefully, he isn't already home and went to bed.

I pull into the driveway and the motion lights come on in his front yard. There's no sneaking around this place.

I'm assuming he normally parks his Jeep in one of the three garage bays, so I don't know if he is home or not. I grab my tote and walk to the front door.

I ring the bell and wait for him to open the door. Headlights coming up the driveway swipe across the front porch, illuminating me like the proverbial deer. I really hope that is Sawyer and not a robber or axe murderer.

The vehicle keeps driving and parks beside Chili. Thank God I recognize that Jeep.

Sawyer hops out and says, "I had a sandwich earlier, but I can always go for a slice of pizza. Or we can skip that part and get right to the good stuff."

"Are you ever going to let me live that down?"

"Nope. What part of best night of my life are you not understanding? I want to relive that as often as possible."

"So you don't care that I'm here?" I hesitate as he steps on the porch and leans down to kiss me.

"Nah, babe. I love that you feel comfortable enough with us to show up on my doorstep at night when you know I will be home shortly. Best part of my day."

"I just didn't want to seem like a stalker. We have plans to meet tomorrow already," I say as he unlocks the door, and we walk through the foyer.

"And this is even better. I'm assuming since you brought the Mary Poppins bag, you are staying."

"I don't have to if you don't want me to."

He grabs me by the wrist and turns me to face him. "Avery, you are always welcome here. I like spending time with you. You understand my life is crazy right now and work around it. I can't begin to tell you how much I appreciate that."

"Well, yeah. Your job is a big part of who you are. I understand that and wouldn't want you to change it for me."

"So what was your master plan? Lure me to my bedroom with this sexy dress that barely conceals your tits as soon as you got here or can we have a beer and decompress first?"

"I'm cool with a beer on the porch. I'm not that much of a fiend."

Sawyer flashes a smile with full dimples, and I almost have to recant my statement. He walks to the kitchen and gets two beers out of the fridge.

"It's nice out tonight. Let's use the upstairs porch instead of the four season."

"Lead the way."

"You can bring your bag and drop it off in my bedroom as we walk through. That way neither of us has to go get it in the morning."

"Is that what you did last time? A walk of shame?" I question.

"Do you see anything to be ashamed about on this body? Didn't think so."

"I didn't even answer."

"I answered for you."

We walk up the stairs to his bedroom. There are two other doors on this floor. I wonder if they are bedrooms or bathrooms or a combination of both.

"I would give you a tour, but what you see is really what you get. The rest of the rooms in the house are pretty much bare studs. I finished most of the wiring, but I am waiting to put up drywall in case I need to add something else. There are two bedrooms up here with a Jack and Jill bathroom on that side of the loft. You obviously know this side of the loft is the master suite."

Sawyer turns on the lights and dims them to a nice ambient glow. We walk through his bedroom that I didn't really pay attention to the last time I was here. It smells like his sandalwood and clove cologne. His bed has a dark wood platform frame and headboard, and it is topped with a light gray down comforter with a charcoal blanket folded on the foot. One wall has the door that leads to the mother of all bathrooms. The opposite wall is covered in floor-to-ceiling curtains a couple shades darker than the bedding.

Sawyer walks over to the curtains and pushes them back to reveal an entire wall of glass accordion doors that lead to a private porch.

He opens one door and motions for me to go through. I place my tote on the stool at the foot of the bed and walk outside.

The black metal porch railing has warm rope lights weaved along the top rail, giving off just the right amount of light to see but not be super bright. There is a small dark, wooden loveseat with cream cushions, two cream rocking chairs, and a dark wooden coffee table out here. I walk over to the loveseat and sit down, and Sawyer follows.

I can't make out where Magnolia Ridge starts in the moonlight, but I can tell it is not far from his backyard.

"This is really beautiful, Sawyer. I can't wait to see what the rest of the house looks like when it's done. You do such good work."

"It's slow going, so you may be stuck with me for a bit if you want to see the finished product."

"I can probably suffer through."

Sawyer pulls me to him and ruffles my hair. "Suffer my ass."

I stay where I am, half on his lap, half on the loveseat. We sit like this for a while, listening to the sounds of the ridge at night and drinking our beers in companionable silence.

"So how did the beginner sailing class go today?"

He gets a big smile on his face. "Not as eventful as the first class, but they are excited to learn. I'm really glad I decided to do this."

"Me too, even though I still can't sail a damn Pudgy."

"You were a pro on dry land. I know you will be fine when you make it to water. I have full faith in your abilities."

"At least one of us does." I drink the rest of my beer and put the empty can on the coffee table. I turn over on my back, lay my head on Sawyer's lap, and dangle my feet over the other end.

Sawyer runs his fingers through my hair and traces patterns on my scalp. "You'll get there. You just have to trust the process."

"We'll see. How was the rest of your day?"

"Pretty good. I think I found a new snorkel location. The water was calmer, and the snorkelers said they saw a lot of fish. The further into the season it gets, the harder it is to find an easy access location that isn't overrun with tourists. I will have to see how this goes."

As he talks, his fingers start to trail farther and farther from my hair.

"Sawyer?"

"Yeah?"

"Can we go to bed now?"

"I was hoping you would ask."

I stand up and Sawyer follows. He picks me up and throws me over his shoulder, his long strides eating up the space between us and the bed.

When he gets to the bed, he tosses me down on my butt like a sack of potatoes.

CHAPTER 27
PLEADING MY CASE

Sawyer

Avery lands with a little bounce, and I take a moment to just look at her sprawled out on my bed. I don't have words to describe what having her in my house, on my bed has me feeling. Is it too soon to be in love? Because that is the only way I can think to describe the feeling in my chest.

The thought leaves my brain as Avery runs her palms up her sides and over her breasts, her mouth open in a breathy moan at the pleasure she is giving herself with that light touch. I can't wait to see what responses I can draw out of her.

I unbutton my Pirate's Life shirt and watch as her eyes get a little darker with desire the more skin I reveal. Her perusal stops on my tattoo for a few seconds before moving on. Her gaze feels like a caress to every dip and valley of my muscular chest and torso I expose. I slide the shirt down my arms and toss it to the floor.

I grab her silky smooth legs and pull her to the edge of the bed, wedging myself between them. The smell of her arousal, thick and sweet, filters up to my nose, causing my mouth to salivate. I can't wait to taste her pussy when she comes.

I have never been more happy that I bought a tall platform bed frame. It is the perfect height for what I have in mind. I lean forward and kiss her as I move my hands from her calves up her thighs. She returns the kiss and places her hands on my chest. She finds my nipples and brushes her soft fingertips over them. The feeling makes a shiver go down my spine and my nipples harden.

My tongue traces the seam of her lips, and she opens to let me in. She tastes like the beer we had on the porch and every good decision I have ever made.

Our tongues slide together erotically as I find the lace edge of her underwear near the apex of her thighs. I slowly slip my finger under the flimsy fabric and find her hot flesh. I part her bare pussy and trail my finger through the wetness coating her inner folds.

She moans as she kisses my jaw through the stubble. I reach down and grab the hem of her dress, sliding it up her body and over her head in one fluid motion.

She is left in pale blue, sheer lace that leaves nothing to the imagination. Dusky pink areolas surround her hard, pointy nipples. She follows my gaze and smiles like a succubus.

"You like what you see?" she coos as she cups her round, perky tits and pushes them together, the fullness spilling out over her hands.

"You know I do." I lean forward and run my tongue through her cleavage, sucking on her soft skin when I reach the top. "These tits are perfect. They are going to look so fucking good wrapped around my cock."

I suck on her pointy nipple. My saliva leaves a dark, wet spot on the lace. The fabric gives a rough sensation to my lips, so I pull her bra down, exposing her breasts fully to my view.

She arches her back, offering me a feast fit for a king. I take her hard peak into my mouth again and suck it with deeper, harder pulls. I comply with her unspoken wish and give her a little nip with my teeth before moving to her other nipple.

"That feels so good, Sawyer. I might be able to come just from this. My nipples are so sensitive."

"We may have to test that theory out another time. I have different plans for tonight."

Avery strokes her hand over the front of my shorts, outlining my hard length with her slender fingers.

"I can see that," she says as she unbuckles my belt and pulls it through the loops. She folds it in half and smacks it on the bed.

"That may have to wait for another day as well." I smile.

Avery laughs and tosses the belt over the side of the bed with my shirt and her dress.

"More promises and you have yet to deliver on one," she jibes as she leans back on her hands, her tits swaying above the shelf that her bra creates.

I grab the sides of her panties and tug them down. She assists by raising her hips slightly. I put these in my pocket for safekeeping.

"I can't wait to start crossing things off that list. I'll start with this first." I kneel down and place her thighs on my shoulders. The smell of her arousal fills the air around me.

I run my finger through her folds, and it comes out glistening with her wetness.

"Look how wet you are for me, Avery." I stick my finger in my mouth to lick off her juices. Her flavor explodes across my tongue. She looks at me with desire pooling in her eyes, and I can't wait to taste more of her.

I place slow, gentle kisses peppered with little nips to the inside of her thighs. Avery groans with unfulfilled desire at my leisurely pace. I slide my hands under her ass to lift her pussy to my face.

Her thighs open wider, making room for me to get closer. She shivers in anticipation of what I am about to do.

I plant soft kisses along her folds then another over the hood of her clit.

She groans and tries to move, but I have her held still with my hands. She crumples the sheets in her fists in her desperation to satisfy her desire.

"I'll decide when you get the pressure you want on that greedy clit. I'm in charge today."

I take my time sliding my tongue through her pussy lips, licking her from bottom to top. When I get to her clit, I draw circles around it with the tip of my tongue, causing her to let out a hitched exhale.

I lick her again, following the same path. This time when I get to the top, I flick her clit with firm strokes before taking it between my teeth for a gentle nip. I draw her nub into my mouth, sucking on it until it becomes pebbled.

Avery moans and lies back on the bed so she can play with her tits as I lick her pussy.

"That's it, baby. Do what makes you feel good. You like your nipples pinched and pulled, don't you? Those little peaks are getting so swollen and sensitive."

Avery whimpers at my words, and I lick her again, this time from her clit down to her hole. I stick my tongue in her tight heat and pull it back out several times, mimicking what my throbbing cock is aching to do.

She pushes her tits together and starts shaking them slightly. The sight of her cleavage jiggling makes my balls draw tight to my body.

I lick through her folds back to her clit and suck on the distended button as I slide one finger into her tight channel, testing her wetness. The spear of pleasure that shoots through her has her back arching in pleasure.

I add another finger and slide them in and out as I alternate between licking and sucking her clit. Her hands grab my hair, and she holds me where she wants me.

Her pussy smashes into my face as she chases her pleasure. She gets wetter and moans louder as I curl my fingers to find the rough area deep inside her.

I make longer strokes with my tongue to lap up all the wetness seeping out of her with every thrust of my fingers. Her taste makes me moan, and the vibration on her clit is enough to push her over the edge.

"Yes. Right there. Yeeesss." She clamps down tight on my fingers as I feel her juices gush out of her and down my hand.

I slow my pace and watch her come down from her orgasm. I pull my fingers out and suck her cream off of them as she watches.

"That was a pretty impressive skill," she says as her chest still rises and falls with her exertion.

"Wait until you experience the next one," I reply as I unbutton my shorts and slide the zipper down. I shove my underwear and shorts down with one move and get on the bed beside her one knee at a time.

Avery's hand comes up to grip my hard cock, her fingers barely touching around the girth. She slides her finger over the tip and swirls. When she lifts her finger away, there is a bridge of precum linking us.

"Scoot up to the headboard," I tell her.

My hard cock bounces against my stomach when she lets go. She scoots up the bed, and I follow her until I am between her widespread thighs. I lean forward to kiss her. She opens to me, and I join my tongue with hers. I know she can taste herself on my lips and tongue, and the thought makes more precum bead at my tip.

I trail sucking kisses down her neck to her clavicle. I lick my way along the prominent bone, smelling her warm vanilla scent.

When I get to her throat, I dip the tip of my tongue in the hollow where the two bones meet.

Her body is undulating under me, like I am already thrusting deep inside her. She wants this so fucking bad. I can't wait to be deep inside her again, but I am going to continue drawing out her pleasure.

I find her nipple with my mouth and suck it into an even longer peak. She arches into my mouth, and I switch to the other one as my rough hands skim up her sides, making goosebumps pop out on her soft skin.

I fist my cock and rub it through her pussy lips, wetting my dick with a mixture of my precum and her juices. I tap the purple head of my cock on her clit a few times, eliciting a loud moan. She raises her arms above her head, her hands grasping the headboard.

That's it, baby. You better hang on. You know this is going to be a rough ride.

I line my cock up with her tight pussy and press just the tip in. I withdraw and smile at the frustrated look on her face.

I enter her about halfway in a slow slide, coating my cock with her arousal. I withdraw again, and she bites her bottom lip to keep the groan inside. I bury my cock all the way inside her this time, my balls brushing her ass.

"Fuck. I will never get tired of how your tight pussy takes my cock."

I slowly pull out until only the tip is left and then slide back in a little faster. I speed up my thrusts when she starts raising her hips to meet mine.

I pull out and run the shiny head of my cock over her clit. The stimulation on her sensitive bud makes her moan. I enter her again with a few slow strokes before I pick up the pace and go deeper, causing her tits to bounce with each thrust.

"Yes. Harder," she says breathlessly.

I change the angle so I can reach where she wants me to. She closes her eyes and bites her lip as I pound her into the headboard.

"Yes. Right there. Fuck this pussy just like that," she demands.

I grab her ankle with one hand and her knee with the other and spread her legs wider. I fuck her with long, hard strokes as she twists her nipples between her fingers.

"Oooh. Yes. Yes. Ohh," she moans. I can feel her pussy getting wetter with every stroke.

I pull one of her legs over my shoulder. I grab her hip and use it as leverage so I can pound that place deep inside her. My cock is getting impossibly thicker with every response she makes.

I'm so close to coming, but I'm not ready for this to end. I let her leg down and lean over to kiss her.

"Roll over," I tell her in a husky voice next to her ear. She shivers and her eyes flare with desire.

She turns over and puts that peach-shaped ass up in the air as she gets on her hands and knees. My cock strains toward her ass, and I rub the head through her folds, catching some of the juices that are leaking out of her.

I stroke my cock to make sure I am well lubricated and to give myself a second to compose myself.

I line up my cock and enter her quickly. She backs up on my dick as I thrust forward. I grab her hips with both hands and guide her along my cock. She bends her arms so her pussy is hiked in the air, and I fuck her hard.

"You going to come again for me, baby?" My chest rises and falls heavily, and I smack her ass.

The nodding of her blond head is the only response I get. I can feel her start to spasm. She is getting close.

"That's it. Come on this hard cock."

I keep thrusting hard and deep. I can feel a tingle starting at the base of my spine. I plant one foot on the bed to change the angle so I can hit the sweet spot deep inside her. My thrusts become frantic and vigorous in my mission to wring every last bit of pleasure from her body. A loud moan escapes her open mouth, and her pussy clamps down on my cock, setting off my own orgasm.

Pulse after pulse of cum fills her pussy as I gently rock to extend our orgasms.

When she is done shuddering and our breathing starts to level out, I lean over her back, and she looks up at me. I give her a long kiss.

I feel her lips smiling under mine, so I pull out and settle back on my heels. My cock is still semi-hard and glistening with cum. She rolls over on her back and puts her legs on the outside of mine. The minx raises her arms above her head, flaunting her killer body.

Her tits are still rising and falling with her heavy breathing, and she wipes the fine sheen of sweat off her forehead with the back of her hand.

"Phew. That was a pretty impressive skill as well. I'll need more demonstrations before I can deem it better than a book boyfriend, though."

"I'll happily plead my case until I can convince you without a doubt that my skills are superior," I reply.

I look down at where we were connected. A mixture of our cum is leaking out. Without thinking, I reach between us to collect the juices on my finger and push them back inside her.

A small gasp escapes her, and my eyes flash to hers when I realize what I just did.

She is mine. Now I just have to convince her of that.

CHAPTER 28
ISN'T SHE A BEAUT

Avery

I wake up to the sun streaming in through the floor-to-ceiling windows. I stretch and roll over to see if Sawyer is awake and wants to start the day off with a bang.

I am in bed alone. I roll on my back and look at the ceiling, trying to decide if I'm ready to get out of bed and go look for him.

Then I remember he said he had a Sunday morning sailing tour and would be back by lunch. I wonder if I am still supposed to meet him at Pirate's Life or if here makes more sense.

My bladder is calling. I look around for the dress I wore last night and don't see anything. I'm not worried about anyone seeing me naked, so I get out of bed and walk across the bedroom and into the bathroom. I do my business and go to the sink to wash my hands.

My tote bag is sitting on the vanity. The toothbrush and paste I used last time are sitting in a pale gray ceramic holder that matches the one on Sawyer's vanity.

The sight makes my inner girl scream, and something warm unfurls in my chest. He is adding me to his home without prodding from me. This is a huge step, but I don't feel any anxiety about it. It feels right.

I wash and dry my hands and walk to the closet to look for one of Sawyer's T-shirts to wear.

Does he even own a T-shirt? I have only ever seen him in Pirate's Life button-ups. He must have twenty of those things.

I'm not complaining, because he looks damn good in them with his golf shorts. He's a cross between a muscular, blue-collar worker and a cavalier billionaire out sailing his yacht.

As I guessed, there is an entire row of Pirate's Life button-ups in various colors hanging up. There are some hoodies and long-sleeved shirts, as well as some jeans hanging on other racks, so I start snooping through the drawers.

Shorts. Boxer briefs. Socks. T-shirts. *Bingo.* I pull the one off the top and slip it over my head. I lift the fabric to my nose and sniff. There is no trace of his sandalwood and clove scent, just laundry detergent and fabric softener.

I walk downstairs and into the bones of the kitchen. There is a single-serve coffee maker on the plywood countertop, so I walk over there. A mug, a new box of cappuccino pods, and a note are placed in front of it. I pick up the note first.

Avery,

Sorry I wasn't here when you woke up. I have a morning sail, so I won't be back until around eleven. I don't have a fancy coffee maker, so I bought you these pods. I hope they are something you like.

Feel free to relax and snoop around until I get back because I know you are going to.

-Sawyer

The smile on my face almost hurts my cheeks because it is so big. Damn right I'm going to snoop around. After I have a glass of cappuccino in the four season room.

I pop the pod in and wait the minute it takes to brew. I walk over and plop down on the sectional. The memories from my first night here flood my brain.

I'm so glad that turned out like I planned. Maybe one day this can be my life. Hot sex, him going to work, and me relaxing or doing chores around the house until he comes home to spend the afternoon with me. Kids running through the house and around the yard. Maybe a dog.

I sigh and settle further into the cushion. Everyone has to have a dream.

I sip my cappuccino and watch some squirrels play in the trees at the base of the ridge. A deer walks by without a care in the world.

I can see why Sawyer picked this location to build his home.

My cup is empty, so I walk back to the kitchen to wash it and set it in the dish drainer.

I rush up the stairs with excitement in my blood. Do I have enough time to take a bath? My Kindle is in my tote. I don't stray too far without it.

I dig through my tote and see I have two hours until Sawyer said he would be back. Perfect.

I turn on the water for the tub. When it gets full enough, I turn on the circulation heater so the water stays this warm for as long as I want to stay in here.

I toss Sawyer's shirt into the dirty laundry and grab my Kindle. I step in the water and sit down. The water covers my boobs and my knees at the same time. Win!

I read for an hour or so and get out. I can't help myself, so I walk over to the shower and turn the knobs to get the hot water going. I grab my travel-sized shampoo, conditioner, soap, and my razor out of my tote and get in the shower.

I place my toiletries on the empty shelf and stand under the shower head for a few minutes, waiting for my hair to get wet. I quickly shampoo and condition my hair and shave all the necessary parts since I am going to meet Sawyer's friends and sister at the beach this afternoon. And maybe come back here later.

I am just walking down the stairs when the front door opens.

Sawyer sees me and a huge grin covers his face.

"Honey, I'm home!" he bellows as he shuts the door. He is wearing his usual shirt, but he paired it with charcoal swim trunks that look similar to golf shorts.

I laugh and keep walking down the stairs.

"You're ridiculous."

We meet in the foyer, and he wraps me in a low hug and kisses me. I am wrapped in a cocoon of sandalwood, clove, sunscreen, and ocean that is uniquely Sawyer.

"Are you ready for lunch, or do you need to do something before we leave?" he asks.

"If we do what I want to do, we won't get anything else accomplished today."

Sawyer groans at my implication and shifts his hips against my stomach so I can feel the rapidly stiffening erection.

"See what you do to me? You can't just say things like that when I come home and you meet me looking like a snack."

"A snack?"

"Yep. I could eat you all day, everyday and not get my fill."

I giggle at his joke and give him a quick kiss.

"We better leave before I decide to put that theory to the test."

"Where do you want to eat? Somewhere in Wild Shore or Magnolia?"

"Normally, I would say Wild Shore, but everywhere is probably crazy busy. I'm good with something in Magnolia if you are."

"Sounds good. We can discuss it on the way over the ridge."

We ate lunch at a fast-food chicken restaurant we both like. Now we are headed to the home improvement store to get the field day toilet.

Sawyer parks his Jeep and says, "Stay there. I will come around to open your door."

I wasn't expecting that, and that says a lot about the guys I have dated in the past. No wonder I haven't found anyone to be serious with.

He takes my hand and helps me out of the Jeep. He keeps his hand in mine until he walks through the door and grabs a cart.

We head to the back of the store to the row of toilets.

"So you picked the wrong one, and the little lady made you come back and get the one with the flusher buttons on top? I told you they were the best seller. At least you realized your mistake and brought her back to pick out the one she wants," says an older gentleman wearing an employee vest walking down the aisle toward us. He looks at me and says, "You can't trust a Squid to make the right decision, ma'am. You gotta hold his hand."

"Now, Dog Face. How am I supposed to keep such a fine specimen if you keep talking about me like that?" Sawyer says with a smile as he shakes the man's hand. "You doing all right?"

"As good as can be expected at my age but still good enough to beat you in a foot race."

They both grin, and even though I have no clue what they are talking about, it is obvious they know each other.

"So what can I help you with today?"

"Avery is looking for a toilet for a field day activity."

He turns his attention to me. "A little odd, but I'll allow it. So you just looking for the cheapest thing I have in stock, or does this need to be fancy?"

"I'll take the cheapest one you have in stock."

He walks over to one on the far end. "Here you go! Isn't she a beaut?"

His sense of humor has me smiling right along with him.

"Looks good to me!"

"Get over here, whippersnapper, and help me load this thing for the lady. No need to be stealing your wife with my manliness when I already have my own."

Being referred to as Sawyer's wife sends warmth through my stomach. Neither Sawyer nor I correct him as they load the toilet in the cart.

"Thank you, sir. I don't know if he could have done it without you. All those muscles are just for show." I grin, joining in on their banter.

He winks at me and asks if we need anything else as his radio calls for him to assist a customer in a different aisle.

"Not today!"

"Then you folks take care. I'll see you next time you come in," he says as he walks off.

"Do you know him?" I ask Sawyer.

"Nope. I was here a few weeks ago to buy a toilet for the half bath, and he helped me then too. He's retired Army, so we connected over our service history."

"That is really neat. Does that happen a lot?" I ask as we get to the checkout.

"Not really, actually."

I pay, and we load the toilet into Sawyer's Jeep.

"Are we taking this straight to Wild Child?" he asks when we reach The Drop.

"Yes, please. I have a key, and we can just leave it in the multipurpose room. Gail will put it away tomorrow."

"Sounds good."

We drop the toilet off and get back in the Jeep when Sawyer gets a text.

He reads it and looks at me.

"They are at the beach and want to know when we are coming. Do you need to get anything or can we just head straight there? I packed a cooler and two beach chairs this morning, so you don't need anything for the beach."

"You didn't have to do that, but I accept your offer. I guess I don't need anything since you have it covered."

He texts back to say that we are leaving Wild Child and will be there in a little bit depending on traffic.

This is really happening. We are officially announcing ourselves as a couple.

CHAPTER 29
DOUBLE P

Sawyer

I turn onto Ocean Boulevard and look over at the water. The sun and blue sky dotted with puffy white clouds brought all the tourists to the beach today. I intentionally had Emily leave this afternoon open in case I could convince Avery to spend the afternoon with me. It just worked out that everyone else was available.

"So tell me about your friends. I have met Pepper, so I sort of know her. Who else are we meeting?"

"Just Mason and Savannah. Mason is a doctor at Wild Shore Memorial. He is usually in the ICU but rotates through the ER and family medicine clinic if they need him. Since you have been to Shipwrecked, you have likely met Sav without knowing it. She spends all her time there. Probably even more than I do at Pirate's Life."

"You guys are very dedicated to your businesses. That's commendable. I love those little kids with my whole heart, but I can't wait for the weekend most weeks. Some days I count down the hours until afternoon pickup. Don't even get me started on the end of school year countdown." She laughs.

Her happiness brings a smile to my lips.

"I don't blame you there. I'm not sure I could do what you do."

"Well, I know for a fact I can't do what you do."

"Give it time. You can't rush these things if you aren't ready. Did you decide what you are doing this summer?"

"Not yet. I haven't really looked around this year. I'm sure I will find something."

"Yep. Pretty much everyone needs help this time of year."

I pull into the lot behind where we usually meet and shut off the engine.

I look over at Avery and ask, "Are you ready? They will assume we are a couple. Are you okay with taking this public?"

"I am if you are. I'm the one who bagged the sexy billboard model everyone has been after. You just got the dorky preschool teacher."

"I think you mean sexy-as-fuck, goes-after-what-she-wants preschool teacher," I flatter as I lean across the console to kiss her.

"I definitely want more of that, but it'll have to be later. I want to meet your friends."

I sigh at being cockblocked. "Then let's go. The sooner we get there, the sooner we can leave and get back to my house."

She just laughs as I walk around the Jeep to open her door.

I grab the chairs and cooler out of the back and take Avery's hand to walk to where Mason, Pepper, and Savannah are sitting.

Pepper notices us first and a smile breaks out across her face. That causes Mason and Sav to look back at us too.

"Avery! I'm so glad you got to join us today," Pepper shouts.

"Drop It Like It's Hot Girl! Sawyer, this is the twerking goddess I was telling you about from the bar. The one I wanted to set you up with. Turns out you were already working that angle. I'm Sav, in case you forgot since that night." Sav laughs.

Embarrassment in the form of a dark red blush creeps over Avery's face.

"Oh, hey. Good to see you again," Avery splutters.

Mason takes pity on her and shifts the conversation away from her night at the bar. "Well, looks like I am the only one you haven't actually met. I'm Mason."

"Nice to meet you, Mason," she replies as she sits her tote bag by her chair. She pulls her tank top off to reveal navy triangles with cream lace trim covering her full breasts, but leaving some side boob out for my perusal. She shimmies her shorts down, and I almost swallow my tongue. The navy bikini bottoms are cut high on her lush ass and held together with a small cream lace band on top.

"Save some of the guys for us, Avery. Damn," Pepper says.

"I'm sure you could have any guy you want from here to New York City," Avery banters as she sits in the chair I opened for her.

I pull my shirt off and sit in mine before my semi-hard cock becomes apparent.

"Too bad all the good ones are taken," Pepper laments, and Savannah holds up her can in a silent salute.

I put a beer in a Pirate's Life koozie and hand it to Avery.

"Look at you. All domestic-like," coos Savannah.

"He came pretrained. I'm just reaping the benefits," Avery jokes, and they all bust up laughing.

"I like her," Mason says, pointing the hand holding his beer in my direction.

We chat, and my friends and I get to know Avery a little more. The way she interacts with them just solidifies my feelings for her that are getting stronger every day.

"So are you guys going with Avyer or Sawry?" Pepper asks.

Mason and I look at each other like she is speaking a different language.

Sav says, "I like Avyer. Sawry is terrible."

"I was thinking Avyer, too," Avery says.

"What are you talking about?" Mason asks.

I'm really glad he asked, so I don't have to look like the dumb one.

"Their ship name. You take half of each of their names and put them together. Then you pick the one that sounds the best," Sav fills us in.

"That is ridiculous, but I like Avyer if we have to have one," I say, looking at Avery.

She leans over and presses a lingering kiss to my lips. "That's because I always come first," she murmurs for my ears only.

"And usually second, too," I breathe before I kiss her under the shell of her ear.

Pepper tosses her empty can in the trash bag and says, "I can't take this lovey-dovey crap anymore. Do you girls want to go pass a volleyball around?"

"Is that a thinly veiled attempt to get Avery to ourselves so we can grill her about what they were whispering to each other that has her looking almost feral? If so, I'm in. I'll just have to mentally picture that she is talking about anyone other than my brother." Sav shivers dramatically.

Avery's tinkling laughter is music to my ears. "Let's go. I'm ready for anything."

They get up, grab the volleyball, and go down the beach a little ways, leaving Mason and me alone.

We watch as the girls pass the ball back and forth for a few minutes. They laugh and joke like old friends. I'm so happy they get along and welcomed her with open arms.

Avery is so fucking sexy. Every time she puts her hands together to pass, her tits squeeze together, making my balls tingle. When she bends over, putting that ass on display, I want to spank it and shove my cock inside her tight pussy.

Mason opens his cooler and pulls out another beer before he says, "So I'm assuming since you got a ship name and you can't peel your eyes off of her for more than three seconds, this is your official announcement that you are a couple. When did this happen?"

"A couple nights ago when I came home to her on my doorstep holding a pizza."

"So she just showed up offering pizza and pussy? Went straight for the Double P? You were toast from the beginning. That was just the cinnamon sugar sprinkled on top. Where can I find someone like that?"

I scoff. "That's not all she showed up offering. She brought homemade muscle rub, too." I chuckle at his disbelieving expression.

"You lucky dog. How was it?" he asks, raising his eyebrows suggestively.

"Best massage of my life."

"That's not what I was talking about," he says, punching me in the shoulder.

"Well, that might have also been the best of my life, but it's hard to compare it to last night," I gloat with a dopey grin that has been plastered on my face more often than not lately.

"You dirty dog. She fits right in with our group, so you better not fuck it up."

"I think I'm in love with her."

"Obviously. I called it the first time you told me about her."

"So you don't think it's too soon? That's a huge step. I have never felt like this before."

Avery and Savannah both dive for the ball and miss. The three of them guffaw as the ball rolls to the water.

"It was bound to happen sometime. Might as well be now with her. She needs saving, and you, my friend, have always been a knight in shining boat shoes," he jeers as he gets up to retrieve the ball before it gets swept up in the surf.

"Who is ready to get beat, and who is on my team?" he calls as he walks up to the girls, bouncing the ball with his fist.

They all raise their hands and shout, "ME!"

"Now how am I supposed to tell which one of you picked me first?"

I get up and walk over to where they are standing. "None of them are calling dibs on you for volleyball or anything else." I swipe the ball from his hands. "Me and Mason versus you ladies."

"We are going to demolish you," Pepper says.

"Prepare for defeat," Sav taunts.

"You're going down," Avery adds.

"Whenever you want me to, babe," I reply.

"Ooohhhhh," Mason and Pepper say while Savannah fakes gagging, and Avery's cheeks get a little pink at the blatant sexual innuendo in front of our friends.

Yes, our. She is one of us. We are officially shipped, and she's not getting out of it.

"Let's go. Losers buy dinner at Shipwrecked," I say.

We play for a half hour or so, and they end up beating us.

Seeing them laugh, smile, and goad us was well worth the price of their dinner.

CHAPTER 30
PHYSICAL THERAPY

Avery

We retrieve our chairs, coolers, and bags from the beach and walk to the parking lot, reliving the highlights of the day. After putting their things in their vehicles, Pepper and Savannah walk over to my side of the Jeep.

Pepper gives me a hug and says, "I'm so glad you made it today. I had such a blast hanging out with you."

She steps back, and Savannah approaches to give me a hug, too. She says quietly in my ear, "I'm so glad Sawyer found you. You guys are good together. He may seem big and tough, but he has a fragile heart. Don't break it."

I nod in affirmation of her request and step back. Sawyer comes around to my side of the Jeep and kisses my forehead before opening the door.

"You ready to go?"

"Yep. Just saying goodbye." I wave as Sav and Pepper walk back to their cars.

When I get settled in my seat, Sawyer reaches over me and clicks my seatbelt into place. He looks up and takes my lips in a kiss that simultaneously hardens my nipples and melts my bikini bottoms.

He ends the kiss with a soft peck and walks around the Jeep to get in the driver's seat.

"So what do you think about them?" he asks.

"They are amazing. You guys are so close and get along so well. I love the way you guys are sarcastic and joke around but are serious when necessary. Riley and I are the same way."

"That reminds me. When am I going to meet Riley? If I recall, that was part of our deal."

"I promise you will meet her and likely regret being so gung-ho about wanting that to happen. She's going through some stuff right now, so she doesn't go out much or have a lot of free time."

"Well, whenever she is ready, I would like to meet the person who is closest to my woman."

"What if that person is my mom?" I ask.

"Then I want to meet her. Your dad, too. I know it's quick, but I'm all in, Avery. I want to work toward a future with you."

I draw in a quick breath. That wasn't an *I love you*, but it felt pretty close. Are his feelings as deep as mine have become?

"I want that, too," I say a little above a whisper.

We get back to Sawyer's house, and he presses a button on his visor to raise a garage door. He parks, and we unload our things from the beach trip and walk through the door to the kitchen.

"Do you have somewhere to be, or can you stay for a little while?"

"I can stay for a bit. These are the last few days of school, so I don't have to prepare anything."

"Good. Let's take a shower and get the beach off of us. I spend enough of my time covered in salt spray. I don't need to be covered in it on my evening off, too."

"Did no one want to sail this afternoon? I thought you were booked almost every available minute for the next few months."

"I told Emily to black it out so I could spend the afternoon with you. Introduce you to my friends. Get to know you a little better."

"You didn't have to do that. I could have met them another time. I don't want you to sacrifice your business for time with me. You know I will work around your schedule to spend time with you."

"And that's exactly why I did it," he says as we walk through his bedroom and into the bathroom.

He turns the showers on and prowls back over to me like a feral jungle cat. "I have been waiting to do this since you pulled your tank top off and these titties practically fell out of that tiny top."

He pulls my tank top over my head and licks a path through my cleavage, sucking on the firm mounds.

He reaches behind me and unties the strings at my neck. Taking one string in each hand, he lowers the small triangles that cover my dusky pink areolas and hardly anything else.

He moves his attention from my cleavage to my nipple. He circles the sensitive peak with his tongue, making it stand up even higher. He pinches my other nipple, causing me to moan with the electricity that shoots straight to my pussy.

I grab the back of his head and pull him closer to me. He takes my nipple into his mouth, sucking while his hands trail down my sides to my hips.

He pushes my shorts and bottoms down, leaving me naked. He trails his fingers back up the inside of my leg and brushes my pussy with one finger.

My legs part automatically, giving him better access.

"You want me to play with that pretty pussy, don't you, baby? Slide my fingers in and fuck you with them until you cover me in that sweet cream?"

"God, yes," I moan as my hips rock onto his finger, trying to make him follow through on his dirty words.

"What do you say?"

"Please, Sawyer. Please finger me until I come. I need it."

He picks me up, and my shorts, bikini bottoms, and flip flops drop onto the tile floor. He takes me over to the shower and sets me down at the door. He grabs his shirt behind his neck and pulls it over his head in the move only men know how to do.

I untie his swim trunks and slide them down his legs. His erection bobs out, long and thick, and stands straight up to his belly button. I take it in my hand and stroke it. My thumb slides over the purple head as a bead of precum forms in the slit.

Sawyer throws his head back and takes a deep breath, releasing it slowly.

I open the glass door to the shower enclosure, and Sawyer toes off his shoes and trunks and follows me.

When I get inside the shower, he turns me and pushes me up against the tile wall between the two shower heads.

He grabs my hands and puts them above my head as his tongue tangles with mine in a deep kiss. I can feel his erection pulsing on my stomach as he slowly thrusts his hips against me.

My core clenches with the memory of what that cock feels like inside me.

I work my hands free of his hold, and he keeps his hands on the wall above me, caging me in.

I sink down to my knees in front of him, taking his length into my hand.

I stroke my fist up and down his length a few times, making another pearl of precum form. I lean forward to lick it, and his breath hisses through his teeth.

I poke the slit with my tongue then lick around the mushroom head. Sawyer growls deep in his throat like the jungle cat I compared him to earlier.

I lift his cock up and trail my tongue from his balls to the head. There is no way I am getting this thing all the way in my mouth. I'm surprised it fits in my pussy.

I circle my tongue around the head, adding light suction when it slips between my lips.

My lips form a tight circle around his cock, and I lean forward slowly, filling my mouth until I can feel him hitting the back of my throat. I pull back, and Sawyer moans. I speed up my strokes and suck him a few more times as he keeps getting stiffer.

"Fuck, Avery. That feels good."

I take my mouth off of him, and a trail of spit and cum connects my mouth to his cock.

I look up at Sawyer and lick my lips to get it inside my mouth and swallow. His brown eyes flare with desire at the picture I make on my knees licking his precum off my lips.

"Fuck, that's hot. I want to paint your mouth with my cum and watch you lick it off while I jack my cock to add more."

The visual makes my empty pussy clench. Arm porn is out. Dirty talking is where it's at.

I lean forward again, this time using my hand to stroke him as I suck him down. When I get him in as far as I can, I breathe through my nose and swallow, taking him down a little farther. I wait a beat before pulling back.

I continue stroking him like this until I feel him harden in my throat. I slow my strokes, and he takes one hand off the wall and puts it in my hair, gripping it hard enough to pull but not hurt.

"You swallow my cock so good, baby. It's so hard to not blow down your throat when you do that."

Taking his erection in my hand again, I stroke up and down his length and rotate my wrist. His grip on my hair tightens, and

I stick my tongue out so he can see his cock rubbing my tongue.

He urges my head forward, so I close my lips around him and take him to the back of my throat until my gag reflex kicks in and I choke a little. He pulls back and lets me breathe a few seconds before doing it again.

My hand wraps around the base of his shaft, and I start pumping harder and faster into my mouth.

I rub my hand up his thigh then between his legs until I cup his tight sac. I take my mouth off the tip and lick his sac while I keep pumping his thick cock.

I take one ball into my mouth and gently suck. When his cock twitches, I switch to the other ball.

My tongue licks back up his shaft then I wrap my lips around it before going back down. I speed up the pace as he grips my hair and fucks my face.

I reach down and run my fingers through my drenched pussy, pulling my wetness up to my clit. I add some pressure and swirl around it a few times, making myself moan.

The vibration makes Sawyer jerk in my mouth, and he pulls out. He grabs me by the armpits and pulls me up.

I slide my leg high around his hip so his dick sits at the entrance of my pussy. My wetness leaks out of me and onto his cock. I start rotating my hips, hoping to find the right angle to get him where I am throbbing for him.

His tongue enters my mouth, and I suck on it like I was sucking on his cock. I know he can taste the salty precum, but he doesn't care. He just keeps kissing me.

"Are you ready, baby? Are you wet?"

"Yes. I need you inside me."

He grabs his cock with one hand and slides the head through my wet pussy lips to lubricate it. Then he lines his cock up with my entrance and slips in slowly, giving me time to adjust to his size.

He is bigger today than he was the last two times. I am so full, it is almost painful. The best kind of pain.

He rocks into me slowly until I can adjust to his size and this angle. I reach up and grab my nipples, pinching each one. The stimulation makes my pussy clench around his cock, and he groans.

"Fuck, that's hot. You playing with your tits and the reaction your body gives to it. Keep playing with those perfect tits while I feed you this cock."

He keeps pistoning into me, lightly pressing on my clit with every thrust. I need more stimulation if I am going to come this way.

I take one hand off my breast and lick it before putting it between our bodies. I rotate my fingers in a circle around my clit without touching the sensitive bud.

Sawyer moans low in his chest. "You don't know what you are doing to me right now. Keep going. Add to the pleasure I am giving you."

I circle a little closer to my hard bud. I know as soon as I brush it, I will fall over the edge, and I am not ready.

Electricity zaps down my spine, making my stomach heat. I start pushing down when Sawyer thrusts up. He is so deep inside me, I don't know where he stops and I begin. I don't want to know. I just want this forever.

"Yes. Keep going. Like that," I manage to pant out between thrusts.

He continues thrusting for a few more minutes before he snakes his other arm under my leg. I jump up as well as I can from one leg and circle it around his hips to lock with the other one right above his rock-hard ass.

He grabs my ass and pushes my shoulders back against the wall. Using his muscular forearms, he guides me up and down his cock.

I slide down his erection, feeling my pussy squeeze every one of the ridges along his eight inches. He bottoms out inside me, his cock brushing my cervix.

He speeds up the pace, bouncing me faster and faster. My voice wobbles on my moan as he continues to lift and lower me. My pussy contracts, and I come with a throaty moan, arching my back as the sensations flood me.

He gives two more hard thrusts, my cum making it even easier to fuck me. He thrusts deep inside me and moans loudly next to my ear.

I can feel the warm cum squirting out of him and coating my walls as I breathe rapidly, coming down from my own orgasm.

He leans his forehead on the shower wall above my shoulder until our breathing slows. His spent cock slips out of my pussy, bringing our cum with it.

Sawyer lets me down, and I stand on shaky legs, from the position or the mind-blowing orgasm, I don't know. It could easily be either one.

"That was…" I start, but I don't have any way to finish it.

"Yeah," Sawyer says, understanding my thoughts without me having to voice them since he is feeling the same way.

We stand under the rainfall shower head for a little longer, letting our bodies relax.

Sawyer is the first to move. He squirts some of the shampoo I left on the shelf in his hand. He brings his hands up to my head and massages my scalp as he washes then conditions my hair.

He pours some shower gel on a loofa then washes every inch of me. My skin is a fresh pink color when he is done.

I find his hair products and return the favor. When it is time to wash his body, I forego the loofa and put the shower gel right in my hands. I take great pleasure in rubbing every inch of his hard body. Some parts I wash twice.

This man is a work of art with his chiseled muscles, SEAL tattoo, random scars from old wounds, and puckered skin on his thigh from a sniper's bullet.

I could explore his body all day, everyday and never tire from the way he feels beneath my hands.

"You better finish what you are doing, or we will be going for round two."

"I'm not sure I would survive another round right now. Honestly, I think you wrecked the ol' girl."

"She'll recover with a little *physical* therapy," he assures me with a smirk.

We rinse off and dress before going downstairs to watch a movie in the four season room.

When the movie is over, Sawyer walks me to Chili and gives me a toe-curling goodbye kiss that will have to hold me over until the next time I see him.

I back out of his driveway and feel like I am leaving a part of myself at the beautiful home on Ridge View Terrace.

Because I am.

My heart wholly belongs to Sawyer Davis.

CHAPTER 31
I ACCEPT

Sawyer

When I get back from an afternoon snorkel, I have a text from Avery.

AVERY: I did it! I finished the school year!

ME: That's an awful lot of enthusiasm for someone who didn't move on to kindergarten with everyone else in the class.

AVERY: That was bad. Is there such a thing as a grandpa joke because that was way worse than a dad joke.

ME: I've still got some time to work on my delivery. Don't worry, I'll try not to embarrass you too bad.

I hit send before I think about what I just implied. She doesn't reply immediately, and I wonder if she is thinking the same thing I am. I basically just told her she is going to be the mother of my children.

AVERY: I won't hold my breath.

I let out the breath I had been unconsciously holding. Thank God she just rolled with it and didn't ghost me.

ME: I need to get ready for the next excursion. I should be back around six. I'll talk to you later.

AVERY: Be careful and enjoy some sun for me!

ME: Always, babe.

I put my phone on my desk and walk to the lobby with a smile on my face.

"Oh, no. Here he comes. Mr. Heart Eyes himself," Emily cajoles.

My smile grows with her candor.

"Is the three thirty here yet?"

"I just saw someone pull in, so they should be coming in any second."

Just as she finishes her sentence, the front door opens, and a small group of kids and a few adults walk in.

"Hey, guys! I'm Sawyer. I will be taking you snorkeling today. The weather is perfect, and the water is warm. It's going to be an awesome trip."

The adults step forward to introduce themselves and shake my hand.

"As soon as everyone gets fitted for a life jacket, we can be on our way. Emily, can you help me with that?"

"Sure thing, bossman."

We walk over to the wall of life jackets, and they all choose one.

"Ahoy, mates! Who is ready to board the Jolly Rodger?" I say in a pirate voice.

The kids all laugh and smile. I hear several "me's."

"Let's go!" I say and point to the back door. They all follow me out to the Jolly Rodger, and we set off for where I last saw the school of fish.

"Those kids wore me out!" I yawn as I walk into the office. "They must have gone down the slide a hundred times each."

Emily runs at me, holding a paper in her raised hand.

"I got in!!! I finally got in!!!"

She wraps me in a hug and jumps up and down, pulling my body with her.

"What? What is going on?" I ask.

She steps back and shoves the paper in my face.

She is still waving it around, so my eyes can't focus on what is printed on the paper.

"The dive school just emailed me. They said they had a last-minute cancellation and asked if I could be there next week for the three-week course. I have waited forever for this!"

"That's great news! I'm so happy for you!"

A weird feeling settles in my stomach. It is a mixture of anxiety, guilt, and regret. I push it aside so I can focus on Emily's excitement.

"When do you leave?" I ask in what I hope is a celebratory tone.

Her celebration comes to an abrupt halt.

"Oh my God, Sawyer. I was so excited, I didn't even think about what me leaving would mean for Pirate's Life right now. I will email them back and tell them I can't this time."

She turns around and walks to her desk.

"Wait, Em. When do they have to know by? Can you give me a little bit to come up with something? Mom may be able to help. I don't know what their vacation schedule is right now."

I scrub my face with my palms and run my fingers through my hair.

"You have waited so long to do this, and I want you to be able to do it. I will try everything to make this happen for you. Maybe Dad can take some of my excursions, and I can stay here to answers the phone and invoice. Maybe I will have to close the office while I'm out. I will come up with something."

"Don't hurt the business so I can do something last minute. This place does so well because of the amount of face-to-face time the customers get. They feel like part of the Pirate's Life crew. It will be okay if I can't go this time. There will be others."

"Just give me until tomorrow. That still gives you enough time to pack and get to wherever. It will just be a little rushed."

She comes back over to me and hugs me. "Thank you, Sawyer, for believing in me. I may give you shit all the time, but I wouldn't want to work for anyone else."

"Well, that's good because no one else would hire you." I smirk as I ruffle her hair.

She pushes me away, and her hands come up to her hair to repair any damage I caused.

"I take it back. You're horrible."

We both laugh at our camaraderie. I am going to miss her when she's gone because no matter what, I will find a way to get her to that class.

"Do you have anything else to do here tonight?" I ask.

"Nope. Just waiting on you to get back in case there were any issues and I needed to come save you." She clicks a button on the phone and picks up her bag. "I'm outta here. See you tomorrow!"

I wave in farewell and walk out the back door as she turns off the lights and locks the front door.

I walk over to the bench and sit down. I stretch my legs out in front of me and let my head hang over the back of the bench. My hands run through my hair and pull at the strands. I try to focus on the sound of the waves hitting the hulls of the nearby boats, but it doesn't calm me. My mind is a whirl of thoughts.

What am I going to do?

I hear footsteps coming toward me and turn my head to look over. Avery is walking down the path, looking like a vision in jean shorts, white tennis shoes, and an orange T-shirt tight across her chest that proclaims her to be a Sutton Star. Her high ponytail sways from side to side as she walks. My chest begins to loosen from just being in her presence.

"You look a little stressed. Luckily, I know the one thing that always leaves you feeling relaxed," she says as she climbs up on my lap and straddles my hips.

She cups my face and tilts it to her so she can press her lips to mine. Her tongue slips inside my mouth and explores. She tastes like sugar and strawberry flavoring.

My hands come around her and grip her ass through her shorts, pulling her closer to me.

She ends the kiss with a peck to my nose. I release a heavy sigh, and her arms come around my neck to hug me close.

"Do you want to talk about it, or do you just need to sit here in silence and decompress? I can leave if you want me to."

"You're fine. Seeing you actually makes me feel better." I release a heavy breath and nuzzle my nose behind her ear to inhale her vanilla and wildflower scent.

"What happened between the time I talked to you and now?"

"When I got back from the last excursion, Emily met me at the door with a paper in her hand. Excitement was rolling off of her in waves. She got into the dive program she has been applying to for over a year."

"That's great news! I'm so happy for her. So why is this a problem?"

"The program starts Monday."

"That's so soon. Will she have time to get there?"

"That's not the problem. She has plenty of time to get packed and get there. The problem is who is going to run the office while she is gone for three weeks. We are in our busiest time, so I can't really just close the office when I'm on an excursion, which is pretty much always. My parents might be able to help out, but they usually help Savannah since Shipwrecked is busy too. The likelihood of hiring someone I trust to run the office in the next two days is nonexistent. I don't really have another option, but I don't want to take this opportunity away from her. Especially since it will help Pirate's Life in the long run to have someone to recertify divers and lead dive excursions. It's just shit timing." I sigh out my frustrations.

I can't ignore the pull of her anymore. I start placing tender kisses and gentle nips along the column of her throat. I love this woman. There is no denying my feelings. One day, I will make her mine. Hopefully sooner rather than later.

"I accept."

"What?" Panic courses through my veins at the thought that I just asked her to marry me again and she accepted. I didn't mean to ask her this time or this way, but a yes is a yes.

"I accept your offer of summer employment. I haven't gotten around to looking for anything yet, so I am available to help you out while Emily is gone."

Oh, thank God. That would have been something I would have to confess after the nuptials.

"Are you sure? This is your summer break. We just talked about how you count down to summer break."

"That's because the closer the last day gets, the crazier the kids get. Not because I want to sleep in and binge-read. Although that does sound wonderful."

"Are you sure, sure?"

"Sure, sure, sure," she proclaims and seals the deal with a kiss.

"Can you start tomorrow morning? Emily really needs to leave Saturday or Sunday. I'm not totally sure what she does, so I have no idea how much training you will need," I admit.

"I guess we will find out. I did just flunk preschool, so no guarantees I will learn it that fast."

I pull her to me for a passionate kiss, feeling the weight of the world lift from my shoulders.

I love this woman. She is the perfect match for me.

CHAPTER 32
BEST THERAPY

Avery

When I get to Pirate's Life in the morning, The Emerald is already gone. That man works way too hard. I glance down to check my outfit again. I hope my jean shorts, teal sleeveless blouse, and leather strap sandals are okay. Emily usually dresses pretty casually, and Sawyer wears his *uniform,* so I think I should be fine. We didn't really talk about what I needed to wear last night. We were both a little more worried about what I needed to not be wearing.

I get out of Chili and walk to the front door. I can see Emily already on the phone and clicking away at her computer.

What time do these people get here?

I walk through the lobby and over to Emily's desk. Her eyes light up when she sees me. Into the phone, she says, "Okay. You are confirmed for a sunset sail. It will be perfect timing for a proposal. I will make a note so Sawyer knows what is going on and can plan accordingly…You're welcome. Bye." She hangs up the phone and comes toward me at a full run, enveloping me in a tight hug.

"Avery! I owe you so big! Thank you a million times over. I could kiss you right on the mouth I'm so happy, but I don't swing that way, and my boss would probably kill me then fire me.

"If Sawyer didn't find anyone to take over for a few weeks, I wasn't going to go no matter how much he tried to get me out of here. We have worked too hard to make this place what it is to let it all go to shit because I can't wait for a good time to go to dive school.

"That being said, I am so excited! I will try to tone it down so you can learn the ropes, but I'm practically vibrating." She sticks her hands up in jazz hands and shakes them.

"I spend my days with a herd of four-year-olds. I can handle your excitement," I say as we walk over to her desk.

"You can put your things in this drawer with mine. I set up your username this morning when I got here. I wrote down the password on the sticky note by the mouse. You should have access to email, chat, the scheduling program, the billing program, and anything else this computer does. This is going to be a crash course, so I left some paper and a pen for you to take notes."

After two hours of nonstop phone calls, switching between programs, and answering questions from people walking in the door, my brain is mush. I don't know how Emily does this.

I am looking over my notes, trying to figure out what I meant, when strong arms band around my middle and lips meet my exposed neck.

Sandalwood, clove, and sunscreen envelop me. My core melts at the feelings he causes in me. I close my eyes and relax into his body as his kisses continue around my exposed neck thanks to my messy bun.

"That's enough of that, you two. This is a place of business, and she has shit to learn. Go play with your boats and leave your girlfriend for later," Emily chides as she comes back from a bathroom break.

Sawyer's breath exhales on my neck with his huge sigh. "Do you know enough that I can tell her to leave right now?"

I laugh and step away from him. "Not even close. I don't know how much you pay her, but it's not nearly enough. This is crazy!"

"I got an email from Emily at HR the other day that said I should sign off on pay raises and fat bonuses. I may have to look into that." He smirks turning toward Emily.

"I mean, she is HR." Emily shrugs.

The relationship these two have is amazing. Even though there are almost ten years between them, they respect each other and get along so well. I feel absolutely zero concern or jealousy over their relationship. He treats Emily like another sister.

"I need to look over some things in my office, so I will see you later," Sawyer says and gives me a kiss before walking away.

The next group starts to trickle into the lobby.

"Hey, guys! Welcome to Pirate's Life. Avery will get you checked in. Today is her first day, so it might take her a minute to get everything squared away," Emily greets the customers.

I need to add that to my list of things to do, also. Everyone who comes through here has a smile on their face. I don't want to mess with the vibe.

Emily and I walk to the counter, and I type in my password, which happens to be Sawyer<3. *Thanks, Emily.* I look up the next excursion and see three families are going on a catamaran snorkel. I use the process of elimination with the names and ages of the people going to decide which family this is.

"Okay, Jones family. Are you ready to see some fish today? Try out the slide? Maybe the swing?"

They whoop and cheer.

"All right. I just need you to fill out this form, and I will get your invoice pulled up."

I click around and can't find what I need. Emily points to an icon, and a light bulb turns on in my brain. I find the right invoice and click print.

The woman hands me the form, and I hand her the invoice.

"Do you take a card?"

"Yes, ma'am. Let me get it ready, and you can slide it out there on that little white box." I click over to the payment program and type in the total. "Okay, it's good to go when you are."

The woman slides her card, and I wait for it to process.

"It went through, so you are all set. Do you need a receipt?"

"No, thanks."

"Everyone, follow me over to the life jackets, and we will get you fitted," Emily says.

Emily told me this would be part of my job but didn't really go over it, so I pay close attention to see what she does and how the jackets are ordered.

"You are welcome to hang out in here, or

.+there is a bench behind this building with a wonderful view of the water. Hopefully, the other groups will be here soon."

They choose to go outside and look at the beautiful water this town is known for.

"You did pretty well. Do you have any questions about the life jackets? We didn't really go over it this morning."

"I think I will listen to your spiel again to make sure I know the high points then I will try it myself for the sunset sail."

"Sounds good. Let's go over some more possible scenarios with the software while we wait for the rest of this group to show up."

I sigh dramatically and walk back over to the counter.

The sunset sail customers come back in to drop off their life jackets while Sawyer tidies The Emerald and stows all the gear.

Emily and I are going over some last-minute questions when Sawyer comes through the back door.

"So how did today go?"

Emily replies first. "She did excellent, way easier than teaching you how to run the place. She knows how to schedule, invoice, fit life jackets, and restock. I think we went over everything, but we had a lot going on today. It's just for three weeks. If she has any questions, she can text me, and I will reply when I get a chance. I don't know how often I will have phone access, but I will check it when I do."

"You're the best, Em."

"Do you care if I take tomorrow off to pack and get my apartment situated? It will give Avery a chance to try it on her own. If she has any issues or gets overwhelmed, I can be here in like five minutes."

"What do you think, Avery? It doesn't matter to me either way. That is between you two."

"I like that idea. I feel comfortable with the software and running the storefront. I'm a little slow still, but I know what I am doing."

"All right then. Emily, have a safe trip and enjoy your diving adventures. You will do great. Now, get out of here. Hopefully, I don't see you for three weeks, but you better be ready to work when you come back."

"Thanks, Saw. Here is my key, Avery."

She hands me an emerald key off of her key ring. "I'm leaving, so you will have to lock the door behind me."

I lock the door when she closes it and walk back to the counter to add the key to my key ring.

"So how did today go for you emotionally? This is a lot of triggers for you, and I have been worried about you pretty much all day."

"Actually, I am fine. I was so busy I didn't really have time to think about much other than what is going on in here. It doesn't bother me when other people get in the water, just me. I think I will be fine doing this."

"If at any time you start to have an issue, promise me you will stop what you are doing and go to my office to relax. If I am out, and you are able, call someone to come here. My parents, your parents, Riley, or even Savannah or Pepper. This place can be on hold until someone gets here. I am more worried about you than a customer hanging in the lobby by himself."

"I'll be okay, Sawyer. This may turn into the best therapy I've ever had."

"As long as you are sure. I have a few things to look over before I can leave. Do you have plans tonight, or do you want to wait for me and we can go grab dinner?"

"The only plans I have involve taking my shoes off and kicking my feet up. I'm beat. I don't know how she does it."

"It's not like this everyday. Just for five or six months a year," Sawyer jokes. "What do you want for dinner? My treat."

"Wild Special. Salty sticks with cheese."

"If you call it in, I will pick it up and meet you at mine or yours."

"I don't want to drive across town in the traffic. Do you care if we go to your house?"

"You going to be naked in my bathtub reading one of your pro athlete fantasy books when I get home?"

I step into him so our bodies are pressed together. I run my tongue along his neck, tasting the salt from dried sea spray, and say, "Only if you promise to rub my feet while I read."

He groans. "Save room for me. I'll be there probably thirty minutes after you."

"No rush. I'm just getting to the good part," I sass as I walk away from him.

He smacks me on the ass. "Don't start without me."

CHAPTER 33

HE'S THE BEST

Sawyer

We are a week into our new working arrangement, and my life has never been better. I spend all day sailing and most nights in her arms, even if we are both so tired we just pass out holding each other.

Every time I walk into my bathroom, a smile grows on my face. I thought Sav and Mom were crazy for designing the bathroom the way they did. Who needs that much space? Apparently, Avery, because she is slowly taking over.

Her makeup and various other bottles are arranged on the vanity. Her hair tools are in the metal holders that line the mirror. Several hair ties and clips in various shapes and sizes litter the vanity and sink basin. The closet is slowly getting filled with the clothes she leaves here and I wash.

Can I just keep collecting her things here until she doesn't have anything at her house and just moves in with me? Is it too soon? Do I care if people think it is? No. I just want her in my life full-time.

I walk in the back door of Pirate's Life, and she is fitting the next group with life jackets. I didn't even think about drowning prevention being part of her job when she said she would help me out. I almost put a stop to it when I walked in on her going over life jacket questions with Emily. I thought for sure that would be a huge trigger for her, but she is handling it like a champ.

"Are you guys ready to set sail?" I ask the group of college students.

"Yeah, man. Let's do this."

"I will meet you outside by the bench in a few minutes."

They file out the door, leaving me alone with Avery.

"Looks like you are going to have your hands full with that group."

"I'd rather have my hands full of you," I reply as I pull her toward me to kiss her.

"Hold that thought until much later. We are meeting Riley tonight at Del after the sunset sail."

I groan and rub my semi-hard cock against her stomach. "Do you feel what watching you take command of this place does to me? Every time I come in here and you are walking around in those sexy shorts and tight shirts, I want to bend you over my desk and fuck that tight pussy. But you're always all *here you go, Sawyer. They are ready for you,* and ruin my fantasy."

"Poor baby. Maybe one day it will come true."

"Don't toy with me, woman. I have a bunch of frat guys outside, waiting to get on my boat and drink all my rum. Don't think I won't make them wait."

She laughs and pushes at my chest. "The longer they wait now, the longer you have to wait later. Get out there, let them drink all your rum, and get them and you back safely."

"Yes, ma'am." I salute her as I walk out the door.

Let's get this party started.

Avery and I walk into Del Mar several hours later. I finally get to meet Riley. Avery talks about her all the time. She is going through something that Avery didn't feel obligated to tell me about, and they haven't hung out as much as they usually do. I told her I didn't want to impose on their girl time, but Avery wants me to meet Riley.

A waiter sees Avery and says, "Avery! Riley is sitting in the corner of the back room."

He walks through the saloon doors before Avery can say anything back to him.

"You are on a first-name basis with the waiter?" I ask as she starts walking to the back of the restaurant.

"Yep! He's the best. Riley and I come here a couple times a month, so he knows us pretty well."

A stunning redhead looks up when we walk through the arched wall that separates the restaurant into two sections. Her face breaks out into a smile, and she stands up.

Avery practically flies the rest of the way to the booth and hugs the woman tightly.

I feel like an awkward weirdo as their embrace continues. Do I stand and watch? Sit down?

Finally, they break apart, each of them wiping tears from their eyes. *What have I gotten myself into?*

Avery turns to me, and the trace of unshed tears in her eyes is my undoing. I walk to her and fold her into my arms.

"It's okay, baby. She's here. You're together. Everything is going to be fine," I say before kissing her forehead.

"Well, I guess that's all I really need to know about you to approve," Riley says, wiping the last trails of tears off her cheeks. "I'm Riley, if you hadn't guessed. Just remember who she loved first, and we will get along just fine," she finishes up with a watery laugh.

"Like I could ever forget. I'm Sawyer. I'm glad to finally get to meet you. Avery talks about you enough I feel like I have known you for a while."

"I've seen your bare chest enough times to feel the same way," she jokes.

"And there it is," Avery says, shaking her head, all tears gone.

We all sit down, and Miguel stops at our table with a strawberry margarita and a lime margarita sitting them down in front of the girls.

"I'm sorry. I didn't know that you were with her or I would have asked what you wanted to drink. These two have the same thing every time," Miguel says.

"I'll take a beer. Whatever you have on tap is fine."

He nods and walks away.

"So he not only knows your name, he remembers your drink orders, too?"

"I told you he's the best," Avery says as she takes a sip of her strawberry margarita.

"Here you go, sir, and some fresh chips and salsa," he says as he places everything down on the table along with a small white bowl for salsa. "Do you know what you want, or do you need a little bit?" he says, looking at me and not the women.

"Let me guess. You already know what they want?"

Miguel just smiles.

Riley answers, "She told you he was the best!"

"I guess I will just go with my normal, chicken fajitas," I say.

"I'll have your food out soon."

We all chime in with "Thanks."

Riley breaks the silence first. "So I see this is progressing. How serious is it?"

She must see the flare of possession in my eyes because she says, "Oh. Okay. Wow. How was your first week working together at Pirate's Life?"

Avery breaks into a story about a group of young kids that came for a birthday party. She knew several of them, and they thought it was really cool to see her outside of school.

Miguel brings our dinner, and we continue chatting while we eat.

Riley is something else. I can see why they are best friends. They complement each other well but also have very similar personalities.

When our dinners and drinks are finished, Miguel brings the checks. I grab all three and excuse myself to go pay. I know they want a few minutes without me to ask the real questions and Riley can give Avery her real opinion.

I'm fairly certain I passed the test, but you never know.

They meet me at the front door a few minutes later. We walk over to where I parked, and Riley grabs the helmet off the motorcycle beside my Jeep. She just gained more badass points from me.

The women hug without tears this time. Riley goes to stick out her hand and changes her mind and hugs me too.

She backs away and says, "Sorry. It felt weird to shake your hand when my best friend practically lives with you. We might as well start like we are going to go on."

I smile. I knew I liked her. "That's fine with me. I'm glad I finally got to meet you, and I hope we get to do this again."

"Definitely," she promises as she puts the helmet on and buckles it under her chin. She throws her leg over her bike and starts it. She gives us a wave and rides off.

"She's something else. I don't think I have ever met anyone like her before," I say.

"She's definitely not afraid to be her full self in front of anyone, and you know exactly where you stand with her."

"I know where I want to stand with you, and that is all that matters. Your house or mine tonight?"

"Mine is closer, so let's go there."

I buckle her in and walk around the Jeep to my door. We make the quick drive to her house, and I park in her driveway since Chili is at my house.

The neighborhood is quiet this time of night. Her house is a cute little Cape Cod with plenty of curb appeal. She won't have any problem selling it when I convince her to move in with me.

It is pretty late and we are exhausted, so we brush our teeth and get in bed. Avery's ass snuggles up against my cock. It twitches at her nearness, but I shut it down. We need sleep.

Avery turns her head back to me, and I press a kiss to her lips before passing out.

CHAPTER 34
AWKO TACO

Avery

Sawyer had a request for a sunrise sail this morning, so he kissed me on the forehead when he left way before dawn, and I went back to sleep. There is no reason for me to open Pirate's Life at that time of day, and I already had everything he would need printed and sitting on the counter.

I stretch and revel in the knowledge that this is my life, at least for another week. The last two weeks have flown by.

Hopefully this arrangement continues after Emily comes back from dive school. I wouldn't care to keep running the office while Emily uses her new certification for dive excursions. I also wouldn't mind continuing to spend the night with a sinfully sexy man who knows his way around my body and wake up satisfied in *all* ways.

I finally get motivated to get out of bed and take a shower. After I dry off, I sit down at the vanity and put a little bit more effort into my hair and makeup than usual. I sort through the bras and underwear that are accumulating on the unused side of the closet. I might as well call it like it is. This side is mine. I may have more clothes here than at my house at this point.

I slip on a cute green sundress and strappy sandals and head for Chili. The old girl probably thinks I abandoned her since Sawyer pretty much drives us everywhere.

I open the door to Rise and Dine, and the smell of coffee beans instantly wakes me up. My mouth starts salivating at the sight of fresh baked scones.

"Hey, Avery! Did you sneak away while Sawyer was out sailing?" Pepper asks jokingly.

"Nope. I haven't even been in today. He had a sunrise sail this morning and did all the paperwork himself. Supposedly. I may have a mess when I go in."

We both laugh at Sawyer's expense.

"What can I get you today?"

"I'll have an iced chai latte and strawberry scone. I might as well get Sawyer a black coffee and bacon, egg, and cheese biscuit, or he will whine all day that I didn't get him anything."

"You know him so well." She cackles as she turns around to make our drinks. "So how is working with him everyday? Still in that honeymoon phase or does he get on your nerves?"

"It's actually not bad. He is either sailing or going over papers in his office most of the day. We hang out for a few hours in the evening then pass out in exhaustion. I don't know how he keeps up with that pace."

"He probably worked harder as a SEAL than he does now. It's all what you are used to," she says as she hands me our drinks in a cardboard holder. "I'll go make his sandwich and grab you a fresh scone. Perk of knowing the owner." She winks at me as she walks through the swinging door to the kitchen.

I sit down on a stool facing the counter and take a sip of my latte as I wait. Pepper is a caffeine goddess.

"Here ya go. I have to get lunch going, so I'll catch you later. Tell Saw I said hi!"

"Will do! Bye, Pepper!" I put some cash on the counter and grab our food and drinks.

I drive the two minutes to Pirate's Life and park Chili facing the coast. The Pudgies are softly bobbing on the water.

I feel like such a failure for not being able to complete the beginner sailing class. Sawyer is teaching the second group, and no one else has had any issues. He keeps telling me to go at my own pace, but I don't like this pace. I want to reach my goals now. I want to be able to go out on The Emerald and see the things the clients gush about when they come back from an excursion. I want to get on with my life.

I sigh as I get out of the car with our breakfast. I am going to sail a Pudgy. Sooner rather than later.

I unlock the front door of Pirate's Life and set our breakfast on the counter. I walk around, turning on lights as the computer starts. I might as well prepare for the next group while I wait for Sawyer to get back. It shouldn't be much longer.

I click print on the next set of invoices and nothing happens. My earlier feelings of failure combine with the printer's inability to do what I want it to, and I explode with frustration.

"Cock sucking, mother fucking, bitch-ass printer! Why doesn't he buy a new printer that actually WORKS!" I am bent over looking for a jam in the printer when hands land on my hips and a nose slides up my neck, bringing Sawyer's manly scents with them.

"I like it when you say those words but maybe not in that tone of voice. I will order a new printer between sails today. Mmm. I don't know what smells better, you or that bacon. I'm starving." He kisses me behind my ear, sending goosebumps down my body. I'm also hungry, but not for my scone.

"Do you want to have breakfast outside or in my office? I think I have a decent break between sails for a change, so I don't have to eat this on the move."

"Let's sit in the chairs out front. I need some sun. I've been cooped up in here too much."

Sawyer grabs the cardboard drink carrier and plastic bag and follows me out the door.

I plop down in a green Adirondack chair and sigh. These things are so comfortable.

Sawyer hands me my drink and scone, and I happily take a sip of the cold beverage.

"I don't know how you can drink that. Coffee is supposed to be hot. And black." He fake shudders at the concoction in my hand.

"It's tea, so I can drink it any way I want it." I take another sip and let out a happy "Ahhhh."

Sawyer just shakes his head and drinks his nasty, black mud.

"How was the sunrise sail?"

"Amazing. I think I like them more than the sunset sails. There is just something special about watching the sun begin a new day. Everything is fresh and quiet. The possibilities are endless."

"You don't have very many on the schedule this summer. Do you normally do more?"

"I just started them this year. I wasn't sure how well they would go over. It's a little chilly, and you have to get up pretty early to be in the best place to see the sun come up over the mountains. A lot of people don't want to get up that early and want to snorkel or see the sights from the boat as we sail past. It takes a certain person or couple to enjoy it."

"The way you describe it makes me want to try it one day even though I'm not what you would call a morning person."

"I could tell. You were practically pushing up daisies this morning when I left. You might want to wash your pillowcase to get all the drool out."

"Stop! I was not drooling!"

"No, you weren't. You sleep like a princess, soft and dreamy." He stands up and kisses me on the forehead. "I have to catch up on some paperwork before the next sail. I'll leave the door open so you can hear the phone."

I watch him walk back inside and settle deeper into my chair. I close my eyes and enjoy the morning sun. The waves hitting the shore and the gulls cawing make the perfect background music to relax and slow down.

The sun warms my muscles, and I find that ultimate relaxation.

My brain starts to wander, and I begin to fantasize about days spent in the sun with a lover. His work-roughened hands trailing up my legs before grabbing my thighs. Sucking kisses on my neck and below my ear. Those same hands sliding up my stomach to fondle my heavy breasts.

I can feel my core getting wet and my nipples peaking. There is a heavy sensation building low in my stomach.

My eyes fly open as I realize where I am. I stand up and walk back inside before I do something totally inappropriate on the side of the street.

When I get to the counter, I can hear Sawyer's deep voice talking to someone on the phone. My body instantly reacts to the sound as I get wetter and clench around nothing.

Sawyer ends the call, and my legs develop a mind of their own. I walk into the bathroom and remove my panties, stuffing them in a pocket of my dress. I walk across the lobby into Sawyer's office and shut the door.

"Hey, Avery. What's up?" he says as he glances up then returns to making notes on a piece of paper.

"Hopefully you," I reply as I walk around his desk.

He slides his chair back as I get closer. I move the papers to the side and sit on his desk, letting my sandals fall off before putting my feet on the outsides of his thighs on his chair.

"I definitely am now." He slides his hands up my legs and grips my thighs, just like in my fantasy. "You're so fucking sexy. I can smell your sweet pussy practically weeping for my cock. Let's see if it tastes as good as it smells."

His dirty talk still surprises me since he is so polite to everyone in public. It has brought out a side of me I didn't know existed, and I love it. It also gets me hotter than I have ever been.

He slides my dress farther up my thighs. I lean back on my hands to give him better access.

"You need this right now, don't you, baby?" He slides one finger along the inside of my thigh.

My teeth bite my lower lip knowing what he is about to find. All I can get out around the desire pulsing through me is, "Um-hm," before I let out a breathy moan.

"Let me hear how needy you are. I love it when you are so turned on you can't hold it in anymore."

He slides his finger higher until he comes into contact with the bare outer lips of my pussy. My hips rock against it to get him where I need him so badly.

His momentary shock of not finding a barrier between me and his finger is replaced with a devilish smile. I whimper as he pulls back.

"Have you been like this all morning or just now?"

"J-Just now."

He smiles at my answer and leans forward to press a kiss on my outer lips. He follows the kiss with a lick from the bottom to the top of my lips, not making contact with my needy center.

He grabs my ankles from beside his thighs and places my feet on the edge of the desk. My legs open wider, giving him a full view of where I really want him. I can feel my juices leaking out of me. I need this so bad, and he is purposely making me wait.

"Show me what you want me to do to you," he instructs as he leans back in his chair, his cock making a tent in his gray golf shorts.

Without any hesitation, I put all my weight on one arm and bring the other one in front of my body.

I slide one finger inside my mouth and suck to get it wet before sliding it through my folds up to my clit.

Sawyer groans and starts unbuckling his belt.

"I'm going to stroke my cock while I watch you play with that wet pussy." He finishes unzipping and pulls his erection out of his black boxer briefs.

It stands thick and tall, ready to bring me to new heights of pleasure. He fists the shaft and lightly squeezes. A pearl of precum appears on the slit, and I wet my lips with my tongue, ready to lick it off.

"None of that right now," he says, reading my mind. "I want to watch you bring yourself to the brink, then I'm going to fuck you on my desk until you come on my cock."

I don't have words to reply, so I do what he says. I slide my finger through my wetness then circle my clit. The little nub is getting harder and more sensitive. I slide back down my folds and inside my tight hole, searching for that place deep inside me.

I pull my finger back out and trail wetness back up to my clit. I press the pad of my finger over it once, then again. The sensations make my back arch and my nipples pebble even harder.

"That's it, baby. Make that pussy weep. Show me what you do when you're alone thinking about me."

His words spur me on. I push two fingers into my channel and pump them slowly in and out. The heel of my palm presses on my sensitive clit, adding to the neediness pooling in my belly, and I moan loudly.

The sight of Sawyer pumping his cock as he watches me pleasure myself turns me on even more. My fingers plunging in my pussy are making a sucking noise I am so wet. I bring some of that wetness up to my clit and circle with two fingers.

I usually make myself come this way, but I'm not ready for this to be over. I continue to alternate between stroking my slit and slipping deep inside my pussy.

Sawyer's strokes are getting faster, and the head of his cock is an angry purple. I can tell he isn't going to last much longer either.

"I'm about to come, and I want to be inside you when I do." He stops stroking his cock and leans forward. "I just need a taste of this drenched pussy before I fuck it."

He laps at my wetness, and I bring my hand up to my breast. I reach inside the low-cut top of my dress and pinch my nipple. The feeling sends tremors down my body and my pussy squeezes around Sawyer's tongue.

He groans and almost sends me over the edge with the vibrations. He gives me one last lick from bottom to top and lightly sucks my clit before standing up.

He fists his dick and runs it through my wetness a few times to lubricate it. He finds my center and sticks the tip in.

We both moan, and I toss my head back, exposing my throat. Sawyer licks the column then places a hard kiss on my lips as he enters me fully.

The fullness makes me clench down on him as he starts to move inside me.

"Fuck, baby. You're clamping my cock so tight I can barely move."

He starts to pump his hips when the door flies open.

Before either of us realizes what is happening, I hear a female voice say, "We're back and here to… oh my God."

Sawyer looks up just as the door slams shut. His head lands on my shoulder as my desire withers away.

"What just happened?"

"Well, you just met my parents while I was balls deep inside you, getting ready to make you have a screaming orgasm."

"What? *That was your mom?!?!*"

"Yep," he confirms as he pulls his deflating cock from inside me.

"Is she still here? Did they leave?"

"I don't know. Why? You want to finish?"

"*What?* NO! We can't just have sex with your parents waiting for us outside this door, knowing what we are doing. Are you crazy?" I whisper shout.

"I'd take some awko taco. I'll take yours anyway I can get it."

My face screws up in horror at what he just suggested. I look up at him and see a huge smile on his face with his dimples shining.

"You look awfully happy with yourself for a guy who's going to have blue balls for the rest of the day."

"You're awfully sassy for a girl who's going to meet my parents without any underwear on."

I reach into my pocket and pull out my underwear. I twirl it around my finger.

"Did you just pull those out of your pocket? What kind of a dress has pockets?"

"The only kind I buy. Now move so I can put these on and go out there to meet your parents with what little dignity I have left. Why don't you have one of those offices with a bathroom attached like in billionaire romance books?"

He just laughs at me as he steps back to put his soft cock into his underwear. I slip on my crumpled panties and sandals.

He is just finishing sliding the end of his belt through the loop when I look up at him. He looks like this never happened. Meanwhile, I can feel my wetness seeping into my panties.

Great. Just great.

CHAPTER 35
DEAD IN THE WATER

Sawyer

Avery veers into the bathroom to freshen up and leaves me to the wolves. I mean, my parents.

"Welcome home! What a surprise!" I say with faux cheerfulness.

"For all of us. Let's keep all future surprises rated PG," my mom says. "Is she going to come meet us, or did I ruin my only chance at grandchildren?"

"Well, if you had shown up five minutes later, your possibility of grandkids would have been a lot higher."

"Five minutes, Sawyer? Really? That poor girl. Todd, give him some pointers before we leave. Make sure you tell him about that thing that makes me go crazy."

I blanch at the thought of whatever *that thing* could be and add memory bleach to the shopping list.

"Can we please stop talking about this?" my dad asks. "I would rather forget this ever happened."

My mom and I say, "Agreed," at the same time Avery walks into the lobby.

"Okay. Let's start over." Mom claps once as she walks to the front door. She turns back to face us and practically yells, "Sawyer, we're here and ready to help! I hope you aren't boning your girlfriend in your office!"

Avery's face practically goes up in flames. I grab her hand so she can't bolt out of here, never to be seen again. Not that she wouldn't have a very good reason to do just that.

"Mom, welcome home! No boning going on here. Just helping Avery with some billing questions. Avery, these are my parents, Crystal and Todd Davis. Mom, Dad, this is Avery, my girlfriend."

My mom walks up to Avery and wraps her in a hug. "I'm so happy to finally get to meet you, dear. Sawyer has been talking about you for weeks."

Avery's eyes go wide and lock with mine, asking for help. "It's…uh…nice to meet you, too, Mrs. Davis. How was your trip?" Mom backs away from Avery to answer her question.

"I feel like we are on a first name basis now. Call me Crystal. The trip was great, but nothing beats Wild Shore in the summer."

Dad walks forward to shake Avery's hand. "You can call me Todd."

"Avery."

I can almost see her mental facepalm.

"Okay, guys. As you can see, Avery has everything under control here. You probably need to go home and unpack and rest from the drive," I suggest as I grab Mom by her shoulders and gently push her to the door.

"The mood is broken, Saw. No need to rush us out now."

"I'm getting you out of here before she decides to leave and never come back."

Mom peers back at Avery. "No need for that, young lady. I was your age once, too. We did some pretty wild things, and Todd wasn't even sexy enough to be shirtless on a billboard."

"But I still sealed the deal," my dad interrupts as he walks up behind her and smacks her on the ass, grabbing her hand as he keeps walking to the door. "Let's go, Crystal. Leave these kids alone." He opens the door and pulls her through.

Before the door shuts, Mom says, "Come over for dinner one night this week! Todd will grill!"

The door shuts, effectively cutting off anything else she was going to say. I exhale deeply and lower my shoulders. I look over at Avery, but I can't read the look on her face.

"Well, those are my parents." I walk to her and pull her close.

"Do you think there is a chance she won't tell your sister what just happened?"

"Absolutely not. Mom probably had her on the phone telling her all about it before they got in the car."

Her forehead lands on my chest as she releases an exasperated sigh.

"Great. Shoot me now."

I laugh and tilt her head up to peck her lips as the door opens.

"I swear to all that is holy, if that is your mom, we are never touching again unless we are behind a locked bedroom door."

I smile against her lips and shift my eyes to the door. "It's just part of the next group."

She pulls away from me and turns to walk over to the counter with a smile plastered on her face. "Welcome to Pirate's Life! I can get you checked in over here."

I turn around and head outside to check the Jolly Rodger to make sure it is ready to sail and everything is stocked.

The Saturday beginner sailing class is about to start, so I check the weather one last time before I head upstairs to start the presentation. I need to decide if I am going to have Avery cancel the Jolly Rodger excursion after lunch or chance it.

The storm chances have decreased for this afternoon but not enough to take a boat full of people out expecting to have a fun time and end up puking over the side from rough seas.

I lock my computer and walk out to the front counter where Avery is talking to one of the beginner students.

"You will like the next couple weeks. Just make it through today, and the rest will be so much fun."

"I'll try my best not to make today as terrible as she is making it out to be," I cut in.

"I'm sure it will be fine," the customer says. "Up the stairs in the back, right?"

"Yes, you can't miss it," Avery answers. She turns to me. "What's up?"

"Can you call the people on the Jolly Rodger excursion this afternoon? There is still a chance of a storm, and I don't want them to drive all the way down here before I have to cancel last minute."

"Sure thing, Sawyer."

"Have I told you how sexy you look today?" I lean forward and kiss her under her ear, making her moan.

"Maybe this morning when I was on my knees in the shower. I can't remember with all the other dirty things that were coming out of your mouth."

"I can think of some other things to do with my mouth other than talk dirty to you."

"Like talking about boater safety and the Laws of the Sea with the class upstairs. Get up there so these people can get out of here before it starts storming."

"Yes, ma'am." I walk up the stairs and think about the first time I gave this speech, the day Avery plowed into my life. It feels like a lifetime ago and yesterday all in one. My life has definitely changed for the better. I don't know what I would do without her. One day soon, I am going to tell her that.

After the beginner sailing class is over, I go back down to my office to look at the weather. The sun is shining outside, and the day looks beautiful. There is barely a cloud in the sky. I hate canceling an excursion due to the weather and then the day turns out perfectly fine, but it is better than the opposite.

The radar looks clear for miles. The storm must have dissipated. I pick up my phone and call the front counter.

"Did you not hear me say behind locked bedroom doors only? I'm not coming in there."

I laugh at her greeting. "Although that sounds like a great way to kill a few hours, I was wondering if anyone walked in this morning to ask about an excursion since the weather is looking much better."

"Nope. You are clear until early evening."

"Good. I need to go scout a new snorkel location. I saw a sea turtle yesterday on the way back from the Twin Peaks. I want to see if I can find it again. The kids love swimming around them, and they are harmless."

"Are you sure? How's the weather?"

"I just checked the radar before I called you, and it is all clear. The storm must have broken up and moved on."

"Okay. Stay safe, and I will see you when you get back," Avery says.

I can tell she wants to say more but stays silent.

"Bye, babe. See you in a few hours." *Love you* sits on the tip of my tongue, but I don't let it slip. One day soon.

I get up and go outside to prepare The Emerald. The possibility of storms this morning left the air humid and muggy. When you add in the brilliant sunshine, it is downright hot outside.

We don't normally have humidity in Wild Shore, so I am not used to almost needing a knife to cut through the air to breathe. I am starting to sweat a little before I get everything checked. Hopefully, this humidity won't be so bad on the open sea.

As soon as I breach the mouth of the cove, I start raising sails. I need some speed to cool off. There is nothing more refreshing than flying across the water at top speed. The wind is blowing through my hair and flapping my clothes against my body.

Until I met Avery, this was where I found my happiness. If someone asked me now what makes me happy, without a doubt my answer would be Avery. Everything about her. Sailing doesn't even come a close second.

I sail around for a couple hours, keeping an eye on the clear, blue water as I cut through the small waves. The water here is the best in the world, and I have seen pretty much all of it as a Navy sailor then a SEAL.

I see several fishing boats but no large schools of fish or any turtles. I check my watch to see what time it is. It is almost three. I better turn the boat around so I can get back in time for the evening sail.

Suddenly, the air turns cool like I just stepped into an air-conditioned house. I glance toward Wild Shore, and what I see sends shivers down my spine that have nothing to do with the chill in the air. A squall is coming straight toward me from the cove. The sky turns dark around me, and I start getting pelted with cold, hard rain.

The Emerald begins to bob over the waves like speed bumps when it was just cutting through the surf like butter a few seconds prior. I open the seat where I store life jackets and pull one over my head.

My stomach turns as I think about the possibilities of what could happen to me in the next few minutes. Adrenaline starts pumping through my veins as I visualize the worst outcome. I prepared for this scenario many times as a SEAL, and my training kicks in to redirect my morbid thoughts. *The only easy day was yesterday.*

There is no way I can put The Emerald in irons. It is already too late. The storm came on too quickly, and I can't ease the sails with the wind whipping against them.

I brace my legs for the next swell and try to hold the helm steady. The wind picks up and starts blowing from all directions as the squall gets closer. The Emerald is being tossed around like a toy boat in a bathtub with a flopping toddler.

Things start flying off the boat as the wind continues to howl, and the water becomes more violent and unforgiving. I am pretty sure I am going to face a knockdown or worse.

Every muscle in my body strains at the helm to keep the bow headed into the waves, but the boat is continuously thrown from one side to the other at the mercy of the elements.

Hail starts to pelt me, stinging my exposed skin. Rain runs down my body in rivers, hindering my vision. The waves are starting to break over the deck and go down the steps to the cabin below.

The bow takes a hard wave. My strength is not enough to rival Mother Nature. The helm pulls through my hands, and the boat turns. I scream my fury into the gale-force winds and brace for the next wave that hits the boat. I know it will hit straight across the beam and roll the boat onto its side, plummeting me into the raging water.

My mind travels out of my body, and it's like I am watching this happen to someone else as I plan what I need to do next.

A huge wave hits the boat, and it takes a knockdown. The force of the boat falling sideways plunges me into the darkest depths of the violent water. I claw my way back to the surface, only to be met by another black wave that fills my mouth with brine before shoving me under the turbulent surface again.

My lungs start to burn from holding my breath, and I try to swim to the surface. The dark, churning depths disorient me, and I don't know if I am swimming down or up.

My thoughts start to spiral, thinking of all the things I should have done, telling Avery I love her at the top of the list.

My hands rake through the roiling water, trying to find something to anchor me to the boat. I come into contact with the mast. My biceps bulge as I try to pull my body to the pole as it thrashes in the chaos, and the water tries to pull me back under.

The wind continues to roar around me so loudly I can't even hear myself think. The rain may be letting up, or it may be coming in from a different direction and blocked by the exposed hull. I can't tell.

I glance at The Emerald. Water is flowing into the cabin. If the cabin fills up, The Emerald will sink, and I will have no way to save myself from predators while I wait for rescue.

My eyes sting from the salt water as I try to assess my situation. Both sails are fully submerged, keeping the boat from righting itself. I have to remove the sails. I reach in my pocket for my knife as the waves slam my ribs into the mast, making breathing difficult.

I cling to the jerking mast with one arm as I slice through the rigging for the mainsail and jib. My beloved emerald canvas is swallowed by the churning sea as it continues to pummel me from all directions. I shimmy down the slippery, bobbing mast toward the hull, and I can feel the boat start its assent out of the murky depths that minutes ago were crystal clear.

The Emerald is finally mast up again. My fear starts to recede at the promising sight. Now maybe my luck will hold, and the cabin isn't full of water, causing the boat to immediately start to sink.

I inch up the deck to the entrance of the cabin, finding handholds as I go. The rain and seawater make walking on the polished deck impossible, and the wind whips my hair into my eyes, causing them to sting more.

Just as I reach the stairs, the hail stops, and the wind dies down slightly. The waves are calming down a little with every passing minute. Relief floods my veins. I am going to survive this.

I need to check the bilge pumps in the cabin and start bailing water. I crouch down and walk to the cabin entrance. The bottom two steps are underwater. I pray nothing electrical is exposed and step down the last two steps.

I walk to the mechanical area and hear only the wind blowing above. None of the electronics are functioning.

"Goddamn it!" I yell to no one and smack the wall.

I am for all intents and purposes, dead in the water.

CHAPTER 36
SAR MISSION

Avery

"Pirate's Life to The Emerald. Come in. Pirate's Life to the Emerald. Come in, Sawyer," I say into the CB radio.

"Damn it, Sawyer. Where are you?" I shriek to the ceiling, since no one else is here.

That squall came out of nowhere and took everyone by surprise. Half the town is without power. Luckily, Sawyer installed a propane generator for this building, and I have electricity. But more importantly, the CB works, and I can keep trying to get ahold of him.

"Pirate's Life to The Emerald. Please, Sawyer. Just answer me." Desperation to hear his voice tries to overtake me.

I don't want to lose two people I love to the water. I barely made it through losing my sister. I don't think I will survive losing Sawyer.

My mind goes through a list of whys. *Why didn't I tell him to stay? Why won't he answer the radio? Why haven't I told him I love him?*

The list goes on but always reverts back to why have I never said those three little words.

I know it is not fear of rejection. Sawyer shows his feelings in so many little ways. I would have to be blind not to notice.

It is not fear of judgment from our friends and families. All of our friends and Sawyer's parents wholeheartedly support our relationship. I know my parents are going to do the same.

Why haven't I told him I love him? Now I may never get to.

I snap my mind away from those negative thoughts. I don't even know where he went. He may be far away from where the storm hit. He might have seen it coming and docked somewhere to ride out the storm. Maybe he's in a shelter and not on his boat, and that's why he won't answer me.

I try calling his mom and dad to see if they know what to do, but the cell tower must be down too.

I groan in frustration at the situation and my inability to do anything.

He knows I would be worried about him and would contact me as soon as the storm was over if he could. That means he probably can't contact me. He must have been caught in the storm. It came right over the mouth of the cove, and he should have been heading back this way right before the storm hit.

I walk to the back door and look at the water. The storm passed through a half hour or so ago. The waves are still a little choppy but still easy sailing for an experienced sailor.

Where is Sawyer?

He was a Navy sailor and a SEAL for years. He has undoubtedly dealt with worse. This was a squall, not a hurricane. He has spent the majority of his life on the water and knows how to handle a storm. He will contact me anytime.

I walk back to the CB. "Pirate's Life to The Emerald. Come in, Emerald. Can you hear me, Sawyer?"

Nothing. The line doesn't even crackle with static. I try calling Crystal, but the phone lines are still down.

Should I drive to Shipwrecked and see if Sav, Crystal, or Todd are there and can help? It's hard telling how much storm damage there is between here and there. I may not even be able to get through town.

I try the CB again, but there is no answer. It is going to be getting dark soon. Someone needs to do something.

Then it dawns on me. No one else knows where he is or that he was even on the water when the storm hit. I am the only one. *I* have to save him. It is up to *me*.

"Holy shit. Can I be the alpha hero in my own smutty romance story?" I ask skeptically.

I'm going to find him. My fear of the water doesn't outweigh my fear for Sawyer's safety. *Yes, I can be the alpha hero.*

I pick up a sticky note from the front counter and write a note.

Sawyer took The Emerald out before the storm and didn't come back. I went to look for him. Took a Pudgy.

> *- Avery*

I stick it to the front door and grab a life jacket as I walk out the back door.

As I hurry down the path to the dock, I put the life jacket on. I reassure myself that I can do this. It's just water. Nothing to be scared of. I take a shower everyday. I swim in a pool. I go to the beach.

I need to stop thinking about the water and think about sailing. I remember the morning we spent on the beach going over parts of the Pudgy and how to sail. Sawyer said he had full confidence in my ability to sail this boat after that morning. I can do this. I *will* do this for him.

I walk down the dock to the line of Pudgies. They all need to be pumped out after the storm, but I am only worried about one. I turn on the bilge pump and get the sail kit out as the boat empties.

The bilge pump kicks off, and I start assembling the mast and rigging. When I get away from the dock, I will be able to raise the sail and head out.

Okay. I can do this. I am closer to the water than I have been in years. Just one small step, and I will be in a boat.

My anxiety begins to peak at the thought of getting in the boat, but my brain overrides the thoughts with a memory of the last time I had a panic attack. Sawyer was there to save me with his warm chocolate eyes and calming presence. Now it is my time to save him.

I get in the boat and sit down.

The boat shifts under my weight, and I close my eyes to bring myself back to the first day I met Sawyer. My heart rate lowers, and I push away from the dock.

I am doing it. I am on a boat. I let out a shaky breath and begin the next step.

I raise the sail, and the wind fills the canvas, sending me off with a slight jerk that almost makes me lose my balance. Through my momentary panic at how quickly that happened, I realize I have to steer. Sawyer's voice floats through my mind, calm and collected, instructing me on what to do next.

I navigate the cove and head to the mouth. The relative stillness of the cove gives way to the open sea rife with small waves. The water has calmed down considerably after the storm, but there are always waves out here.

My mind brings up a memory of Sawyer's voice instructing me to steer into the waves to avoid taking a wave to the side of the boat.

I am doing it! I am sailing! I can't believe I am doing this. I can see Sawyer's sexy smile in my mind, cheering me on.

The next step is trying to figure out where to go. How do I find a single sailboat in someplace so vast? I scan the water for a few minutes before I remember Sawyer said he was going to look for a sea turtle off of the Twin Peaks.

I have seen the Twin Peaks from Riley's shop, but I'm not sure how to get there by boat. I adjust the sail to get me going in the right direction. I will just follow the coast until I see the identical rock formations then sail to them. Hopefully, Sawyer didn't change his mind and go somewhere else.

I keep my eyes peeled for boats or anything floating as I glide slowly through the water. Sawyer wasn't joking when he said these things are snail fast. I have plenty of time to make decisions on which way to move the sail to correct my course, and I feel capable of making the adjustments.

The ocean has returned to its idyllic atmosphere. The sun is shining, and the gulls are floating on the wind, swooping to nab a fish here and there. It is shocking how quickly nature can change.

The wind blows through my hair, and the sun feels amazing on my face. I can totally see why so many people come to Pirate's Life for this experience. This is very invigorating.

I sail for almost an hour before I see anything. Off in the distance, I can see a single mast sticking up.

My heart rate kicks up at the possibility that I found Sawyer. I can't see the hull of the boat, and the sails are not up, so I can't be sure who it is until I get closer.

I tack the sail to get another knot out of the Pudgy. It won't go any faster no matter how desperately my heart, body, and mind want it to. These things just weren't made for speed.

When I get close enough, I can read the name written in elegant green font on the side of the charcoal hull, and my heart speeds up and drops out of my chest simultaneously. *The Emerald.* I found him!

As I get closer to the boat, I don't see Sawyer or any movement. The mainsail and jib are gone. Debris floats around the boat, telling a horrifying tale that I won't let myself listen to.

Was he flung into the water with the debris? He may be a ways away from the boat if he is still alive.

No negative thoughts. Only positive thoughts.

I continue sailing in that direction and scan the water around the debris for any movement. I don't see anything.

I will the boat to go faster, but it is at maximum speed. I can't imagine in what universe I would have wanted to go faster in a boat, let alone be solo sailing on a SAR mission to save an ex-SEAL.

When I get close enough, I cup my hands around my mouth and yell.

"Sawyer! Can you hear me? Are you on there? Saw-yer!"

Nothing moves on board. Maybe I'm not close enough for him to hear me. I refuse to believe anything else could be the reason he isn't out on the deck welcoming me to him with a huge dimple-laden smile.

I shriek again. "Sawyer! Sawyer! Where are you, Sawyer?"

Unbidden, tears come to my eyes as I continue to sail closer to The Emerald in slow motion.

I blubber out, "Sawyer! No, Sawyer! I did it. I got in this damn boat to save you. I conquered my fear to save you. You better be on that boat and tell me how amazing I am! Saw-yer!"

Snot starts running unhindered from my nose. I can't be bothered to wipe it or my tears as I continue to sail closer to The Emerald.

I yell again, but nothing moves on the deck.

He can't be gone. I have to tell him I love him, and he has to tell me how proud of me he is for coming out here.

"Sawyer! Get out here now! Where are you? I need you!"

I lower the sail to stop moving and break down into full-on body wracking sobs when I don't get any response.

CHAPTER 37
SEA NYMPH

Sawyer

I am trying to hot wire the battery to the radio so I can call for help when I hear a voice that sounds like Avery's. I don't think I have been out here long enough to be delusional, but I probably hit my head when I fell off the boat when it turned over. I didn't think about starting concussion protocol, which in itself probably means I have a concussion.

I hear her voice again.

"I know, baby. I'm trying to get back to you. I didn't serve in the Navy then as a SEAL to die on a sailboat five miles from my dock. Hell, if I can't get this figured out, I might just take my chances and swim back to shore. The only easy day was yesterday."

I go back to splicing wires when her voice comes to me again. "I'm trying to get back to you, but I'm not great with electronics."

Avery's voice comes closer or gets louder. I'm not sure. Neither is likely, but at this point I'm willing to go see what kind of sea nymph my mind is conjuring. I set the wires down and go above deck.

I hear sobbing and look around until I see a sight that makes me seriously consider beginning concussion protocol.

"Avery." I say her name on an exhale. I can't believe my eyes. She is here in the middle of the water, captaining her own vessel.

She must have heard me because her head whips toward me.

"Sawyer? Sawyer! Oh my God! You're alive! I couldn't get ahold of you, and I got in this boat and found your boat, and I yelled for you and you didn't come out and I thought you were gone before I could tell you I love you…" She drags in a huge breath of air as sobs continue to rack her chest.

She said it. She said she loves me. I will do anything in my power to make her mine. Nothing will stop me. Not even a broken-down boat in the middle of the water with no way to signal for help.

"Baby, I am so proud of you! I love you more than you will ever know. You conquering your fear to look for me means more to me than everything else combined. I love you, Avery Sutton."

Her watery eyes look up at me standing on The Emerald.

"This wasn't exactly how I pictured this going. This is actually exactly the opposite of how I thought this would go. I thought we would be together the first time you went on the water so I could show you how proud I am of you."

"We can be together now. Just help me get to you," she says through quivering lips.

"That's not exactly doable right now. I don't want you to have to go from the Pudgy to The Emerald."

"I'll do it. How do I get up there?"

"Are you sure?"

"Yes. I'm not scared of the water. I thought you were dead. Convince me you are alive and you love me."

"You will have to paddle over to the stern, and I will pull you up."

Avery pulls an oar out from the hull of the Pudgy and starts paddling to me like she has been doing this her entire life.

She gets to the stern and throws a rope to me. I quickly tie the Pudgy to The Emerald and extend my arms toward her. She stands up on sturdy legs and steps over the side of the Pudgy into my waiting arms.

My mouth slams down onto hers hard and fast. She moans, and I deepen the kiss, darting my tongue between her lips to tangle with hers. She plasters her body to my slightly damp one. I reach down and grab her ass as she jumps and circles my hips with her legs.

My cock goes from semi-hard to full mast, pushing against the seam of her jean shorts. She groans into my mouth at the pressure.

"Unless you want me to fuck you standing on the deck, we need to move. Everything below deck is wet, so this is going to be the worst introduction to sex on a boat you could have."

"I don't care. Stop talking and get inside me," she pants between sucking kisses and licks to my salty throat.

My cock agrees with her and strains against my shorts at her words. I walk us to a bench in front of the helm and lay her down.

She pulls her shorts and underwear down and throws them on the deck, exposing her glistening pussy. She slides a finger through her slit as I lower my shorts just enough to pull my cock out. The sight makes me groan and fist my erection. I replace her finger with the head of my cock before slowly pushing inside her wet hole.

She is so tight, but her wetness makes it easy to slide in until my balls hit her ass. We both moan at the fullness, and she clenches down on my cock, causing me to throw my head back and release a feral noise from my open mouth. She repeats the internal movement, and I can't hold back anymore.

I pull out and slam back in quickly. My thrusts are so deep and hard she starts to slide up the seat until her head is stopped by the armrest.

"Oh God, Sawyer. Yes. Aaaaahhhhh. Keep giving it to me. Like. That."

She continues encouraging me through her moans and panting breaths as I get closer to the edge. I need to slow down, or I will come before I want to.

I reach up and push her shirt up her chest, exposing her pale pink lace bra. Her tits are bouncing wildly on her chest in time with my deep thrusts. Her nipples are so hard they are almost poking through the delicate fabric.

I lean down a little farther and take one in my mouth. I feel a rush of wetness on my cock that only allows me to fuck her harder and faster.

Her hands come up to my shoulders, and her nails score the skin of my back as she tries to find something to hold onto.

"I'm not going to last much longer, baby. Are you getting close?"

"Uhhh-huh," she lets out between moans.

I reach down and circle her clit with my finger. The sensation has her crying out as she clamps down on my cock so hard I'm slightly worried she may cut it off.

The pressure and warm juices flowing out of her pussy put me over the edge. I roar as I come deep inside her.

"I love you, Avery," I yell as jet after jet of cum leaves my cock. I keep rocking into her, pushing our combined juices out of her pussy and between her ass cheeks.

I lean forward onto her chest as we both pant from our exertions. I know I need to get off her so she can breathe easier, but I am physically drained.

My limp cock slides out of her pussy, letting more of our cum flow through her ass cheeks and down her thighs.

She doesn't seem to mind as she focuses on recovering. I look up at her face, and her smile is blinding.

"Well, I can say that wasn't the most comfortable sex I have ever had, but it might have been the best. I'm not sure if my pussy or the top of my head got the hardest pounding."

Her bubbling happiness makes me happy, and I return her smile.

"Only the best for my woman on the day she faces her fears and rescues the man of her dreams."

"I love you, Sawyer." She sighs contentedly.

"I can't believe you came out here. I am so proud of you," I say before kissing her on the lips. "I hate to break up this moment, but we really need to get back to shore so I can radio help to get this boat before it gets dark. The electrical system must have been damaged, and I can't get the radio or electric motor to work."

Avery exhales loudly through her lips. "Let's go then."

"Let me lower the anchor so it doesn't drift off."

With The Emerald as secure as it can be, we sail back to Pirate's Life in the Pudgy hand in hand. I keep looking over at her, trying to convince myself that this is real, and she is here with me on the water.

She catches my stare and smiles.

"I know. I can't believe I did this either," she says as she squeezes my hand.

We get back to Pirate's Life, and I radio the Coast Guard. They say they will be at Pirate's Life in a few minutes.

"I'm going with you to get The Emerald," Avery informs me.

"Are you sure?"

"Yes. You are not leaving my sight. Maybe not even for a few days."

"I understand that, but are you certain you want to go back out right now? You were fueled by adrenaline and worry the last time. It's not like that this time."

"Yes, I am certain. I can handle it. I just pictured your calming eyes and heard your encouraging words while I was out there, and it all went away. I know it will be fine to go out again because you will be there in real life if I have any problems, which I won't."

"Ahhh, baby." I pull her into a hug and kiss the top of her head. "Let's go outside and wait for them to get here. It shouldn't be much longer."

I take her hand, and we walk outside to sit on the bench. She tucks herself tight into my side, her ear above my heart, and we just relax as the events of the day wash over us.

I lead the Coast Guard to The Emerald, and they pull my boat to Peak Mechanic, ironically the shop Riley owns.

Riley comes running out when she sees the Coast Guard pull into the cove in front of her garage.

"Sawyer? What is going on?" She glances at Avery, then back at me.

"Avery! What is going on? Oh my God, Avery! You are on a boat!" Riley screams as she runs down the long dock to get to us.

The Coast Guard pulls up beside the dock, and Avery jumps off their boat. The two women hug tightly, and a tear or two are shed.

Avery quickly tells Riley the story about what happened.

"I can't believe it. I am so proud of you!" Riley practically yells and gives Avery another hug.

"Where do you want this boat, ma'am?" the coastguardsman asks.

"Get it as close to the front as you can. I'll take it from there. Thank you."

They maneuver The Emerald up to the dock, and I secure her.

The coastguardsmen wave, signaling they are done here, and I return the gesture.

Riley asks about the electrical system, and I tell her what I did.

"Electric motors and systems aren't really my forte, but I'm pretty sure I can fix it. Give me a few days to look into it. I should have it done by the time the new sails get here. Just ship them here when you find replacements, and I'll get them installed."

"Thanks, Riley. I appreciate it."

"No problem. You're practically family now."

We turn to walk the rest of the way to the shore, chatting about Avery's heroism. Riley slips on some loose gravel, and I look back at her to see if she needs help.

Over her shoulder, I see a white fishing boat floating in with the tide, listing heavily to one side.

"Hey, stop! There is a boat out there!" I exclaim.

Riley and Avery turn just as the boat crashes into the rocky shore this end of town is known for. We all run to that side of the cove to see what is going on.

"Oh no," Avery says sadly. "That is the Bro and Tell. I've seen this boat at the wharf before."

We look around the boat and don't see anyone.

"Where's the guy who owns it?"

Want to find out where the captain is? Find out in the next book in the Wild Shore Series!

Thank you so much for reading *Sail With Me*! Do you need to know more about the people of Wild Shore? *Stay By Me* releases in mid-2024!

An Interesting Note

I never set out to write an actual book. I was looking through editing jobs online one night and came across a posting for a ghostwriter needed to write a twenty thousand word adventure story. I wasn't finding anything to edit, so I decided to see if I could write twenty thousand words.

When I hit the twenty thousand word milestone, I knew the story wasn't over. Avery and Sawyer hadn't even gotten to the "good" part yet! They deserved a full book to tell their story. I backtracked and added the first five chapters then continued with the rest of their story.

Six months later, I am writing this note before uploading the finished manuscript. I hope you enjoyed my first attempt at writing an actual novel and found me as funny as I find myself!

Acknowledgments

Thank you to my husband, Timmy, for going with the flow when I told you I was going to write a spicy romance, even though I'm one hundred percent certain you had no idea what that meant. You have since morphed into the best hype guy and salesman around.

Thank you for everything, Jordin. I'm not sure that word even encompasses how much input you had in this book. What's the word that means more than everything? You probably know it.

Thank you to my two sons for providing endless sarcastic comebacks, one-liners, and random AirDrop videos. Those your mom jokes hit a little different when you're the mom they are bashing.

Thank you to my editor, Emily. Also, sorry. I apparently don't understand English grammar. I'm a work in progress.

Lastly, thank you. I will be forever grateful you took a chance on an unknown author and allowed me to share the characters inside my head with you. Hopefully you found a few you like!

About The Author

LJ Makenzie is a chemist by day and writes explosive chemistry at night. She is of the small percentage of people who believes the best ideas and spiciest scenes flow from the brain at 2:00 a.m.

She lives on a small hobby farm in Indiana with her husband and two feral, preteen boys, who provide endless writing prompts with their nonstop sarcasm, humor, and overall ridiculousness.

Become a member of the Mak Pack to stay up to date on all things LJ Makenzie!

Scan the QR Code to get links to my author pages and the Mac Pack or email me at lj@ljmakenzie.com